ALL YOUR SHIPS AND STORMS CALLED SHE

Geonn Cannon

Supposed Crimes LLC • Matthews, North Carolina

www.supposedcrimes.com

This book is typeset in Goudy Old Style.

All Your Ships and Storms Called She

CLIO LANDAU

"I was born in your arms, blood in my eyes, aboard a ship of mutineers. Your eyes were the first thing I saw in this world.

Water washed the blood from my face while the wounds were still pouring. I thought it was raining, but it was just spray crashing over the gunwales of our ship. You were on your knees, face tilted toward the commotion I was still too dazed to understand. Your face was lit by a flash of gunpowder and you turned away, held me closer to you, and I reacted. I grabbed for your arms. That was when you realized I was conscious.

You look down at me with eyes the same color as the clouds overhead. Your raven's wing hair fell on either side of your face. It was so long it almost shrouded me entirely. Spots of blood marked where tiny splinters of shattered boards had embedded themselves in your cheek and jawline. Your long fingers touched my cheek and you offered me a pained smile.

'Thank God. You're alive.'

A whisper, but I could still hear it over the raging sea, the fight, the shouting of men. I saw blood on your clothes but didn't know if it was mine or yours. I heard shouts of pain, and how quickly they were cut off as the suffering was ended. The world beneath me rose toward the clouds and then dropped down so quickly that I felt it in my stomach.

Another wave crashed over the side of the ship and we both tumbled. You refused to release me and I clung to your arms as we were carried on the water. You twisted so that you took the impact against the wooden wall on your back but I felt it rattle the whole of you, ever bone shaken in the act of protecting me. The sea was in my eyes and mouth and I was still bleeding, and there was no chance of making sense of the world when there was no direction, no gravity, no center.

You saved my life, Harriet. As I was born into a storm, surrounded by killers, you put yourself in harm's way to keep me alive. You spilled your blood, you bruised and marked your porcelain skin.

How could I do anything but fall in love with someone like that?

And how could I do anything but fall to pieces when that person is taken away from me?"

CHAPTER ONE

INES RANZI slumped in her chair at such an angle that she could keep one eye on her cards, the other on Clio Landau. Her captain had spent the last two hours on a stool at the end of the bar with one arm folded in front of her as a pillow, the other gripping a mug. The bartender made frequent stops to ensure the mug was never less than half-full. Her hat had been tossed aside, and her short white-blonde hair stuck up in wild weedy spikes. For all intents and purposes, Landau was comatose, and Ranzi wanted to be sure she didn't slump backward off her stool. The captain didn't need that kind of humiliation.

"You paying attention?"

Ranzi focused on her table in front of her. She added three more bills to the pot. She barely acknowledged her cards; it was easier to bluff that way. The man across from her sneered and fanned his cards out wider, lip curling as he considered what he was holding.

To Ranzi's right, Fausta Gittens chewed on a toothpick. The first mate of the *Banshee*, Fausta had thick waves of dark brown hair threaded with a lighter caramel color. Her eyebrows were thick and heavy, shading her eyes so that it was difficult to tell that they were locked on the last man seated at their table. Their fourth and fifth players were long gone, having folded early, but this man seemed determined to defeat them. Five empty bottles formed a barricade around Fausta's winnings. The sixth bottle, which she held on her thigh, was half-empty. Despite the amount of liquor in her, she had a sharp focus on their only remaining opponent.

Ranzi looked down at the hand she'd been dealt. The cards were well-worn cardboard with edges that had become worn and cottony from years of drunken games like this one. There was no way of counting the cards because, going by the various designs on the back, they were playing with four different decks of various completion. So it really was all about outmaneuvering the other player.

Ranzi arched one eyebrow. She tapped her smallest finger against the back of her cards.

"They aren't going to change no matter how much you stare at them," the man said. "Make a decision, *tarado*."

"Patience, boy, patience." She chose half a stack of coin and tossed it to the pile in the center of the table.

The man leaned back, clearly surprised. He grunted and tossed his cards down, revealing he had only been bluffing with a pair of hearts. "I'm skint enough as it is."

Ranzi put down her cards and stood to gather her winnings. "Don't be glum, Dodds. Plenty of other players here ain't as good as me. You can get your money back from them."

Dodds reached out and grabbed Ranzi's arm before she could pull the cash toward her. "Hold on now." He nodded at her cards. "Show what you had."

"It doesn't matter." Fausta sat up straighter, the movement of her toothpick the only indication of her tension rising. Her eyes were locked on Dodds. "Pair doesn't beat nothing."

"A pair actually *does* beat nothin'," Dodds said, still staring at Ranzi. "And if she's got nothing, then *I* win."

Ranzi, the picture of calm, smiled. "It doesn't matter what I had. You folded."

"I don't trust Africans."

Fausta hissed through her teeth. "She's half-Spaniard, half-Indian, my friend. And I'm Persian, which is almost the right continent. Well done for that. And Africa is a very, very big place. I would think twice before you besmirch an entire continent." She leaned forward to look him in the eye. "The game ended when you folded. My friend Ines was the only one still in when that happened, so she wins regardless of~"

"Shut your mouth." He tightened his grip. "Show your cards."

A sword came down between them. Its edge came to rest on Dodds' wrist just above the ragged cuff of his sleeve. He and Ranzi both looked at the shiny metal, then followed the blade up to the woman holding it: a fully awake, seemingly sober Captain Clio Landau.

"Is this really the last thing you want to do with that hand, Mr. Dodds?"

He tightened his jaw and narrowed his eyes.

"Kindly remove it from my friend before I end its usefulness to you."

Dodds looked at Ranzi again and finally, with a disgusted grunt, flung her arm away from him. The movement caused her arm to swing away from the table, and a pair of folded cards fluttered out of the sleeve. Dodds, Fausta, and Clio all watched them tumble to the floor like snowflakes.

"Aw, fuck, Ranzi," Clio muttered, wincing as if physically pained.

Fausta hooked her foot around the leg of Dodds' chair. She jerked it toward her, pulling it out from underneath him. Clio grabbed Ranzi and shoved her toward the door. They burst out into the sunlight as Dodds shouted for others to join him in pursuit. Normally he wouldn't have had much luck gathering a mob, but the two men who had folded earlier would likely be eager to make amends now that they knew she was a cheat.

Clio kept one hand curled in the Ranzi's coat, guiding her through the narrow streets by the shoulder. Fausta followed them at a trot, half turned and gun drawn, keeping an eye out.

"You don't have to cheat at every game, Ines."

Ranzi laughed. "And play by the same rules as everyone else? How is that even a game?"

Clio grunted. Fausta fired once, twice, and Ranzi knew the chase had begun in earnest. She twisted away from Clio's grip and pointed down a side street.

"Roundabout," was all she said, but it was the only instruction Clio needed.

The captain cut right, down the street Ranzi had indicated. Ranzi went left, ducking into the next alleyway. Ranzi knew that Fausta would stop and turn to face their pursuers. She would draw the second gun at her hip and then... She heard five gunshots, most likely aimed at the feet of the drunk men, and knew to expect five opponents.

When she reached the back of the building, she shoved through the open back door, weaved through a storage room, and burst through the front room of a clothing store. One customer screamed at her sudden appearance, but Ranzi didn't slow down. She hit the front door with both palms, shoving it open and delivering her onto the main street behind Dodds and his gang of drunks. Clio appeared out of the alley opposite and drew her own pistol.

Ranzi whistled. The drunks turned. Clio gave a ferocious yell and charged forward. She ducked down at the last moment before impact and hit the lead man with her shoulder. He fell back into the others, toppling them like ten-pins. One of the men grabbed the collar of Ranzi's coat, and she chopped her hand into his throat to make him release her. He gagged and she leapt over the still-sprawled Dodds to rejoin Fausta.

"If either of you ever show your face in that pub aga~" Dodds didn't have a chance to finish his threat, interrupted by Clio's boot connecting with his jaw to lay him flat.

Ranzi took the lead for the rest of their retreat. Clio was behind her, and Fausta brought up the rear to make sure the drunks were truly dispatched. A crowd had gathered to see the cause of all the fuss, and Clio shoved Ranzi to make her move. Where crowds and gunshots converged, authorities were never far behind.

Fausta only relaxed when they were back at the dock, climbing down into the launch that would take them back to the ship. There was an unspoken rule among certain elements that disagreements ended at the waterline. Pursuing anyone back to their ship ran the risk of an all-out skirmish with a heavily-armed crew, and no one was willing to cause that much of a headache over a lousy card game.

Ranzi dropped down onto the center bench and rolled her shoulders, stretching her arms, basking in the successful escape. Clio hopped down from the ladder and aimed a finger at her.

"You're rowing, Ranzi."

"Small price to pay, considering~" Ranzi's smile fell as she put a hand to her pocket and made a horrifying realization. "Oh bloody hell."

Fausta looked at her and immediately sussed out what happened. "You didn't clear the table. You left the money just sitting there when you ran."

"I had three hundred pounds of an angry Sam Dodds bearing down on me!"

Fausta and the captain looked at each other, sharing silent disbelief, and then Fausta threw her head back and laughed. Clio joined her and slapped her hand across the top of Ranzi's thick dark hair. Ranzi scowled and squeezed her eyes shut, trying to erase the memory of the paper and coins and that damned signet ring she'd left behind.

"You're still rowing." Clio settled on a forward-facing bench. "Since you made us run."

Ranzi exhaled, more of a grunt, and reached for the oars. It was a fair and well-earned punishment, even if she didn't have any spare coin to show for it.

"You left your own money behind too, then?" Clio reminded her. "Since you'd helped build up that pot. So it's not just losing the winnings. You're poorer than you were before we got here."

Ranzi froze, considered the question, and tightened her grip on the oars until they risked splintering. "Bloody hell!"

Clio and Fausta laughed the entire way back to their ship.

The *Banshee* was a full-rigged frigate, a forty-gun ship of the line. Just over fifty meters from bow to stern and fifteen meters at its widest point, it stood stately in the harbor. It towered above the launch as they approached. The sails hung limp and waved gently in the breeze. When the winds were good, those sails could carry this beast all the way across the ocean and back again. When things were still, there were a hundred oars and a hundred sailors to use them. Clio leaned back to appreciate the sheer size and beauty of the ship, *her* ship, the only home she'd ever known. Past the ship, she could tell from the waves riding into the harbor that they'd have plenty of push when they raised anchor.

The crew hauled up the launch and helped the three women onto the deck. Aravanis, the third mate who'd been left in charge, descended from the quarterdeck. She raised her hand to her brow in a salute, spine straight and shoulders square. Clio returned it the way the tall Greek woman had taught her.

"The ship is yours, Captain Landau," Aravanis said in her heavy accent.

"Thank you, bo's'n," Clio said. "Anything to report?"

Aravanis clasped her hands behind her back, shook her head. "Everything was smooth, ma'am." She watched Ranzi stomp off, still muttering under her breath as Fausta trailed behind her with what could only be described as a shit-eating grin. Aravanis' face remained emotionless. "And on your end?"

Clio laughed and clapped the Greek's solid bicep. "You'll most likely hear the whole story by the day's end. I don't want to ruin whatever embellishments Fausta puts on it."

"Understood, ma'am." She saluted again and headed off to resume her other duties.

As far as Clio knew, Aravanis had never served in any sort of actual military. And God knew Clio didn't demand that level of strict severity from her crew. But the formality seemed to make the big woman happy, and Clio had no problem with anyone who tried to put some order in the chaos. So she went along with it, even if she felt silly every time she saluted.

She went below, tugging at the collar of her shirt on the way to her cabin. She supposed she owed Ranzi a debt. If not for the skirmish, right now she would probably be facedown in a puddle of spilled ale. She'd already been half-unconscious when she realized there was a potential calamity brewing at her crew's table. She'd opened one eye and seen the intention in Sam Dodds' face. There was no doubt Ranzi could handle herself in the brawl and come out of the scruff intact, but it would have cost a lot of property damage in the process. And all it took was one lucky blow for her best fighter to be blinded or crippled for life. It was easier to just stop the fight before it began.

But gods, her head was pounding. She untucked her shirt and pulled it over her head without bothering to undo the tie at the collar. She dropped onto her bunk, a too-thin mattress crammed into a nook in the wall. She held her arms out in front of her and examined the scars carved into them. Long slashes along her forearms, as if she had used it to stop the strike of a sword. Smaller wounds that could have been from shrapnel or any number of other sources. Slashes, gouges, a possible bite...

She had other old scars across her body. Three whip lashes on her back across her shoulders. Ghosts of being stabbed, slashed, burnt. There was a gnarled knot on her shoulder that a doctor told her was, without question, from a bullet. He had examined it, then looked at her with concern.

"Who's been shooting at you, Miss?"

"I really wish I knew," she answered him then, and she whispered it again now in the silence.

Every one of her scars was a story told in a language she didn't speak. Most of them had already been present when she regained consciousness in Harriet's arms aboard a ship in distress. Harriet kept her alive during those first chaotic minutes and hours, putting her own body at risk to protect Clio. In the aftermath, lying next to each other in the ship's infirmary, Harriet had reached out into the space between their beds.

"We went through all that," her savior said, *"and I don't even know your name."*

Clio opened her mouth and the word died in her throat. She felt it fade away, just like a dream she was trying to remember. She saw the basic shape of it but then it became mist.

"I don't know it either," she finally admitted.

Harriet pushed herself up on one arm. Blood was trickling out of myriad wounds on her face and throat. "You don't know your own name?"

Clio moved her mouth but didn't speak. "I don't... think I know much of anything."

"Head injury," the doctor said from across the room, where he was tending a patient in much more dire circumstances. *"A little fog is to be expected. It'll clear up."*

It had been thirty years since that day, and the fog was stronger than ever. Clio remembered as much as anyone else from that day forward, but everything leading up to that day, that hour, the second her eyes snapped open in the storm, was lost. An inquiry to the purser revealed her room had been registered under the name of Mrs. Jane Noakes. Dozens of searches in the decades since had turned up no such soul. The information was as useful as if she'd called herself Mrs. An Onymous.

She remembered her fear in the moment, coupled by the tender weight of Harriet's hand on her shoulder. She was nothing. Nobody. There was a panic rising in her chest until that light touch and the gentlest of whispers.

"We'll sort this out. Someone must know you."

And yet, a thorough excavation of her cabin had only yielded clothing, newspapers, a little bit of cash, and a book which was inscribed "To Clio, For Her Long Journeys and Overdue Homecomings."

So she had a true name. It meant nothing to her, and it led her precisely nowhere in her quest to learn her origins, but it was something she could hold tightly to.

Clio stretched out on her bunk, feet flat and knees bent,

resting her hands on her stomach. Thirty years since she woke up. She and Harriet deduced she had lived an equal number before the fog erased everything. A life split in half, sixty years all told. She didn't feel like she was over half a century old. She raised her hands to look at them. Hands that had lived a life, hands that had reached out for others, which had hurt people or wiped away their tears.

She'd given up on trying to find answers about her previous life when Harriet died. It didn't seem to matter after that. Everyone on the ship knew her as Clio Landau, as their captain's wife and right hand. Her past life didn't matter to them any more than their childhoods mattered to her. They only wanted to know if she could keep their ship afloat, their bellies full, and their coffers full of riches.

Clio dropped her hands and closed her eyes. If she got to sleep now, in the comfort of her own bed, she could possibly avoid a hangover and the blinding headache that came with it.

The mysteries of her past were unnecessary. She had a life to live now, a life and a name that she'd built and earned, and she wasn't going to waste it looking backwards.

Chapter Two

The commotion in the main drag told Delfina Pendergast it was time to leave as surely as church bells meant the pious needed to get to church. She extricated herself from the arms of the lovely blonde barmaid who had saved her the cost of renting a room, slipped out of bed, and retrieved her clothes from the pile on the floor. She was cinching her belt when the barmaid, Cadence, realized she was about to be left alone. She propped herself up and let the sheet fall away, her bare chest an enticement to stay.

"It's not like they'd leave without you, is it now?"

Delfina grinned, tilting her head to admire the curves. "I'd hate to tempt them. But if anyone would be worth it… ah, love." She bent down and gave Cadence another kiss that lingered.

When they parted, Cadence let her fingers drift through Delfina's thick black curls. "Take my blouse with you." She winked and raised a shoulder. "Add it to your other trophies."

Delfina stooped, retrieved the shirt, and pressed the material to her nose. She sighed and then slipped her arms into the sleeves. She left her own shirt on the floor next to the bed. If there were going to be trophies, it might as well go both ways.

"I'll remember you always, Cadence."

Cadence dropped back onto the pillows and raised her arms over her head. "You better. Keep me in mind on those quiet nights at sea."

Delfina blew Cadence a kiss and finished buttoning the shirt on her way out the door. She did have a collection of trophies, and she tried to choose women she didn't think would mind that fact. Sometimes she did better than others, but most women in towns like this were happy to lay with a woman instead of a hairy, dirty, rowdy man even if their tastes didn't normally swing that way. If Delfina wanted to grab a keepsake on her way out the door, whatever she took was sure to be less than they'd have risked taking a man home for the night.

She left the building and strolled toward the harbor. The *Banshee* really wouldn't leave without her, but Ranzi would be pissed off if she had to wait for one wayward crewmember to get back aboard. Cadence's shirt was a little too big for her so she tucked the tails tightly into her pants as she walked, the sleeves billowing around her arms.

"Excuse me," someone behind her said. "Are you with the pirates?"

Delfina ignored the question and kept walking. She rolled her sleeves up past her elbows, head down, focused on her destination.

"Excuse me, you. Ma'am? Miss?"

The other woman had caught up with her. Delfina glanced at her from the corner of her eye but didn't slow down, despite the trouble the pest had keeping up. She was a tall drink of water, someone who would have been called black Irish if it weren't for her sea-green eyes. Most of the other color in her face came from the scattering of freckles that spread across her cheeks and down her neck. The strap of a bag crossed her chest, the bag itself banging heavily against her hip as she walked.

"What's someone like you want with pirates? Don't you know they're rough and tumbles?"

"But that ship is different, right? The crew is all women?" The woman raised her eyebrows beseechingly. "At least that's what it looked like. The three what caused the trouble in the bar, they were all women. People 'round town are saying everyone on the whole ship is. Not a beard to be seen."

"Mostly women, that's true. We got a few menfolk, and some who are welcome not to choose either way." Delfina finally stopped and faced the woman fully. "What's your name?"

The woman looked grateful as she caught her breath. "Cariad Baillie."

"Well, Cariad Baillie, don't go asking strangers about pirates. They're a very private folk and don't tend to like people scraping around their hull. Savvy?"

"I have work for them. Potential work. I was working up the courage to say something in the bar after their game, but things got a little noisy 'fore I could. And then they were gone. I thought I saw you with them when you first came ashore. I just want you to take me to the ship so I can talk to the captain myself. If she says no, put me on a rowboat and send me back here. And, in exchange..." She dug in her pockets until she found a bag heavy with coin and possibly jewelry.

Delfina raised an eyebrow at the sight of it. "Where'd you get *that?*"

"Ain't mine. Your friend left it behind, the dark-skinned one with the tricorn hat. It was on the table when she and your other friends made scarce. I gathered it up. She'll probably be wanting it back."

"Ranzi." Delfina chuckled and shook her head. "Yes, I bet she's looking for it."

Cariad raised her eyebrows. "Well? Is that enough to get me a ride to the ship? A conversation with your captain?"

"Aye, come on." She smacked the bag of coin against her palm and slipped it into her pocket. She started walking again and motioned for Cariad to follow her. "I'll take you."

Cariad was forced to trot after her. "You didn't tell me your name."

"Delfina."

"And, um, what's your job on the crew?"

"Physician."

Cariad made a sound of confusion. "Wait, you're a doctor? What's someone respectable like you doing at a place like... Oh no. There's not an outbreak or anything is there?" She gestured over her shoulder at the inn Delfina had just left. "Is someone sick?"

"No, no, no," Delfina laughed. "Let's just say I was brushing up on my anatomy."

Fausta knew from experience the captain would need to sleep off her drunk. Being called into action to save Ranzi's hide had interrupted her body's natural attempt to heal itself, so she would likely be out of commission until dawn or later. That meant she had the whole night to get an idea of what had happened aboard the

Banshee while they were ashore. Her own drunkenness had been soured by the fight, and she was far enough on the side of sober that she could deal with the mundanity of an inventory.

She was pleasantly surprised by what she found. Ammunition stores were fully supplied, decks were swabbed, dinner had been prepared and served up, and there had been no reported incidents of fighting amongst the crew. Fausta was pleased, and she knew that the captain would be as well. Their time on the island might have ended poorly, but this small vacation had been days of well-needed rest and recovery. They'd even managed to restock their pantry enough that the cook, a lovely young Spanish lass named Estacia, had clapped her on the back when she revealed the haul. She was confident they could head back to sea with a healthy and fit crew of sailors.

The watch had called down that a boat was on its way from shore. Fausta slipped her spyglass from her belt as she crossed the deck. She recognized the dark black hair of the sawbones, and there was someone in the boat with her. Intriguing. It wasn't like Delfina to bring one of her conquests aboard. Whatever had prompted the guest was sure to be interesting.

Fausta waited at the gunwale until the boat was hauled up and the doctor came aboard. Once the doctor had her feet firmly on the deck, she held out a hand for the other passenger's bag. The woman handed it over and Delfina hauled it over the railing.

Delfina hooked a thumb over her shoulder to indicate the passenger, who was struggling to find an elegant way to climb over the railing. "That's Cardamom Baker."

"Cariad Baillie," the other woman corrected. "I'm here to see the captain."

Delfina held up a purse. She hooked her finger around the drawstring and let the bag swing, giving Fausta an idea of how full it was. "She paid for her passage with this. Ranzi left it behind after some kind of scuffle, apparently."

Fausta laughed. She took the purse and stuffed it into her pocket. "I'll see that it gets to her. Eventually." She turned her attention to Cariad. "The captain is a very busy lady."

"I'm sure she is. But I also know this ship has sat idle for several days, and that can't be very lucrative. I have potential work for your crew. Long-term. But I'm only supposed to talk details with the captain herself."

Fausta and Delfina looked at each other, and the doctor gave a subtle shrug. "Okay," Fausta said, "come on. I'll take you to her."

"Much obliged," Cariad said with a relieved sigh.

Fausta walked away with the grace of a much more sober woman, avoiding the sailors preparing to set out and sidestepping the piles of ropes and tools that scattered the deck. Cariad watched her go, then turned to see Delfina walking in the opposite direction.

"Where... wh-who..."

"Captain's waiting," Delfina said without turning around.

Cariad quickly grabbed the strap of her bag, slung it over her head, and hurried after Fausta with much less grace. She tripped and muttered apologies to anyone she collided with. Fausta made sure she didn't fall too far behind but also didn't adjust her pace much to accommodate her. When Cariad caught up, Fausta looked the woman up and down.

"So can you tell me who you are, or is that also for the captain's ears only?"

"I'm a journalist."

Fausta bared her teeth and narrowed her eyes. "Don't tell the captain that unless it's absolutely vital, all right?"

They arrived at the cramped, narrow corridor that led to Clio's cabin. Fausta held up a hand indicating Cariad needed to stay at the stairs while she continued on. She rapped her knuckles on the door and waited patiently for a response. After a minute, she knocked again, louder.

"Sorry to disturb you, Captain. But I got a paying passenger here, needs to speak with you. Says it's about a potential job."

There was a pause of nearly a minute. Finally a shadow darkened the four fogged glass panels in the door. Clio swung the door open and peered out, first at Fausta, and then beyond her to where Cariad waited. The captain's white-blonde hair was mussed as ever, and she was wearing a shirt she had clearly just thrown on. Her brows were arched, half anger and half curiosity, but the thin line of her lips could only mean irritation.

"Didn't know we were taking passengers this trip."

Fausta shrugged. "Ask Delfina. Her name is... I don't remember, something Scottish."

"Cariad Baillie."

"Yeah, that. Said she'll only explain her business to you, personal-like."

Clio drummed her fingers against the door once, then nodded. "Okay. Fine, not like we have anywhere else to be. Take her to the map room. I'll be up in a minute."

"Aye."

Clio shut the door again. Fausta turned and motioned Cariad back up the stairs.

"Back the way we came," she said, "take a left and it's the big room at the front of the ship. Can't miss it. Lead the way."

They walked up together, this time with Fausta lagging behind. She checked the woman's clothes for evidence of hidden weapons. The shirt was baggy enough that she might have had something strapped to her arms or torso, but she wouldn't be able to get at them quickly if she did. No holsters, no tell-tale bulges in her pockets. But there was no telling what she had in that bag over her shoulder so Fausta had to remain on her guard. She had no plans to leave this woman alone with the captain unless she was formally dismissed.

The map room lived up to its name. A representation of the Atlantic Ocean took up a large central table, printed on parchment on rollers so it could be cranked to show the Indian Ocean. Smaller maps, atlases, and insets were posted on the walls, the majority of them darkened by pencil marks from previous journeys. It was a cramped room with low ceilings, the exposed beams nearly brushing the top of Cariad's head, but the far wall contained a window that looked out on the sun-dappled waters of their current harbor. Two globes stood on plinths underneath the window.

Fausta leaned against the wall next to the door and crossed her arms. "She shouldn't be too long."

Cariad nodded nervously. She went to the wall and began examining one of the maps at random. Fausta watched her for signs of nervousness, twitches, anxiety, anything that might indicate she had ulterior motives. She did look apprehensive, but she didn't give off assassin vibes.

Clio arrived a few minutes later in a pressed blouse under a vest, clean trousers, and boots that added an inch to her height. Fausta also noted the pistol on her hip and the way her vest shifted due to the weight of a knife in its inner pocket.

Fausta said, "Cariad Baillie, allow me to introduce Clio Landau, captain of the *Banshee*."

"So you'll only speak to me? Here I am." She walked to the other side of the map table so she'd be backlit by the window. "Speak your peace."

Cariad cleared her throat. "There've been rumors going

around for a while now. Whispers, really, about someone looking for a crew. Whoever sent the message is very clear that the offer should only be made direct to captains, no middlemen or messengers. And word is the person doing the hiring is not just a person, it's the leader of country. They're looking for a partnership. And ongoing sort of thing. They have something they need done, like a test run, and if you succeed, they'll put your ship on retainer. In return, you get safe harbor on their shores. Somewhere you can go when the pressure is too heavy."

"What's the test run?"

"There are no details."

"And no one else has taken advantage of this deal?" Fausta asked. "It seems pretty swell."

Cariad said, "A couple of ships have headed out to hear details about the mission, but they always come back empty-handed. I tracked them down, captains and crew both, and I asked them about it. They were pretty tight-lipped but basically whoever they met with deemed them unworthy and sent 'em away. They said the country is looking for a specific sort of crew. Women. They want a woman captain, that much seems pretty much confirmed. I saw you in the bar and was waiting for the right chance to bring it up. And now that I've seen your crew, I'm positive you're going to be accepted."

Clio looked at Fausta and raised an eyebrow. "Thoughts?"

Fausta had a lot of thoughts, but she posed a question to Cariad first. "Which country?"

Cariad opened her bag and took out a slip of paper, offering it to Clio. "It's not a country you'd recognize by name. But these are the coordinates."

Fausta intercepted the note and read the coordinates. She frowned and looked up into the rafters as her mind worked. After a moment she went to one of the maps to double-check her numbers. After a moment she dragged her finger out away from Gibraltar, south along the coast of Africa, then jabbed her finger at a spot northwest of the Canary Islands.

"What's there?" Clio asked.

"Whole lot of water," Fausta said. "Nothing else."

Cariad shook her head. "Something *is* there. The people who have gone and come back used the same information I just gave you. They said the same thing before setting out. Some of them only went to prove there wasn't anything to find. But every single one of them confirmed there's an island, and they all described it the same way. Big, mostly forest, with one obvious settlement. They were forbidden from giving any specific details of the mission to anyone who wasn't willing to offer their services. So I thought if I could find a crew that fit what they were looking for, I could find out for myself."

"It's a trap." Fausta seemed bored already. "And a lazy one, from the sound of it. Lure in ships with the promise of a safe harbor, throw in enough mystery to make it enticing. Then you rob them blind and send them home. People are going to be too humiliated to admit they got tricked, so they make up an oath of secrecy." She shrugged. "I don't see any reason to risk it."

Clio was watching Cariad. "Why did you bring this to us?"

"Well, there aren't a whole lot of ships out there with female captains. You have the best shot of not being sent away."

"Sure, sure," Clio waved her hand dismissively. "You said all that. But what do you get by telling us about it? What are you gaining out of handing over this information to a crew of strangers?"

Cariad shifted uncomfortably and glanced at Fausta before answering. "Passage, and a story. I plan to go there with you. To see it for myself."

Clio grimaced and leaned forward, resting her hands on the map table. "God, you're a *journalist*."

"I don't know what that has to do with anything. If you're worried about me exposing your identities, I can use fake names or–"

"You can make all the promises you want, but you can always change your mind right up until you set ink to paper. I'm not going to ask my crew to sail with someone who might take every word they say and put it in front of every eye in London."

"I would never do that," Cariad said. "You have my w–" She cut herself off, realizing Clio had just told her how much that would mean. She cleared her throat and changed tactics. "A dozen crews have gone after this treasure, Captain Landau. All crews mostly made up of men, and captained by men. Men who would see that a woman and her crew of women had succeeded where they had failed. I'll change your names if you deem it necessary, whatever you ask. But I've been following this story for years without knowing the end. I need to know the end, ma'am."

Clio narrowed her eyes and worked her jaw.

Fausta watched her and could already tell which way she was leaning. "Might be nice to have a place we could go when the seas get rough."

"A place no other ships seem able to find," Clio added thoughtfully. "How long would it take us to reach those coordinates?"

Fausta did the math quickly. "Half a week, if the winds are amenable. We've got enough in the stores to make the trip twice over, and we've nothing else planned that might interfere."

Clio stood up straight and faced down Cariad. She crossed her arms over her chest and waited a beat before she spoke again.

"I guess we might as well go and see if we find anything. I have to admit, you've gotten me more than a little curious myself."

Fausta smiled and pushed away from the wall. "I'll let the crew know we've got a new heading." She looked at Cariad. "And a new passenger."

"Welcome aboard the *Banshee*, Miss Baillie," Clio said. "Hope you're ready to earn your keep."

Cariad was breathless and wide-eyed. "I-I'll pull my weight, you have my word. Just let me know where I can be most useful."

Clio stepped around the table and left the room. Fausta fell into step beside her, and they headed back up to the main deck together.

"Promising?"

Fausta shrugged. "Could be potential. Could be a whole lot of nothing. But if it does turn out to be a trap, I reckon we can handle ourselves well enough."

"Let's not get too cocky, though. Tell Ranzi and Aravanis to prepare like we're sailing into enemy territory. Prepare for the worst and cross our fingers."

"Aye," Fausta said. "You sure you want to bring her along with us? She might just be hoping for excitement."

Clio laughed. "Well, the next week should be greatly disappointing to her, then. Might as well let her see for herself, right?"

Fausta smirked. "As you say, Captain."

They split off in different directions once they reached sunlight. Fausta had hidden her excitement in the map room, and with the captain, but now that she was alone she allowed herself a smile. She'd been certain the next few weeks would be a dull stretch of days and weeks until they found something to get the blood boiling. Now this had dropped into their laps, and she honestly didn't care if it was a boondoggle or a trap. It was true, traveling to the coordinates would be dull and likely dissuade Miss Baillie from ever setting foot on another ship. But once they arrived at their destination, whether trap or treasure, it would certainly be an adventure.

And Fausta was always ready to dive into adventure with both feet.

Chapter Three

SHE WAS on the boat. On the boat, with a promise to go follow the coordinates and find the truth, once and for all. Once Cariad was back on deck, she went to the railing and opened her mouth so she could breathe as deeply as possible. The air off the water was icy cold, jarring, delicious. She wasn't seasick because they weren't yet at sea, and harborsick wasn't a thing. So whatever was swirling in her gut, just below her stomach, had to be nervous excitement about the fact she'd finally succeeded in her goal.

This was her story. She had taken threads of a mystery and weaved them together until they formed a picture. There was something incredible out there in the ocean waiting to be found and she was going to be there when it was revealed.

She would see it. With her own eyes. Whatever or whoever was there, she would see it and she would finally know. And she would tell the world.

Someone farther down the deck started singing. Cariad turned and watched the rest of the crew. As Delfina had promised, they seemed to be mostly of the feminine variety, though she spotted a few men. They were moving like pieces of a machine as they prepared to move out, and a few of them on the far side of the deck had started singing.

One by one, everyone on the deck picked up the song. Some

mumbled the lyrics until they were confident of the verse and then started singing in full voice. The dark-skinned woman who had escorted Cariad to the captain's cabin descended from the quarterdeck and joined in, raising her voice above the others to draw in anybody who wasn't already singing.

> *"...and when daylight's gone*
> *And the night coming on*
> *You rest upon your oar,*
> *And oh boys, you wish that you was dead*
> *Or snug with the girls ashore*
> *Ashore, ashore! Snug with the girls ashore*
> *Oh boys, you wish that you was dead*
> *Or snug with the girls ashore!"*

She had no idea what in the world they were doing, but it was awe-inspiring to see people move like they knew what the woman beside them was about to do. And the ship came alive in response, a beast waking from sleep and called into service. The boards groaned beneath her boots, the sails expanded as if taking a deep breath, and the deck shifted almost imperceptibly under her feet as the ship turned leeward. A small group of men and women pulled on ropes and shouted incomprehensible orders to each other beneath the cadence of the song.

Cariad moved to go belowdecks, unsure of where she was going so long as it was out of the way. She had to keep her hands out to either side, braced against the walls, because now the ship was definitely moving. The queasy feeling in her stomach stirred again and she took a deep breath, let it out slow, ignored the beads of sweat forming on her brow, and continued on until she found herself in a relatively spacious room that seemed to be a public space.

There were tables and benches, and she dropped down at the nearest one. Sitting helped, and so did focusing on the edge of the table. She heard a door swing open.

"I don't serve food while we're getting underway." The new arrival sounded stern but amused. "From the look on your face, I think you already know why."

Cariad sat up straighter and wiped her hands over her face. "I'm fine. It's just nerves."

"Sure, sure." The cook chuckled and retrieved a cup and pot

from the cabinet. Cariad looked over at her and saw she was Spanish and petite, currently dressed in a white shirt under a well-stained apron. She brought it over and sat down across the table. Up close Cariad could see that her eyes were jade green flecked with gold, almost distractingly pretty. "Here, drink this for your 'nerves.' Ginger tea. It'll steel you right up."

"Thank you." Cariad took the cup and sipped it, grateful for the opportunity to end the staring contest.

"You're new," the other woman said, crossing her arms on the table in front of her.

"Mm." Cariad nodded around a mouthful of the tea. The damn woman had dimples, too. She looked around the kitchen to avoid staring again. "My name is Cariad Baillie. I gave the captain, um, there's a job she might be interested in. Benefit the whole ship. She agreed to take me so we could go take a look, see what we see."

"Exciting!" The woman extended her hand across the table. "Estacia Navarro. I'm the cook. If you need anything to eat let me know."

"Right now I'd settle for a place to leave this bag. It's killing my shoulder."

"They didn't assign you a place to sleep?" She clucked her tongue. "Who have you met?"

"I'm not very good with names. Um, I met the doctor, and a woman that I think is the first officer. Delfina and, and, um..."

"Fausta. And I am E-stay-shah." She winked as she enunciated the name. She bumped her foot against the side of Cariad's bag. "Don't worry. Finish your tea and we'll find you a place to stash this. Plenty of space on the ship."

Cariad smiled. "Thank you. It's nice to know at least one person aboard is friendly."

Estacia smiled back, and her eyes shone like gems, almost enough to distract from her dimples. And those apple cheeks... Cariad closed her eyes and ducked her chin. Normally she could control her eyes around even the most beautiful women. She must be particularly vulnerable at the moment, what with all the excitement. And the swaying of the ship. And the tea had really been soothing. Very... very soothing.

"Oopsie," Estacia said as she plucked the cup from Cariad's hand, her limp fingers giving no resistance as they uncurled from its handle. "Easy, easy," Estacia said. Cariad felt hands on her head, guiding it down... No, not guiding it. Just cushioning it so she wouldn't hit it on the table. That was nice of her. She opened her mouth to say so. Her mouth was suddenly so dry. She smacked her lips together and forgot what she was going to say.

When Cariad regained consciousness some time later, alone in the galley, it took her a moment to realize she had been drugged. It was another thirty seconds before her head was clear enough to realize her bag was gone and for her to figure out who had taken it. She half-turned on the bench to look toward the door as if she could still catch the thief making a getaway, but the corridor was dark and empty.

She put a hand over her face and slumped against the table.

"God damned pirates..."

Aravanis brought the bosun's whistle to her lips and blew a long, trilling note that carried across the whole of the ship. They had passed through the Strait and now had clear sailing for a while, long enough for the crew to be informed of their current goals. Once a crowd had gathered between the two flights of stairs leading up to the quarterdeck, Clio stepped forward to address them. Most of the swabbies, powder monkeys, and cabin girls were relatively new and had known her as captain. But others... those who had been with the *Banshee* set sail... even after seven years, she wondered if they looked at her and saw the shadow of another captain over her.

Harriet's shadow.

She spotted Fausta and Ranzi near the mast. Estacia made her way over to them with a large duffel bag, which she handed to Fausta. The cook leaned over to whisper something in Fausta's ear, and Fausta laughed, nodded, and took the bag. She set it at her feet and turned her face back toward Clio, awaiting to hear what she had to say despite the fact she already knew what would be said. Delfina was at the gunwale, back to the ocean with her elbows resting on the railing. She winked one startling blue eye at Clio, forcing the captain to look quickly away.

"I wish I could tell you more about our current heading," she said, raising her voice to be heard above the sails and the waves. "The truth is, I don't know much about it myself. We're responding to an offer. It's an offer that promises steady employment and a safe harbor. I cannot support that promise, as there is every chance it's a trap. But those who have followed this rumor in the past returned to tell the tale, and I am confident we have nothing to fear. I want to ask every sailor aboard to be prepared for either eventuality. We may be forced to fight. We may be boarded. Don't let your guards down. Don't be blinded by what we're greeted by when we arrive. Any questions?"

The crew murmured amongst themselves, but no one voiced concerns.

"What ship this be?" she said, raising her voice slightly.

"*Banshee!*"

She slapped her hands on the rail in front of her. "Then let me hear your siren call!"

Every head on the deck below leaned back and let out a battle cry, a long howl that varied in pitch and volume until it rivaled the sound of the sea. To any ships nearby it would sound as if the ship itself was a beast come to life and roaring into battle. She saw Fausta, Delfina, and Ranzi joining the cry, despite the fact their position as officers didn't require it. She nodded her gratefulness to them, then looked at the muscular woman standing silently at her side.

"Uninspired?" she asked in Greek.

Aravanis allowed herself the smallest of smiles and responded in the same language. "Quite inspired, ma'am. But someone must maintain decorum."

Clio smiled and smacked her palm against Aravanis' back. "Let's hope that excitement carries us all the way to whatever awaits us at the end of this journey. Keep her true, 'Vanis."

"Aye, captain."

Clio looked down at the deck again, at the crew scattering back to their stations, to Fausta leading Ranzi below with the mysterious overstuffed bag. She had no doubts this crew could handle whatever was waiting for them out in the middle of nowhere.

But now, even after every trial they'd faced together, she could only hope they had the same confidence in her.

Fausta and Ranzi were quick to examine the clothing, which made up the bulk of Cariad's bag, but carefully thumbed through everything else. They were in Ranzi's cabin, a space that reminded Fausta of a prison cell with slightly fancier decorations. A bed along one wall, a basin for water so she could clean up, and a shelf above the bed for weapons and books. There was more of one than the other; Ranzi wasn't much of a reader.

Ranzi was cross-legged on her bed with the bag open in front of her. Fausta had dragged a stool into the room and squatted on it as she catalogued everything their new passenger had brought with her. Four books, only one of which had a pre-printed story in it. The others were filled with notes and drawings. Pages torn out of other books had been folded and stowed between the covers of these, but there were no clues to their significance that Fausta could see. The fourth book was an official journal which detailed Cariad's many attempts to find a ship to take her to the mysterious coordinates mentioned in the offer.

"She was really determined to get to that place," Fausta said, "whatever it ends up being."

"Hope it's worth it for her in the end." Ranzi held up a small cloth bag and shook it next to her ear, grimacing at the meager clinking within. "It's no wonder she didn't try buying passage on a ship. There's not even enough coin here to make it worth stealing."

Fausta smirked. "Are you sure you're not just feeling generous since she returned your loot from the card game?"

"Might could be. Good deeds being their own reward and all that. Besides, it's bad luck to rob a person the same day they return your riches."

"So tomorrow...?" She found a bottle in the bag, uncorked it, sniffed the contents. She took a swig and licked her lips. She set it aside to finish later.

"We'll see."

Fausta snatched the coin purse away from Ranzi before she could change her mind and tossed it back into Cariad's bag. The bottle of liquor notwithstanding, theft wasn't their goal. They were only looking for evidence to either support or damn Cariad's story. If there was an ulterior motive behind her request, or if there'd been information she held back, she hadn't kept any written record of it in her personal belongings. It was either very smart of her, or there was just nothing to hide.

"Alcohol aside, I think we can agree there's nothing here worth stealing."

Ranzi lifted one shirt and curled her lip in disgust, letting it fall back into the bag. "Without question."

"And there's nothing to indicate she's lying about her intentions. So I think it's safe to take her at her word for the time being." Fausta repacked everything into the bag and cinched the top shut again. "I'll see that it gets back to her."

Ranzi relaxed against the wall, stretching her legs out in front of her. "Does the captain really think there's something worth finding at the end of this trip?"

Fausta stopped and leaned against the doorway. "I'm sure she has no idea one way or the other. But the way she sees it, if nothing's there, we wasted a week there and another back. Slightly irritating but easily forgotten. But if there *is* something to be found, and someone else gets there first? That's a regret you don't get over easy."

Ranzi raised an eyebrow and nodded her understanding.

Fausta put the bag's strap over her shoulder and went in search of Cariad. It was dusk, and they were far enough into their journey that only open ocean stretched out to either side of the ship. The sun seemed to be balanced on the horizon, just waiting for that last gust of wind to topple it over the side. Fausta took a moment to appreciate the never-boring sight before she resumed her search for Cariad.

She didn't have to look long; the little Irishwoman had become a wraith, standing on the deck and baring her teeth as she snapped at a sailor whose name Fausta didn't remember right off. She was so caught up in her rage that she didn't see Fausta approach, didn't see her wave the sailor away. He nodded his thanks for the rescue before he fled off toward the stern.

"Hey! Get back here! I'm not done with you!"

Fausta gripped the bag's strap and held it out between them. "Looking for this, Miss Baillie?"

Cariad spun on her, looked at the bag, then focused her fury on Fausta. "Your cook *drugged* me and *stole* my bag!"

"We had to be sure you weren't a threat. You could've been smuggling anything at all in a bag that big. We were just being cautious."

Cariad snatched the bag from her. "You went through my things?"

"It's nothing I haven't seen before."

"I want that cook punished." She was holding the bag against her chest like it was a baby. "She drugged me, knocked me out."

Fausta shook her head. "No."

"That's it? Just no?"

"Do you see this situation as one where I have to explain *any* ship decisions to you? You're not a client. Even if you were, no one on this ship answers to you. That man you were yelling at a minute ago? He outranks you. Estacia did what she did to protect the crew, and I hope she'd do it again the next time we have a petulant child onboard. We don't know you, Miss Baillie. We're sailing off into the middle of nowhere on your say-so. This information could be sent by another crew to lure us into a trap, or pirate hunters, or any number of authorities who would be glad to see one more ship of corsairs and buccaneers taken off the sea. You'll forgive us for being cautious."

Cariad worked her jaw, her eyes hard and cold. "So long as it doesn't happen again..."

Fausta shrugged. "I don't see any reason to knock you out again. Your bag wasn't very interesting. But if we have any other questions, I'll politely suggest just having a conversation with you instead of going through your things. Will that work?"

"I... I-I suppose..."

"Good. Did you ever get assigned somewhere to bunk?"

Cariad shook her head, and Fausta started walking, waving for her to follow.

"Come on. We'll find you a good one."

"What, um..." Cariad tripped over something but found her footing again. "What counts as a 'good' cabin on a ship?"

Fausta held up a finger. "First off, you're not getting a cabin. You're getting a bunk. It will have a bed. You won't be able to see the people sleeping around you. That is what counts as a good one. I won't hold my breath waiting for a thank you. Just promise me you won't scream at any of the crew when you find out just how crummy the accommodations on this boat are."

"I'll try to keep my expectations at bay. After all, it's just a couple of days. How bad could it be?"

Fausta grinned knowingly over her shoulder and led her down into the darkness below.

HARRIET LANDAU

"You were a drowned, lost doll being washed toward the sea when I found you. You would have looked peaceful without the blood on your face. I don't know what possessed me to catch you, to anchor your limp body with mine. I saw you from a distance when we boarded, but we'd never spoken. So why did I risk my own safety to secure yours? Did I sense who you would become? How precious you would be in my life, or how many things you had yet to do?

Or did I simply find you beautiful and know what a waste it would be losing you to the Atlantic?

Whatever my intentions, I was grateful for the decision every day thereafter. First you became invaluable to me, with your keen navigational eye and intuitive fighting skills. You were strong and clever. You knew how to handle a sword and pistol, occasionally at the same time. I watched you in moments you thought you were alone, staring out over the water, trying to find those lost parts of your life. I was desperate to unlock those secrets for you. I asked at every port, sent messages to everyone I could think of, but it seemed as if somehow you'd managed to pass through this world without making a mark.

Sometimes I think that is the most unbelievable thing about you, Clio.

But time passed. Your guard lowered. I saw you smile, heard you laugh. I fell in love with the way your eyes sparkled in lantern light. The chasm of your past and all those missing years still haunted you, but I saw when you began focusing on your current days rather than always looking backward. You chose to become a new person, to forge your identity. I taught you everything I knew.

On the anniversary of your first memory, I asked the cook to make you a cake. Your first birthday. One candle, one wish. You asked for a life worth remembering.

I kissed you then, the first time our lips had touched, and your fingers curled at the nape of my neck. We both knew the kiss was the start of something new, even if neither of us were sure exactly what it was. That was the moment, my love, that I swore to share the rest of my life with you, to dedicate all my energy to ensuring you never lost another precious second.

I intend to keep that vow, Clio. You have my word.

I shall remain by your side until the day I die."

Chapter Four

She was still on the fucking boat.

Cariad woke with that realization and rolled onto her side, drew her knees up toward her chest, and wrapped the paper-thin pillow around her head. It was a futile attempt to block out reality. The sounds of shouting broke through the pillow's pathetic barrier, and the way the ship leaned and swayed kept its grip on her stomach so there was no chance of forgetting where she was. At least with sleep she could disappear into memories and fantasy worlds. Being awake meant being imprisoned in this hell.

To entice herself to get out of the bunk, she reminded herself that it wasn't all bad. After dinner on her second night aboard, a group of pirates gathered together under the quarterdeck to play music. Those who weren't immediately involved with keeping the boat on track gathered around and joined their voices in song.

On her first full day aboard the ship, she'd never strayed from the bunk she'd been told was hers. She watched the crew wake and go about their business. When dinnertime arrived, though she was starving, she refused to return to the galley.

Her boycott was proven useless when the cook appeared at her bunk with a bowl of the most delicious-smelling stew Cariad had ever been offered.

"A peace offering," Estacia said, sensing Cariad's wariness. "We have to look out for each other, you know. When you finish, I'll take you up on deck. You can be my guest for the festivities."

Cariad's fingers brushed Estacia's as she took the bowl from her but she ignored it. She refused to allow this woman to distract her again, no matter how gorgeous her eyes were. Oh. And the dimples...

"Is it required to be someone's guest?" she asked to change the subject.

"No," Estacia admitted. "But it gives you someone to sit next to." She winked and turned away. "Come find me when you finish eating."

Cariad watched her go and then climbed onto her bunk, devouring the first meal she'd had since they left the harbor.

She had indeed joined Estacia at the festivities. Lanterns had been hung from the yardarms and cast orange light down on a group of sailors who had formed a circle around a man playing the fiddle. Everyone clapped along to the beat, stamping their feet, some of them singing and some laughing. When the fiddle player finished, someone took her place and led the group in a round. Cariad remained silent until Estacia nudged her, prompted her with the right lyrics, and raised her own voice to encourage her.

Liquor flowed freely, which may have helped Cariad enjoy herself. She thought the pirates were remarkably good singers but she had to admit she wasn't a sober judge. Good or bad, the whole night had been a joyous occasion.

She took the opportunity to surveil the people she would be trapped with for the next few weeks. Delfina was there with her hair down, joining in the festivities but not the alcohol. Cariad was grateful to see their surgeon wasn't also a drunkard. But she sang as loud as anyone else, she grabbed hands and danced with anyone who offered to be her partner.

The tall, quiet woman Aravanis was at the helm, but Cariad could've sworn she'd even seen her moving her head to the music a few times. Estacia had casually mentioned that Aravanis hadn't been off the ship since she'd known the woman. It seemed impossible for Cariad to believe, but she'd heard and seen so many stranger things where the sea was concerned. Nothing would surprise her now.

Fausta and Ranzi were standing together near the gunwale passing a bottle back and forth. Fausta seemed to do most of the talking, but Ranzi was an energetic audience for whatever the story was. Cariad found the women extremely similar. They were strong, took no guff, and both seemed eager for a fight. It made sense they would be thick as thieves to the exception of everyone else on the crew. If they hadn't been from such different parts of the world, she would have thought they were sisters.

Maybe that was the point of this ship. Bringing together people who should never have crossed paths and forcing them to interact, to get friendly, to know each other. Ranzi and Fausta might have killed each other if they met in a barroom. Maybe it was the lawlessness of the profession. Maybe it was the fact they'd been through hell and back together, faced death together.

Or maybe it was just a side effect of the crew Captain Landau had brought together. Singing, dancing, laughing, drinking. Cariad hadn't felt this relaxed in ages, maybe in her entire life, and she was amazed to discover that feeling on a ship of criminals.

The night came to an end when the musicians and audience had both started falling over in drunken stupors, and Estacia offered to walk Cariad back to her bunk.

"They find somewhere nice for you?"

"That bunk where you brought me dinner."

"Oh! That was a bed?"

"It's better than the alternatives I've seen."

She knew that a great many of the crew slept in a single room on cots or hammocks that were so close that occasionally the sleepers would touch or roll over onto each other. Limbs drifted from one bedroll to another, pillows were accidentally snatched from underneath a neighbor's head. Once she saw the alternative, her tiny and cramped bunk seemed like a godsend.

Estacia examined the small space when they arrived back there. She tilted her head and nodded with something Cariad couldn't quite identify. Not approval, but something close to it. She leaned against the wall and pushed her hair out of her face, letting her hand drift down to rest on her shoulder.

"The officers get much nicer digs."

Cariad chuckled. "Well, something to aspire to, I suppose. But I don't intend to be aboard long enough to get a promotion."

"Well, sure." Estacia dragged both words out, letting them soak in her accent. She rolled her head to the side and teased the collar of her shirt with her fingers. The material sagged open just enough to hint at her cleavage. "There are other ways to get into an officer's bunk."

Cariad couldn't help but look at the flat expanse of Estacia's chest, the beads of sweat on the skin, rolling down toward the swells, and the way hairs stuck to the column of her throat...

"With y~" She cleared her throat and shook her head. She'd only had one drink, but her head felt swimmy. She didn't think she could blame Estacia for it this time. Or at least, not something she'd slipped into her drink. "I don't know what you mean."

"No?" Estacia raised an eyebrow and smiled. "You don't know what I mean? No? She chuckled and pushed away from the wall. "You sure?"

Cariad looked down at her boots. "I don't suppose th-there are male officers on the ship who might be willing to make the same offer."

"Not on this ship, not now, no," Estacia said. Why did her damn voice have to sound like singing? "The men who make officers tend to be rough. But I don't think you like rough, Miss Baillie. I think you like... gentle." She made the last word a whisper, and her fingers brushed Cariad's knuckles, which made her jump.

"I like the men," she blurted.

"Okay." Estacia backed up a step. Her whole demeanor had changed, like a candle had been snuffed. "Okay. Just thought I'd let you know the offer is on the table. Good night, Miss Baillie."

"Goodnight."

Estacia leaned in and kissed Cariad's cheek. Cariad didn't dare move, didn't look back to make sure the cook had really left. She just waited, stock still, eyes closed and breath held. When she finally felt confident she was gone, Cariad scurried into her bunk and pulled the blanket up over her head.

And now here she was, this bleak and bright morning, this start of another tedious day at sea. She didn't know how she was going to bear it. Her queasiness had never developed into a full-out seasickness, for which she was grateful, but it also hadn't gone away. The one meal Estacia brought her had been the only food she'd managed to finish. In a way she was grateful. The kitchen was where Estacia was. It was a minefield Cariad would rather avoid if at all possible.

She finally left her bunk, put on the same dirty clothes she'd worn the day before, and headed up. The sun was a needle to her eyes and she raised a hand as a shield until they adjusted. She almost bumped into a large shadowy shape and muttered an apology as she stepped to one side to let it pass.

"Dangerous place for you to be if your eyes are closed."

Cariad cracked an eye to confirm she recognized the voice. It was the poker player, Ranzi, who Cariad recently learned also served as the ship's gunner.

"I heard some pirates wear an eyepatch to prevent this sort of thing."

"Might be true," Ranzi admitted. "I heard you were responsible for getting my coin back to me. Haven't had a chance to thank you for that."

Cariad shrugged. "I had ulterior motives. It got me on the ship."

"Motives don't matter in my book, honestly. You had a choice and made the one that benefitted me. So I appreciate it. Let me know if you need anything."

"Okay." Her vision had cleared enough that she noticed something over Ranzi's shoulder. "You could tell me that isn't anything to be worried about."

Ranzi turned to starboard. The entire shoreline was gone, obscured by a mountain range of storm clouds. The air underneath was a hazy gray of falling rain and the occasional flicker of lightning. It was still too far away for them to hear thunder, but Cariad couldn't gauge distance over water. Ranzi didn't seem overly concerned by the sight.

"How do you know the storm isn't coming this way?"

"It might be. Common's got an eye out."

"Who?"

"Teresa Common." She tilted her head back to look straight up, then pointed. Cariad followed her finger and saw an oblong basket attached to one of the masts. "We call her Tis. Tis Common." She grinned at her joke, shrugged when Cariad remained stone-faced. "You definitely haven't met her yet. She's our navigator and lookout. If she's not holed away in the map room, she's up there acting as lookout. She's definitely been watching that storm since it started brewing up. Right now she's probably calculating things like wind speed, watching to see where it's going and how fast, and if we've got a chance of outrunning it 'fore it gets here. If it *is* coming here, of course. Sharp eye and quick wits. She'll let us know if we need to be worried. The good thing is, storms like that push wind out in front of them. So if we have to run, it'll help us move fast."

Cariad swallowed the worry in her throat. "I suppose that is a good thing."

Ranzi nodded and continued to whatever task she'd been pursuing when Cariad ran into her. Cariad continued as well, even though she didn't have a destination or purpose in mind. She was hoping to run into the captain, even though there was no chance of an update yet. What could she say other than 'still sailing, we'll be there when we get there'? They seemed to be making good time, as far as she could tell. Not that she was any kind of expert. Maybe they were lagging~

"Storm!"

Cariad jumped at the voice and looked up. A woman she assumed to be Common was climbing out of the box Ranzi had pointed out. Her long legs and arms seemed to flail and grab at handholds on the mast without looking, but Cariad knew she was seeing the ease of long practice at work. The lookout skittered down the mast like a monkey, her hands and feet barely resting upon each rung before she was stretching for the next one.

Then she was on the deck and Cariad didn't even have time to register the lookout's clothes or features before she was darting toward the captain's cabin.

"Storm!" Common shouted again, and now a crowd was gathering. "Storm to starboard!"

Clio came up from below with her spyglass already in hand, raising it to her eye when she saw where Common was pointing. She examined the leading edge of the front and pressed her lips together in a tight line.

"How long do we have before it hits us?" the captain asked.

"Hour, more or less," Common reported. "Depending on if it keeps steady."

The towering Greek woman had appeared at Clio's shoulder. "It will grow stronger before it gets here. Gain speed over the water."

Ranzi also joined the growing crowd. "La Llama is just east of us." The captain closed her eyes and she turned her face toward the sky as if imploring Heaven for help. Ranzi shrugged. "It's the closest safe harbor, unless you think we have a half-chance of outrunning that monster."

Clio opened her eyes and screwed her lips into a crooked line. To Common, she said, "How steady has she been rolling?"

"Steady and sure, ma'am. Looks like she's chasing us down, almost. Like we're trailing it."

Clio took a deep breath, then rolled her eyes and smacked the spyglass into Ranzi's hand. "How long do I have to make a decision?"

Common chewed her bottom lip and looked toward the sea, wincing almost as if it pained her to give an answer. Finally she shrugged.

"Quicker is better than slow."

"Understood." Clio turned and retreated again.

Ranzi saw Cariad watching. She hurried over, wrapped an arm around her shoulder, and guided her back toward the door that led to her bunk.

"You're not going to want to be up here while we're going pell-mell. You definitely don't want to be here if that storm gets here before we're safe in the harbor."

"Wait, are you saying this ship can't manage a storm?"

"Of course it can," Ranzi said. "But a storm like that? It'll clobber you, tear your sails, make you blind. Turn you around a half dozen times. Better to just wait it out if you can." She gave a sigh of disgust. "I just wish it was anywhere else but La Llama."

"What is that?"

"Lots of things. It's an island named after fire. And a llama is also a desert animal known for spitting on people. But first and foremost, relevant to your interests and the concerns of every damned fool on this ship, it's the kingdom of a lady that Captain Landau would rather not see again."

"Why not?"

Ranzi shoved Cariad onto the stairs and answered just before she closed the door behind her.

"Because Captain Landau got her daughter killed."

Clio could see the storm from her cabin windows. She told herself not to look, but her eye was drawn to the glass every few seconds. They were making good speed, but she could see the waters churning at the storm's leading edge. The thunder rumbled and carried across the water now, a quiet roar promising it would get to her soon enough. It was just a matter of time.

She knew it wasn't the same storm that had cost her half her life. In her heart she knew that, in her mind as well. But her soul didn't know the difference. It wore the same face and had the same voice, and suddenly she was back there. Cold and alone and afraid. Why couldn't storms invoke Harriet, the strong arms of a willful stranger who was determined to keep her alive? Why did she only remember the terror of that moment? Why was her brain such a stubborn fucking bastard?

And of all the potential safe harbors, they just had to be closest to La Llama? The fiefdom of Aldoncia Reyes, the one person in the world she would have been thrilled to never lay eyes on again. Reyes most likely felt the same way. It didn't matter that Clio blamed herself for what happened, that she carried the guilt with her every hour of the day, or that Aldoncia's daughter was as permanent a fixture in Clio's dreams as Harriet. Aldoncia believed only a death could repay the debt, and Clio wasn't about to just lay her head on the chopping block for anyone.

"Save me from memories of storms and angry women," she muttered with a grimace.

Her decision made, she slapped the top of her desk and went to the door, swinging it open to find Aravanis waiting in the corridor.

"Change course," she ordered. "We're taking refuge on Llama."

"Aye," Aravanis said.

She pivoted and marched back outside, and Clio followed her. She shouted to a group of crewmen nearby and they jumped to work.

Clio walked to the gunwale and looked at the storm behind, close enough now that she felt the first icy droplets of rain on her cheeks. Ahead, a harbor that was safe in name only, ruled over by a woman who would happily see Clio swing from the neck until dead.

"For on the rocks it bore where Scylla raves," she quoted under her breath, "and dire Charybdis rolls her thundering waves..."

Chapter Five

Though Captain Landau commanded every other inch of the ship and her word was gospel to the crew, there was one compartment where even she had to answer to someone. The sick bay, a narrow stretch with a gunpowder store room on one side and the scullery on the other, was Delfina's domain. She ruled supreme there and held enough power to detain any officers she considered unfit for duty. She kept the room as sterile as humanly possible, given the conditions of being aboard a ship, and she made sure every crewmember knew better than to question her decisions.

Her four beds were currently empty, their clean white sheets pulled tight over the mattresses, and she was busy doing an inventory of her medicine cabinet when someone rapped on the door. She turned to see Ranzi leaning in.

"Just wanted to give you fair warning, Doctor. Storm's coming up fast on starboard. We're heading somewhere to wait it out, but it might catch up to us before we get there."

Delfina was already calculating the kinds of injuries she could expect. Scrapes, bruises, broken and dislocated bones... She turned back to the cabinet to begin gathering the items most likely to be required. She picked up a pair of tweezers for splinters and held them, her brain catching up with reality. The length of time they'd been sailing, and the direction...

She looked back to Ranzi. "This place we're going to wait out the storm..."

"La Llama," Ranzi said with the smile of a demon.

Delfina closed her eyes and muttered a string of her favorite curses in Italian. She began collecting other medicines, other instruments, tools she would need to dig out bullets or stitch closed a knife wound.

"I don't suppose she plans to stay on the ship."

"She doesn't want to look like she's hiding," Ranzi said. "She thinks it's better if she goes ashore and meets Aldoncia face to face. Respectful-like."

"She's going to respectfully get her throat slit," Delfina said.

Ranzi snickered and bobbed her head, then shrugged. "Damned if she do, damned if she don't. I guess she doesn't want anyone claiming she acted cowardly."

"Fair enough. But I'll be sure to remind her the cost of saving face the next time I need my supplies refreshed. We're low enough as it is."

"Anything you need immediate?" Ranzi asked, coming into the infirmary and tilting her head to look into the medicine cabinet. "If we're going to La Llama anyway, we might see if they have any pharmacies or doctors we can trade with."

"Nothing dire, so don't go out of your way. But if you happen to see anything..."

"I'll keep you in mind, Doctor."

Delfina sighed heavily and looked for anything she needed to do in order to make the room ready for an influx of patients. Just because Captain Landau and Aldoncia were going to be sharing space didn't mean there would be casualties. Maybe they would just snarl and pace around each other from a distance and decide that a stalemate was the best course of action for everybody given the storm. Stranger things had happened.

She still wanted the infirmary to be ready. Just in case.

Some wounds didn't heal. And Delfina had seen enough loss and suffering to know losing a child was a cut very few people even wanted to heal.

Aldoncia's daughter Dulcinea had been a crew member on the *Banshee* back when they sailed under the first Captain Landau. Delfina allowed herself a moment of quiet reflection at the thought of Harriet. Speaking of wounds that didn't heal... She swiped a hand under her nose, sniffed, and went back to her inventory, focusing instead on thoughts of Dulcinea. Young, trusting, and as excited about the sea as Delfina herself had been when she first came aboard.

She looked down at the tweezers in her hand, twisting them so the metal caught the light. The first time she'd used these had been on Harriet...

"It'll be all right," Delfina said, trying not to let laughter color her voice. "It will only hurt for a second."

"It doesn't hurt," Harriet said indignantly, though the set of her jaw and the fact she'd come to the infirmary in the first place proved it was a lie. "I'm just embarrassed. How can I expect anyone on this bloody ship to respect me if I'm laid out by a splinter in my hand?"

"Splinter?" Delfina said, faking shock. "This is no splinter, my friend. This is a plank of wood, half a tree, this is a significant slab of lumber." She looked knowingly at Harriet as she flipped down the magnifying glass from the strap she wore around her head, leaning in so she could get a better visual of the offending foreign object.

Harriet chuckled. "So we can keep this between us?"

"Aye, no reason to go spreading your business around. Just a little..."

Harriet tensed, then hissed as the splinter was removed.

"There we are."

Delfina dropped the splinter into a metal tin, flipped up the glass, and retrieved the ointment to prevent infection. There was only a little dab of blood, since the splinter had only barely broken the surface of the skin, but it was better to be safe than sorry. Then she applied a bandage and, only because she remembered her mother doing it to her when she was young, she brought Harriet's hand to her mouth and kissed the palm.

"All better," she muttered. She looked up to see Harriet was staring at her with the strangest look. She laughed nervously. "I'm sorry, that was something–"

Harriet cupped the back of Delfina's head with her uninjured hand, pulling her in as she leaned forward. Their lips met in a kiss, passionate for Harriet but stiff and awkward for the doctor. Delfina's heart stopped, her eyes wide open and lips tightly shut. She could almost hear her brain asking if she wanted to retreat, but the last thing she wanted was for this to end. So she parted her lips, she closed her eyes, and she returned the kiss. She kept her arms out to either side, but she shifted her weight to the balls of her feet, leaning awkwardly forward, pressing her mouth hard against Harriet's.

This was an option? All those boys her mother had paraded through the house, all those fumbling and sweaty young men who didn't seem to understand how their bodies worked, let alone someone else's body, when the entire time, she could have been doing this?

Harriet started to pull away. Delfina made an unnamable noise in her throat and quickly brought her hands forward, grabbing Harriet's head, keeping her in place for just another second, just a little bit longer. But after a second she had to breathe, she needed to remove herself from the situation to process what she'd just done, and she released Harriet's head. She took a step backward and spun away, putting the back of her hand against her mouth. She heard Harriet shifting on the bed behind her.

"I'd ask if that was all right," Harriet said, "but I think I got your answer."

"I've never done anything like that before." Harriet's cheeks were burning, and she could only look at the floor.

Harriet said, "It can just be a kiss."

"I'll take that into consideration." Delfina's heart skipped again. She turned and looked at Harriet. "But what if it was more?"

And it was more, after that. So much more. She went to Harriet's cabin that night, their first night together, and she learned what she liked and how to ask for what she wanted. Harriet was gentle with her, and patient, and Delfina went to sleep that night certain she'd not only found her calling in life. She'd found her person.

And now here she was, nigh on twenty years later, serving under the late Captain Harriet Landau's wife.

She held no ill feelings toward Clio. She hadn't stolen Harriet away, there'd been no affair or contest for affection. Harriet let things carry on for about a year and a half before she very kindly sat Delfina down and told her there was no way they could continue on as a couple. Delfina's feelings were stronger, and more intense than Harriet's. The captain had been looking for some fun. Delfina had confused it with love.

It took time, but eventually Delfina understood. She was still very young. Harriet was the first woman she'd ever even kissed, let alone gone to bed with. When she got over feeling sad and rejected, she realized there were islands and port towns and ships full of other women she had yet to experience. There was a whole world out there waiting for her to figure out exactly what and who she liked.

What she discovered was that she didn't want to settle down. She didn't want to make one choice and be stuck with it forever. Around a year or two after Harriet and Delfina stopped spending their nights together, Harriet returned from a mission with a washed-up rat of a woman who didn't know who she was or where she came from. Harriet took the amnesiac under her wing, and Delfina saw what was happening long before either of them did.

She was sad when Clio started using the last name "Landau," but not because of a broken heart. It was only because the idea of Harriet being tied to a single person for the rest of her life seemed tragic at the time. Eventually she got to know Clio, and she got to see the two of them together and understand how perfectly they fit, and she knew they'd made the right decision.

And when the end of Harriet's life did come, Delfina was happy she'd spent so long with someone she adored and who adored her in return. It made her rethink her own ideas about romantic entanglements and spending her life with somebody. It might actually be nice to have someone...

She jumped when someone knocked on the infirmary's doorframe. How long had she been standing there staring at the tweezers like some sort of entranced fool? She turned to see Fausta in the corridor.

"Ranzi tell you where we're heading?"

"La Llama," Delfina said, nodding. "Aldoncia. And something about a storm."

"It's coming up faster than Common predicted, so we're bracing for that to catch up with us before we reach the island."

Delfina sighed and shrugged. "Well, I didn't sign up to be bored."

Fausta laughed and slapped her hand against the door again. "Try to keep stable, sawbones."

"I always do," Delfina said.

The island was in sight when the storm finally overtook them. A gale swept across the deck as if trying to wipe it clean for the wall of rain following right behind it. Fausta had just returned topside and almost got thrown off her feet, but she found a rope and gripped it tight in her left fist. She planted her feet shoulder-width apart and scanning the deck for anyone who didn't absolutely have to be present. She grabbed a crewman and half-threw him toward the hold. He might get bruised, but it was a far sight better than what he'd suffer if he was washed overboard.

Aravanis stood on the quarterdeck like she was carved from the same wood as the deck below her, the wheel gripped tightly in her hands, knees bending and arms stretching as if the ship was just an extension of her body. Ranzi was shouting for the deckhands to stow the sails. Fausta didn't know why it hadn't been done before, but then she figured Clio and Aravanis had weighed the risk of keeping them up with the chance it would help them outrun the weather.

Fausta kept her head down as the rain lashed against her back, her clothes weighing her down as she climbed to the quarterdeck to stand next to Aravanis. The muscular woman's eyes were squinted shut and water dripped off her lashes, pouring over her carved features, but she otherwise seemed unconcerned by the weather.

"On the bright side," Fausta hollered over the wind, "now we don't have to go to the island!"

Aravanis shook her head once and leaned her massive frame toward Fausta. "Just the first wave! Common saw more stacked up behind!"

The blood drained from Fausta's face. "We're not going to try to reach the island *during a storm* are we? That's suicide! We'll be blown aground!"

Aravanis shrugged, straightened, and focused on steering again. Fausta searched the deck and then slapped Aravanis on the shoulder before she went below to find the captain.

Clio was in her cabin, hunched and dripping over a map spread out on her desk. "Going toward land is suicide," she said without preamble. "Winds like these will dash us to pieces if we're even lucky enough to get that close. We need to drop anchor..."

"Common said this first wave won't last long. It's narrow and moving fast. That's one reason it caught us so off guard. We'll ride it out and then we'll have plenty of time to reach the harbor before the full brunt of the storm. But we have to gain as much distance as possible while we can. Otherwise we run the risk of being caught. This is the best course of action, even if it seems a bit crazy in practice."

Fausta came deeper into the room and took note of Clio's hands, the way her fingers drummed against the desk, and the paleness of her cheeks. Her skin was nearly the same color as her hair, blurring the lines between the two. Her eyes were wide, darting across the map in a way that revealed she wasn't actually looking at anything. In that moment, Fausta knew the captain wouldn't have given the order to ride through a storm like this if she thought there was any other option.

"What do you need?" she asked gently.

Clio looked up at her, noticing the change in her tone. She swallowed the lump in her throat and looked down at the map again.

"Eyes and ears," Clio said, then gestured at the door. "Out there. Until this is... until it's... quiet."

Fausta nodded. "Any orders I should pass along?"

Clio shook her head. "You'll be acting in my stead. I defer to your judgment."

"Aye, captain."

She turned and went back out into the gale, pausing to take Clio's tricorn in the hopes it would provide some protection. She mashed it down onto her head and held it in place as she returned to the quarterdeck.

The wind caught her clothes and pulled at them, threatening to kite her up into the rigging and then out to be dashed on the waves. She clapped her free hand on Aravanis' shoulder, the other still holding her borrowed hat in place, and planted her feet against the deck, trying to emulate the Greek's posture.

"We'll get through this!" Aravanis shouted over her shoulder. The damn statue actually sounded calm despite the raised volume of her voice.

Fausta nodded and ducked her head as another sheet of rain hit her like a solid sheet of water. Thunder rumbled above. The deck seemed to rise, forcing her knees to bend, and she was grateful for the anchor of Aravanis to keep her steady. Crewmen on the deck weren't as fortunate, and she saw their feet leave the ground as they went airborne. They were only saved by their grip on the ropes, cables, or chains they were within reach of as the *Banshee* crested another wave.

"Ship's strong," Aravanis shouted again.

Fausta pressed her lips together and wished she knew if the bosun was reassuring her or trying to convince herself.

Either way, they were now in the thick of the storm. The only way out was through. Fausta set her eyes on the wall of water ahead and trusted in the captain's plan and in their ship.

CHAPTER SIX

"TELL ME this isn't normal," Cariad asked to no one in particular. She was unsurprised when no one stopped to respond. The fear was evident in her voice as she pressed herself against the wall.

The ship careened again and she was suddenly aware of its mass. A huge beast of wood, held together by nails and tar, pushed into movement by huge sheets of cloth. It was a madness to think such a thing could keep them safe on a calm day, let alone in this maelstrom. She squeezed her eyes shut as the world suddenly tilted the other way. Her feet skidded across the floor and she struck out her arms to brace herself against something, anything, to stop this slide.

She should have just gone back to her bunk. She would have been safe there. She would have been able to plant her feet against one wall, her hands against the other. It would have made her like part of the ship, just another piece of lumber.

Someone put a hand on her shoulder and she clung gratefully to them. "Thank you," she muttered.

"Sure. Just relax. This trip isn't doing you any favors, is it?"

Cariad opened her eyes to see Estacia smiling down at her. She tensed and leaned away from her, but the cook tightened her arm and shook her head.

"No, no, don't be like that. I apologized, right? We had that lovely night, I invited you to fuck me. An invitation you haven't take up yet, I noticed. But my feelings aren't hurt. You've had a lot on your mind. We're friends now, and that means I'm looking out for you. I'm going to take you somewhere and help you with that twisty stomach of yours."

"More dodgy drinks?"

Estacia laughed. "I was thinking dryer. Much dryer. I'm a marvel in the kitchen, but even I have yet to figure out a way to fuss with saltines."

The deck rolled under their feet again and Cariad wrapped her arms around Estacia's waist. She groaned in surrender.

"Fine. Lead the way."

Estacia guided her down the corridor and into a small supply room. The walls were lined with shelves outfitted with closed drawers, leaving only enough room for two stools in the center. Estacia motioned for Cariad to sit down, then unlatched one of the drawers and reached inside. She withdrew a box of crackers, turned, and handed it to Cariad.

"Thankee."

"Sure." Estacia sat across from her. The space was so cramped that she had to spread her legs so Cariad's knees fit between them.

"I remember my first trip to sea. I was bent over the rail the entire way, getting rid of every meal I'd ever had in my entire life to that point. It was truly..." She caught the color in Cariad's cheeks and stopped herself. "Ah, it was truly not the sort of story you want to hear right now. But talking does help."

Cariad munched on a cracker and thought about topics of conversation. "Ranzi said Captain Landau wouldn't want to go to this island because she killed the daughter of its ruler. Is that true?"

Estacia chuckled. "Ah, that was before my time. But I've heard the story. I may not be the best person on the crew to tell it, but I'll give it a shot if you want."

"Sure."

"Well, it happened about ten years ago. This was back when the first Captain Landau was still alive."

"There was another Captain Landau?"

"Oh sure. This one's wife. Clio was her first mate, and we elected her to take over when Harriet died. But that's not part of this story. Which one d'ya want to hear?"

"The one about the island woman's daughter."

Estacia nodded. "Okay, like I said. About a decade back, we were transporting some cargo for La Reina Aldoncia Reyes. That's the woman who runs La Llama. Her daughter, Dulcinea, was on board to keep an eye on it, keep track of the money, make sure everything was on board and honest."

Cariad said, "Wait, Aldoncia and Dulcinea? I think that's from a book."

"I don't know about that, but that's their names. The *Banshee* took the money to the seller, picked up the supplies, was taking it back to the island. Now, they hadn't been told what the cargo was, and they were smart enough not to ask. You don't hire a ship like this for an aboveboard exchange of goods and services. But everyone who was there swears everything went perfect with the transaction. But one night when they were at sea..." She drew in a breath and let it out slowly. "See, this is where it would be better if you could ask someone who was actually there. Ranzi or the sawbones, or..."

"I think they're all busy at the moment."

Estacia ducked her chin and chuckled and, for a moment, Cariad saw her as a cute young woman rather than the sly vixen who had drugged her.

"Well, from what I've managed to piece together, one night when they were at sea, someone got into the hold and tried breaking into the cargo. Depending on who you believe, Dulcinea did it and Clio caught her. Or Clio did it and Dulcinea caught her."

"Clearly Harriet believed her wife."

Estacia shrugged and nodded. "Sure, of course. But even Clio understood there had to be a proper investigation into what happened, so she surrendered herself to the brig. Dulcinea didn't go so easily. She demanded Clio be punished immediately. She attacked Clio, who took her wife's dagger to protect herself from the girl's attack. The doctor, Delfina, insists that most of the blows Clio made were defensive. Shallow cuts on Dulcinea's arms, deflecting blows, that sort of thing. But Dulcinea was going for the kill.

"Clio basically got lucky. A twist of her wrist at the wrong time and her blade slid across Dulcinea's throat, opened a vein. Things got extremely bloody on the deck, from all accounts. Clio tried to stop the bleeding and Delf did everything she could, but in the end..." She shrugged and held her hands out palm-up. "Harriet delivered the goods to La Llama, along with Dulcinea's body, and tried to explain what happened. But Aldoncia refused to believe Clio's version of events."

Cariad said, "It does beggar belief a little, doesn't it? Why would Dulcinea try to steal her mother's cargo?"

"There are two lines of thought on that." Estacia leaned forward. "The cargo turned out to be flintlock pistols. Ranzi and Aravanis believe that Dulcinea was under orders to use the pistols to take the ship. They think maybe she had a few mutineers among the crew who were going to help her, and they would sail the *Banshee* home as a prize. But Fausta and Delfina say that it's more likely the Reyes women weren't exactly as close as Aldoncia pretends. Fausta believes Dulcinea was in the dark about what she was escorting home and really just wanted to take a look, or maybe dump the guns and take out the crew, then take the ship home and take over the island from her mother."

"So why would Aldoncia be so angry if she didn't like or trust her daughter?"

"Because if Clio took her daughter, that's a personal attack. It doesn't matter how she felt about the girl. Blood is blood."

Cariad made a considering sound and nibbled on another cracker.

"Whichever theory is true," Estacia said, "they got rid of everyone who might've been a mutineer at the earliest possible convenience. That included the cook. And that's when I came aboard." She beamed and lifted her chin as if posing for a portrait.

Cariad smiled and admired the line of Estacia's throat, the way her hair fell away from her face, her cheekbones. Those sparkling green eyes, the tan of her skin, the dimples. Estacia probably only held the pose for a second, but Cariad felt like she was stuck in that moment, holding her breath, waiting for her body to act on its own accord without waiting for her brain to catch up.

The trance was broken when Estacia finally relaxed her pose, the smile going away and taking its power with it. But the damage was done.

"Are you ok~"

"So," Cariad said quickly to interrupt the question. She cleared her throat. "So, um, going back to the island now is a pretty desperate act."

Estacia nodded slowly. "Yes. The most desperate." She ran her tongue over her lips. "Can I ask you, why are you here? I know you brought the job and all that. You're the reason we're on our way to God knows where. But why is it so important to you, mm?"

Cariad looked down at the crackers. "I'm... a journalist, and~"

"You're after a story? Yeah, we heard that but none of us buy it. You're looking for something~"

The door to the supply room opened, interrupting Estacia again, and they both looked up to see Ranzi looming in the hallway. She was out of breath, soaked to the skin, her shirt practically transparent and hanging like rags from her shoulders. The gunner swept her seaweed-limp hair out of her face, looked at them both, and furrowed her brow.

"You're still dressed."

Estacia raised her eyebrows. "Should we not be?"

"Every other time I've walked in on people in here, they've been some sort of naked. Are you just getting started?"

"What did you need?" Estacia said brusquely.

"We're out of the first wave of the storm, bit of calm. Fausta wants us to move quick-like, but a couple of deckhands are down with the seasickness. Delf asked me to get some saltines."

Cariad held up the box she was holding and Ranzi took it.

"Thanks." She stepped back and put her hand on the door. "Open or closed?"

Cariad stood and hurried past. "We were about to leave anyway..."

"We were?" Estacia said, following her out.

Ranzi shut the door and went to deliver the crackers.

Cariad moved as quickly as she could in the tight corridors of the ship, occasionally pressing herself hard against a wall so a group of sailors could rush past in the pursuit of one duty or another. When she finally reached the stairs and climbed back up onto the main deck, she recoiled back into the darkness and held a hand up against the unbelievably sharp sunlight. It was almost as if the storm had polished the air and the sun was shining off every gust of wind, sending the heightened beams directly into her eyes.

Waiting to adjust to the brightness gave Estacia time to catch up with her.

"What happened?" She put a hand on Cariad's shoulder. "Are you okay?"

"I'm fine. Please don't touch me."

The hand vanished, but the ocean despised her. It lifted the boat and made her tumble backward. Estacia was blocking the door to the stairs so Cariad fell into her. One of Estacia's arms went around Cariad's waist, her hand flat on Cariad's stomach just above her belt buckle, and she lashed out with the other hand to grab the doorframe. Cariad's breath died as she was very aware of the warm body behind her, taking her full weight, and the surprisingly muscular arm stretched out next to her. Estacia's hand on her stomach was small but felt like a hot iron, the fingers splayed to cover as much space as possible.

"Cariad, I can't... you've got to step up, girl..."

And then Estacia was pressing her forward, the arm next to her flexing as the cook used her body to push Cariad upright again. Cariad realized she'd been dead weight, and Estacia had probably been moments away from tumbling down the stairs.

"I-I'm sorry," she said when she was back on her feet again.

Estacia let her go and straightened her clothes. "You don't have to apologize." Her voice was flat, not with anger, but frustration. "Can I offer you some advice, Cariad? I'm pursuing you because I like you. I think you're cute and you have a nice body and I'd like to take you to bed. But I'd never be this adamant about anyone I thought wasn't interested. You've obviously got an itch, some kind of feeling, and you need to take care of it. Because it's a distraction. Just now, you ran away from me and then you froze when I was holding both of us up with one arm. You can't be distracted like that on a ship. You just can't. So you need to either decide to let go of those weird feelings or indulge in 'em. It doesn't have to mean anything. Just an itch got scratched. Clearing up the fog."

"I've never done anything remotely like... what I'm feeling," Cariad said.

"So?" Estacia chuckled. "I'm not going to grade you, darlin', we're just talking about having a nice time together for a night, maybe more."

She brushed her hand down Cariad's forearm, squeezed her hand, then looked out over the deck. She gave Cariad one more smile, then disappeared down the stairs.

Cariad watched her go. When her brain finished processing what she'd said, she turned away and focused on taking in the state of the ship.

A thin layer of water sloshed across the deck, leaving everyone up to their ankles in miniature waves of salt water. Everyone looked half-drowned, even Aravanis at the wheel looked like she'd been through the wringer. The sky above them was clear and sunny but, in every direction she turned, thick black thunderheads seemed to roll and breathe with imminent threat.

Captain Landau came out from belowdecks, her clothes damp but otherwise untouched. If anyone resented the fact she seemed to have missed the storm, none of the sailors gave any indication. She walked out far enough that she could turn back and see Aravanis, who nodded ahead.

The captain went to the railing and took out her spyglass. She confirmed what Aravanis had conveyed with her head nod, then sprinted up the stairs to stand in front of the wheel.

"La Llama is directly ahead of us. We'll be there within the hour. We don't have to outrun the storm anymore, we just have to keep up with it. We stay in the eye and pray it doesn't close in on us. Think we've got it in us?"

Every deckhand shouted and lifted their fist in response. Captain Landau smiled and nodded her chin, smacking her hand on the rail in front of her.

"That's what I like to hear. Let's show this fuckin' weather what a banshee can do, ey?"

Another cheer went up, and the crew went back to work.

Cariad, seeing that she would only get in the way, turned and fled back to the relative safety belowdecks. At least down there she only had to worry about Spanish cooks with jade eyes.

DELFINA PENDERGAST

"It's a good life, and I don't hold it against none who may choose it for themselves. Fine clothes washed by someone else, hung and waiting in your wardrobe when the day begins. A feast every day, more food than we wanted or could even eat. The only concern weighing on my mind being whether to choose an escort for that weekend's ball or hope to find someone there. But I preferred going to my father's classroom and listening to his lectures about medicine, surgery, sickness, healing. The human body was this amazing thing that could be broken so easily, and mended like magic. I spent ten years sitting under his desk while his other students came and went. I stayed up after he'd gone to bed and go through his books to see what he hadn't gotten to yet.

When I turned sixteen, my mother started trying to pawn me off with the desperation of a woman holding a sizzling stick of dynamite. She would have no old maid in this house, no sir! She braided my hair so tightly my scalp felt like a drumskin. She cinched my waist in corsets until I couldn't breathe. She pranced me in front of boys from reputable families, with prospects, with riches. None of them seemed very interested in finding out I wanted to be a doctor, but to their credit, only a few of them laughed in my face. Those were the ones I let go without a slap or a kick.

Then, on a rainy Saturday morning, one of the boys came running to my house in the clothes he'd been wearing the day before. One eye was swollen shut and there was blood on his collar. He dropped to his knees on my front stoop and begged me to loan him some money, a shocking sum, insisted it was life or death and he would repay me as soon as humanly possible, but he needed the cash immediately.

That's when the pirates arrived.

He'd been playing them in a card game, winning at first before sliding headlong into a valley. By the time the sun rose, he was tremendously in debt and the pirates were due to ship out. They wanted what was owed them, and they had no interest in his family's credit or promises of favors. The boy begged me, bruised and on his knees at my feet, and I knew I held his life in my hands. More than that, I was holding my own life in my hands.

The lead pirate was young and beautiful. Long black hair and ice blue eyes, pale skin. She wore a tricorn hat which funneled the falling rain out to either side of her face so it looked as if she was watching from behind a veil. She held a blade in her hand, but its gleaming tip lowered when she saw me.

'We're not trying to rob anyone here, miss. The man owes us a debt, that's all it is. If he pays what we're owed, we'll be along on our merry. But reputations are at stake here. Ours and his. I'm sure he wouldn't want it known he's a cheat and liar, now would he?'

'I can't give you the money,' I said, which prompted a whine from the boy at my feet, 'but I can give you something equivalent. Take me.'

Everyone on my front lawn was confused by my meaning.

'I'm a doctor,' I explained.

The boy said, 'You ain't a doctor,' as if I wasn't handing myself over to save his sorry hide.

'I've never heard of a girl doctor,' the lead pirate said.

'You likely never will. But I've been sitting in my father's classroom every day since I was six years old listening to him teach boys how to be half the doctor I am. I may not have a degree from an institution, I may not be allowed to practice, but I'm sure I'll be a damn sight better than whoever you've got on your ship.'

The woman pirate lowered her blade and looked at the men behind her. She looked back at me and lifted her chin to look fully at me.

'And what do you get out of it?'

'I get to be a doctor. I get the ocean. And I get to burn this fucking dress.'

The pirate grinned and sheathed her blade. 'I think we can all agree that's a fair trade. And if we change our minds later, we'll take you on anyway and come back later to settle our debt with this one.' She kicked at the boy's rear end, which made him yelp. The pirate laughed. 'What's your *name, Lady Doctor?'*

My heart was pounding and my hands wouldn't keep still. 'Delfina Pendergast.'

She grinned and motioned with her head for me to come along. 'Harriet Landau. Stick with me and I'll give you the whole ocean.'

I pulled the boy's hands from my skirts and left him kneeling in the mud, left him to tell anyone who cared where I'd disappeared to. I tore at the confining stays of my dress as I followed Landau, the woman I would soon call friend, briefly call lover, and who will always be my captain."

Chapter Seven

The map revealed how the island of La Llama had gotten its name, and confirmed which definition of the word was intended by the settlers. The southern tip was almost perfectly rounded with a series of jagged inlets that Fausta could now see led to precariously tall cliffs. The island narrowed in the middle stretching out toward a pair of northern spits with a gradually widening straight between them. It looked like a dancing flame, and the harbor was one of the most protected Fausta had ever seen. The southern cliffs would take the brunt of the storm's force, and the spits would protect them from wilding seas.

They'd managed to stay ahead of the second storm front, sometimes just barely. Now Aravanis was carefully threading the needle between the two northern reaches of the island. It was a tight fit but Fausta was already confident they could make it. The main concern was that reaching La Llama's harbor would require turning around, back toward the rain and wind they had just spent an hour evading.

At least Clio was back in command. Fausta was relieved to have her leading the way for this part of their journey. Given her history, she didn't begrudge the captain a phobia when it came to tempests. She just hoped the captain had spent the time in her cabin constructively. Perhaps thinking up what she was going to say when she was face to face with Aldoncia.

Fausta couldn't imagine any words that would prevent that cold, stoic woman from having them killed on the spot. But just as surely she knew there were no better options. The storm would have eventually overwhelmed them. They needed this harbor. And there was no way they could simply squat there and hope the ship went unnoticed. Going ashore and officially requesting sanctuary was the only possible chance they had to survive the day without bloodshed.

Rain swept the deck again. The crew ignored it, at most tucking their collars up against the icy water that threatened to run down their necks. Fausta walked to where Clio was standing and raised an eyebrow at her.

"Do you still think this girl's mysterious coordinates are still worth checking out?"

Clio sighed heavily and then lifted her shoulder. "We were bound to find ourselves here sooner or later. In a way, we're fortunate to have this opportunity to get it out of the way on a job where time isn't of the essence."

Fausta laughed. "Ever the optimist, even in the darkest storms."

Clio smiled and clapped Fausta on the shoulder. "I'll take optimist. Sounds so much better than foolish or suicidal."

"Oh, that's wrapped up in the definition as far as I'm concerned. So I assume you'll be wanting me to go ashore with you."

Clio's smile faded and she rocked her head back and forth, like she was trying to work out a kink. "Sort of. I may be a foolish optimist, but I still believe in planning for the worst. Find Ranzi and bring her to my cabin. We have some logistics to work out before we drop anchor."

"Aye, captain."

Fausta descended to the main deck and looked past the bow. The rain veiled most of the way ahead, but she could make out torches and lantern light, markers indicating the star of La Llama's harbor. She pressed her lips together and turned away from the sight.

She prayed La Reina de Llama was in a good mood.

They brought the ship as close to the harbor as they dared, then turned broadside to the shore. Clio used the spyglass to keep an eye on the town. It was barely visible through the veil of rain, a blue-black blur of stone buildings clustered around forested foothills. Lanterns and torches burned in a handful of windows, giving her an idea of the town's shape.

Within twenty minutes of their arrival, a pair of guards had arrived at the shore. They walked to the end of the dock and watched the ship. They kept their swords and flintlocks sheathed, but she could tell they were prepared for the eventuality of violence. Clio had made doubly sure their cannons were stowed and the ship looked completely harmless, no whisper of a threat. The rain was still falling but, as promised, La Llama's unique structure protected them from the worst of the winds.

Clio had a pocket watch clipped to her belt. When she wasn't watching the guards, of which there were now four, she was checking the time.

After forty-five minutes, with six of Aldoncia's men waiting, Delfina appeared at the captain's shoulder.

"We've got everyone patched up," she reported. "They may not be a hundred percent, but they're back on the line."

"Good. Good to know. Thank you, Delf."

"Mm-hmm." Delfina squinted at the people waiting on shore. "Waiting for them to get tired?"

Clio made a quiet noise of amusement. "Not a bad idea. Just waiting for the right moment."

Delfina scanned the deck. "I assume Ranzi and Fausta are gunning up?"

"They're not coming with me."

"Then who are you taking?"

Clio shook her head. "No one. Aldoncia wants my head. If I show up surrounded by guards, she can claim it was an attack. She can have all those men on the dock respond with brute force."

"And this way she can claim it was suicide."

"Maybe," Clio said. "Or maybe she'll be intrigued about why I'm willingly walking into her stronghold unprotected and unarmed-"

"Sorry, 'unarmed'...?"

"-and keep me alive long enough to ask me why."

Delfina blinked. The rain had plastered her hair against her face and she pushed it back over the top of her head. She exhaled and looked to make sure there were no weapons hanging from Clio's hip.

"Huh."

"You think it's a bad plan?"

"I think…" Delfina considered, then said, "I think it's a plan Harriet would've come up with."

Clio smiled. "I'm not sure if you mean that as a compliment. But I'll take it as one regardless."

"Good luck, Captain."

"Thank you, Doctor."

One hour after dropping anchor, Clio handed command over to Aravanis and climbed into the launch. The deckhands lowered her to the water and she rowed herself slowly toward the docks. She watched as the waiting guards - eight now - reacted to the sudden activity. One of them broke away from the group and ran back into the town proper, clearly to alert Aldoncia of the development. The others formed a line.

Clio was unhurried. She didn't overexert herself, didn't rush, but also didn't let the guards get the impression she was frightened. The rain pelted her the entire way. When she arrived at the dock and removed her hat, shook water from the brim, and ran her hand through the short white-blonde spikes of her hair before she approached the lead guard. He puffed out his chest and squared his shoulders. His jaw was set behind his graying beard, and his hooded eyes were impossible to read in the overcast light. Clio only came up to his chest, but she tilted her head back and offered him a confident nod.

"I assume you're my escorts, gentlemen. Lead the way."

"We're supposed to disarm you," Beard said.

Clio held her arms out and leaned back. "Feel free to take any weapons you find. They'll be yours to keep."

One of the men stepped forward. With thick, overly roaming hands, he confirmed she didn't have any weapons hidden on her body. He gave a nod to Beard and returned to his spot in the line.

"Miss Reyes is quite interested to speak with you," Beard said.

"I'm certain she is. As I said, lead the way."

The men surrounded her. Beard turned around and began marching up the main drag. When Clio followed, the rest of the group maintained their defensive shield around her. She clocked all six pistols, the eight swords, and the four knives strapped to the men who created the mobile prison cell. She was aware that those were only the weapons they wanted her to see, and they certainly had more concealed.

They arrived at their destination, a walled compound right at the edge of the wooded area, its back completely shrouded in vegetation. It was separated from the rest of the town by a wide road currently spanned by a makeshift bridge made of wood and stone. They had to form a single-file line to get across, and Clio was forced to take the center position.

Once inside, Beard dismissed the rest of the guards. He motioned for Clio to follow him down a short corridor. The interior of the house was warm and lit with the soft glow of candles, enhanced by a few lanterns strung up in strategic places. Clio smelled evidence that a dinner of beef, carrots, and potatoes had recently been cooked here, and her stomach rumbled in reaction. Beard, if he heard, chose to ignore it and pushed open the door to a lavish dining room.

Aldoncia Reyes, la Reina de Llama, sat at the head of the table. She wore a silk blouse and her black hair was done up in a complicated style that Clio couldn't help but think had been done for her benefit. The entire setup could have been thrown together in response to the *Banshee*'s arrival, accomplished during the hour Clio had waited before coming ashore. Beard indicated Clio should approach but, when she reached to pull out a chair, he grunted to let her know she was to stand.

Aldoncia picked up her wine glass and took a slow drink. She let her dark eyes linger on Clio, taking in the wet clothing and her short, dripping hair. She finally put the glass down and folded her hands in her lap.

"Miss Landau. I was beginning to fear you wouldn't be doing me this honor."

"We both know that if I'd waited much longer, this gentleman would have been sent out to retrieve me."

"Hm." Almost a laugh, almost amusement, but not quite. She steepled her fingers. "It is unseemly to darken someone's threshold without a formal greeting."

Clio nodded and put her hands behind her back. "I understand. My purpose in coming ashore is to assure you my only intention is shelter from the storm. Once it passes, we'll be on our way."

"And what if I require recompense?"

"Naturally, as we're taking up space in your harbor, you would be more than welcome to ask for some sort of fee–"

Aldoncia said, "I ask for blood. Specifically your blood. Spilled on this table by Matias' blade."

She heard the hiss of steel against leather behind her. She raised an eyebrow and lifted her chin, a defiant gesture. Or perhaps foolish, given what had just been said.

"I offer you gold. A fair price for what we are asking. I will not give you my life."

"You owe me nothing less," Aldoncia hissed, leaning forward.

Clio shrugged. "On that point, we disagree. But slitting my throat will not even the score. In fact, it shall only complicate matters. If your man Matias kills me with his sword, my crew will be forced to respond."

"By the time your crew even learns of your death, we will be ready for them. I have a hundred men heavily armed men in this house. I will summon them to form a gauntlet, and they will cut down any pirate who dares leave your ship."

"You don't have a hundred men in this house."

Aldoncia arched an eyebrow. "Are you certain of that fact, Captain Landau?"

"Honestly, no." She raised her voice and projected enough to be heard outside of the room. "Ranzi? What was your count?"

The door to the kitchen opened and Ines Ranzi walked out. She had a peeled potato speared on the end of her knife and she finished chewing a bite of it as she approached.

"No more than forty-five. But that's including the chefs and servants, and honestly I wouldn't put any of them in a fight. At least not a fight I plan to win."

Aldoncia's entire body was rigid with tension, her eyes wide as she cringed away from the unexpected arrival. "Who...? Where did this woman come from?"

Matias stared at Ranzi, wide-eyed in surprise and rage. "No one else came ashore with the captain."

Ranzi took another bite of her potato. "No, that's true. Don't blame him. We went the long way."

"We?" Aldoncia said, sounding breathless.

"She means Fausta Gittens," Clio said. "My first mate. Now, if you truly want a hundred men to guard your house? Fausta is the next best thing for my money."

She pulled out the chair Matias had stopped her from taking earlier. She sat down and reached for Aldoncia's bowl of stew, dragging it over in front of herself. Aldoncia stared down, rage behind her eyes but fear preventing her from reacting. Clio scooped up a generous amount of the stew and took a big bite. Her delay in leaving the ship had been to give Ranzi and Fausta time to drop down the seaward side of the ship and swim to shore well away from town. Once they were on land, they only had to stick to the forest and infiltrate the stronghold from its lesser-defended southern entrance.

She chewed thoughtfully and then raised her eyebrows at Ranzi. "The stew is damn good."

"Very damn good," Ranzi confirmed. "I tasted some in the kitchen. I might steal a few bags of their veggies, see what Estacia can do with the same ingredients. I bet it'll be magnificent."

"Fucking magnificent," Clio agreed.

Aldoncia sat up straighter, her posture seeming to indicate her growing rage. "It would appear you have me at a disadvantage, Captain."

"I only want a fair deal. If you accept the offer, I'll take my crew members back to the ship and you'll never have to see hide nor hair of us until the storm passes and we go about our way. Everyone comes out of it intact... oh." She furrowed her brow and looked at Ranzi. "Are the guards intact?"

Ranzi made a so-so gesture. "Them that aren't, they'll probably heal."

Aldoncia was taking deep, measured breaths. She struggled to keep her voice even. "And what exactly is your destination, if I may inquire? There isn't much out there of interest to the likes of you."

"Do you interrogate everyone who arrives in your harbor so thoroughly?"

Aldoncia said, "I think we can both admit you're not just *any* passerby. In the past year, I've watched close to a dozen ships sailing out to the middle of nowhere for seemingly no reason. I even had Matias stop a few and board them to see if there's some new shipping lane I'm unaware of. But he found nothing of interest. No interesting cargo, nothing to justify the long trip out to the nothingness. The crew seemed downtrodden, definitely not conquerors fresh of a payday.

"And now here comes you, and your blasted ship. Traveling toward the same nothing. Only you're in need of a favor, not to mention the debt you owe me. Answering my question won't clear that debt, of course, but it may make me inclined to accept your offer of payment. So tell me, Clio Landau, what in blazes is so fascinating out there?"

Clio considered the question. She looked down at the bowl of stew. Behind her, Matias was still waiting with his sword drawn. Ranzi's clothes dripped on the stone floor of the dining room.

"Ranzi, where is Fausta?"

"At the front, keeping an eye out for reinforcements."

Clio kept her gaze locked on Aldoncia, who returned the stare without blinking. Clio narrowed her eyes but the flame queen didn't respond.

"Two heavily armed intruders and you don't call for help."

"I place much trust in Matias to protect me."

Clio pushed her chair back and stood. "I'm sure he's more than adequate, but you wouldn't take the risk. There's only one reason you would let me walk in here without a dozen blades following me."

Aldoncia laughed and shook her head. "I think you overestimate my terror, Captain Landau. Matias is only here as a formality. I have no doubt I could handle you both myself if the situation arose."

"Mm, let's not test that theory."

Clio drew her own sword and spun around with the same motion. Matias lunged at her but she had all her weight on her left foot. She effortlessly leaned away from his sweep and thrust her sword arm forward as if she was throwing a punch. Matias' failed strike meant that he fell directly onto the tip, and his weight sank him down onto it. Clio withdrew her arm before the sword could be irretrievably buried in his gut.

As Matias fell, Clio turned back to the table. Aldoncia was still seated, watching in horror. It was a terrible reaction to violence and Clio was certain it would one day lead to the queen's downfall. But not today. Clio reached out, grabbed the bowl of stew, and flung it toward the head of the table. Aldoncia screamed, the sound twisting into a shriek as the hot broth splashed over her face and clothes.

"They're attacking the ship," Clio shouted, nodding for Ranzi to follow her from the room.

"Damn it," Ranzi said, running apace next to Clio down the vacant main hall toward the front exit. "I knew I should have stayed behind."

"You might as well have for all the help you were back there," Clio joshed.

"Someone had to witness your daringness," Ranzi said. "I'm already composing the epic song in my head. I shall put pen to paper once we're safely back to sea."

"Once we get our ship back."

"Aye, Captain, once we get out ship back."

They burst out the main doors to see Fausta standing in front of the muddy road that cut across in front of the house. She was watching the town. Clio approached her left, Ranzi to the right, and Clio noticed every lantern in every window had been extinguished. The entire island looked completely abandoned now.

"They started blinking out a few minutes ago," Fausta said. "I just thought people were going to bed. But they're not, are they?"

"No," Clio said. "They're going after the *Banshee*. They might already be there."

"Then why aren't we?" Ranzi asked, drawing her sword.

Clio scanned the streets. At least some of Aldoncia's men had to be waiting for them to make this attempt. There were ambushes waiting in every shadow. She could almost hear the shine of their blades and the sizzle of gunpowder waiting to be sparked.

"That's a damn good question, Ines," Clio said. "Let's go get our ship."

CHAPTER EIGHT

SOMETHING THUDDED against the side of the ship. Aravanis turned toward the sound, just barely audible over the wind and the rain and muttering of the deckhands. It could have been a random piece of debris knocking against their hull. She walked toward the source of the thud, brushing past a crewman and taking his gun from his holster with such a smooth grip that he didn't even notice it was gone. At the gunwale she paused, the gun at her side, and scanned the waters around the ship. There was some debris floating in the harbor. Branches and the like. Nothing heavy enough to have produced what she thought she'd heard.

Another thud, and this time she could pinpoint its origin. She motioned a deckhand over and put a finger to her lips to indicate silence. When he was in place, she stuck her borrowed gun in her belt. She went to the rigging and used her knife to cut off the weighted iron at its end. She handed the rope to the deck hand, who had to quickly brace himself to keep from behind tugged into the air.

Aravanis crouched down and carried the weight to the gunwale. She kept low, listened carefully, then palmed the weight and raised it up over her head. She gently tipped it over the side and let it fall.

Less than a second later she heard it hit something fleshy. The victim managed a brief "Fu~" before she heard his weight tumbling against the hull as he fell. She drew her gun as her body unfolded to its full height. She leaned over the railing and fired at the first movement that caught her eye.

Blood gushed from the man's shoulder as he let go of his rope with one hand, then succumbed to gravity and fell after the man she'd hit with the iron.

"*Boarding party!*" she shouted, firing again at one of the other climbing men.

There were four more men climbing the ship's own ropes and chains. They had stopped where they were, just outside of arms' reach of the railing, and were fumbling with their own weapons as the deckhands responded to Aravanis' call and came to join her. She checked to be sure the port side of the ship was also being checked. One of the deckhands, a man named Paul, climbed over the railing and jumped down out of sight.

"Six men over here!" someone shouted. "They got a launch! Trying to sabotage *Banshee!*"

Aravanis' lips curled back from her teeth. She stalked across the deck and looked down the other side of the ship. Paul had jumped down into their launch where he was taking on three men single-handedly. All three were bloody and it was difficult to tell who, if anyone, had the upper hand. She was more focused on the man in the stern of their boat with a hatchet. He clearly meant to use it against the *Banshee,* but their launch had drifted too far for him to get close. The fight was also making it difficult for him to strike. He bent and straightened his legs to keep from stumbling, swaying and using the hatchet as a counter balance to keep himself from falling into the water.

Aravanis was up and over the railing before anyone knew what she planned. She dropped like an anchor, her boots striking the hatchet man, crushing him down into the boat. The landing caused her to fall backward, but she was quick enough to grab his hair with one hand, his shirt with the other, and she pulled him over the side of the boat with her.

He fought her, and she wrapped her arms around his chest, pinning his arms to his sides so he couldn't get the blade up to use it against her. This meant that she wasn't able to swim and keep them afloat, and their combined weight dragged them quickly into the deep dark. She kicked her feet but it did little to slow their descent.

She held her breath and clung to the furious man. Drowning was not how she intended to die. But if it saved the *Banshee* from being damaged or scuttled, she would consider her life a small price to pay for its survival.

They moved faster than their ambushers anticipated. Clio let Ranzi and Fausta take the lead, leaving herself to watch their backs. They had passed two alleyways before the men emerged from the shadows with surprised grunts. Their boots slid in the mud as they advanced, swords and cudgels raised high. Clio stopped running and ducked under the first man's swing, thrusting her sword forward into his side. He folded in on himself. She pulled her arm to free her weapon and sent her follow-through into the second man. He dropped his weapon to clutch his wound. She shoved both men to the ground to serve as roadblocks to the men coming behind them.

She looked and saw Ranzi chop down another man, then stoop to take his sword for herself. Now swinging with both hands, she advanced and sliced at the back of the man trying to take on Fausta.

Any hope of an ambush was gone, so now the townspeople were emerging all at once, shouting to distract or disorient the invaders. Clio pulled the knife from her boot, used her sword to redirect the strike of someone's sword, and swung the smaller blade into his chest. As he fell she turned to see Fausta throw a limp body down to the mud. The rain had plastered her hair to her face and she wondered if it had been raining when they left Aldoncia's palace or if it was a new development. It seemed like ages ago she'd been relaxed, mostly dry, and not beset by a gauntlet of swords.

"How are things going?" she called.

"Never fought an entire town before," Ranzi said. "I wish we'd started with somewhere populated by people who actually knew how to use swords."

"Next time, maybe," Fausta said, then hissed as someone's sword slid across her bicep, leaving a spray of blood behind on her sleeve as she spun and thrust her blade into his stomach in return.

Clio deflected a sword's downward arc and kicked its owner away from her, jabbing at him once he was clear. Ranzi surged ahead and stepped left, sliced, ducked right, chopped, and kicked a man's leg out from underneath him.

They were nearly to the dock. Flashes of light sparked on the *Banshee*'s deck, followed seconds later by the crack of gunfire echoing over the water. Clio saw two pistols tucked into Fausta's belt.

"I'll row, you and Ranzi keep anyone from coming after us."

"Aye!" Fausta said.

Ranzi leapt down into the launch and had it prepared to shove off by the time they caught up. Clio waited until Fausta was safely aboard before she jumped off the docks. Someone tried to follow them and Fausta dissuaded him by clipping his ear with a bullet. The standard unspoken rule about leaving disagreements at the dock wouldn't help them here.

Clio stood to her full height, such as it was, and aimed a sword at the men racing up behind him.

"I don't want to burn your dock, but I will. I'll blaze every boat in this harbor if you come after us, so I'd consider that the end of this chase. Agreed?"

The men didn't reply, but they remained where they were. One of them knelt down to help the man Fausta had shot, his ear now bleeding freely. Ranzi started rowing while Fausta kept her pistols at the ready. Once they were confident no one was going for a boat, Clio sheathed her sword and took over rowing. Ranzi took one of Fausta's guns and turned toward the ship.

"Anything interesting in that direction?" Fausta asked.

"A few scattered boats around her," Ranzi reported. "Men in the water. Some swimmin', most not. I think I just saw that deckhand with the wooden eye throw a body overboard."

Clio smiled. "Nicolo."

"Well, he's certainly pulling his weight. He just dropped another one."

Fausta chuckled but without much humor. "So I guess we lost our bid for safe harbor. D'ya think we're close enough to the end of the storm to risk heading back to open ocean?"

Clio shook her head. "We'll stay until the weather passes."

Ranzi and Fausta both looked at her. Fausta was the first to accept the captain was serious. "In case you haven't been paying attention, Reyes made it fair clear we aren't welcome."

"And asking permission was just a courtesy," Clio responded. "This harbor is the only thing between us and shipwreck. We're using it. We'll move out of her way so as not to be a nuisance, but we'll stay within cannon range. If she keeps sending her people to try and board, we'll consider it an offer to make an exchange. We'll send them a lead ball for every man she puts on *Banshee*'s deck.

Sound fair?"

Ranzi smiled and shrugged. "Seems reasonable enough to me, Captain."

"Aye," Fausta said, chuckling again.

Clio rowed as fast as her back and shoulders allowed, eager to get back to her ship as quickly as possible. The deckhands saw them coming, and she heard one of them shouting orders to the others.

Their launch was hauled up and Clio went over the railing, ready to continue the battle she'd left behind on shore. One of the attempted raiders was on his knees near the mast, and a deckhand was holding a blade to the man's throat. Clio stalked over and glowered at the prisoner. Clio recognized the deckhand and searched for the young woman's name as she approached.

"Preparing to send a message back to the flame queen, Danae?"

"Was trying to decide how to word it," Danae said. "I didn't know how you'd want to send the message. Verbally or..." He pressed the blade harder against the man's skin. "Otherwise."

"Aravanis didn't weigh in?"

"Haven't seen her in a bit."

Clio's stone face shifted at that, but she resisted the urge to search the deck for the missing woman. She crouched down so she could look the captive in the eye.

"What were your orders?"

"Cripple your ship," the man said. "Take down as much of your crew as possible."

Danae said, "Failed miserably on both counts, Captain. Only a couple injuries to report, so far, but he's lost quite a few of his folks. Probably have their blood painting the hull if it weren't still rainin' so much."

Clio nodded. "I think Aldoncia has lost enough of her people. So you'll be sending her an actual message. I won't have you tell her I didn't kill Dulcinea, because I believe she knows the truth of what happened there. Instead, I want you to tell her that I have no intention of being her enemy. I will defend myself against attack, as any captain would. Tell her that if she comes for my ship or my people again, I will not hesitate to strike her down. Understood?"

He sneered, which was good enough for her. She gestured for Danae to dump the man over the side of the ship. She'd seen their boats bobbing in the water on her way back, most unmanned or occupied by injured men, and she was confident he could get himself to one without much trouble. More accurately she didn't much care if he could.

Ranzi came up from below, having done a quick circuit during the interrogation. "Minor injuries. A couple of people will have some new injuries and an exciting story to tell next time we're at a bar, but it seems like we're mostly unscathed."

"Aravanis?"

"No one's seen her for a while," Ranzi said, setting her jaw firmly as she scanned the deck. "Doesn't have to mean anything dire."

Clio shook her head. If there was a fight, she knew Aravanis would be at the center of it all. "We'll find her. First we have to get any of Aldoncia's remaining men off the ship and--"

She was interrupted by the anchor chain rattling. She and Ranzi both pulled weapons - pistol and sword respectfully - and ran to investigate.

The ocean seemed to add a hundred pounds to Aravanis, water pouring from her torn shirt as she reached for a higher link on the chain. Her boots were firmly braced against the hull sliding only a little as she surfaced. She took a step. She stretched, grabbed hold of the steel, and ignored the agony in her bicep and shoulder as she pulled. There were deep cuts on her forearms where the man she'd killed had tried to cut off her hands. The saltwater had gotten into the wounds and made them sting like demons, but she could push back the pain if it meant getting herself back to safety.

Another step. Higher on the chain. Breathing was difficult, almost impossible, but her body knew what it had to do. She didn't look up, didn't want to know how much further she had to climb. If it was too far, she was afraid her brain might rebel and just open her hands, sending her tumbling down into the water to meet her end.

Higher on the chain. Another step. Her hand slipped a little on the metal, and her thighs burned as she pushed her foot down on the curved wood of the hull to keep from falling. She grunted, bared her teeth, reached up for another length of chain--

Someone grabbed her.

She looked up and saw the captain's hand clasped around her forearm, just above where the cuts started. Ranzi was also leaning over, counterbalanced by two deckhands holding onto her other arm, and she reached down to hook her hand under Aravanis' other arm.

"*Heave!*" Clio shouted.

Everyone leaned backward onto the deck, and their combined strength hauled Aravanis the rest of the way over the railing. Ranzi crouched down and let the bosun lay across her lap, leaning against her chest. Aravanis shuddered and closed her eyes, her hands twisted into cramped claws as if they were still trying to grip the chain. Once she was rolled onto her side, she immediately threw up a tide of water that splashed over Clio's boots, but Clio didn't step back.

"Ship," Aravanis said hoarsely. "Attacking the ship..."

Clio had ripped off her own sleeve and was using it to bind one of Aravanis' arms. Common, who had appeared as if from thin air, was doing the same with the other.

"You did it, Penelope. You saved the ship." Clio looked past Ranzi and saw Delfina rushing toward them with a leather bag of tools. "Now it's our turn to save you. Just hold on, sister."

Delfina examined Aravanis' wounds. "What the hell happened to her?"

"She was overboard," Clio reported, "apparently fighting someone who had an axe or a hatchet. That's all we know."

"Let's get her out of the weather."

They recruited three deckhands to help them lift Aravanis. As they carried her below decks, Clio spotted Fausta.

"Get us to the entrance of the harbor. Show off the cannons. I want Aldoncia to be looking down every starboard barrel when she gets the message we just sent her."

"Aye, captain."

Clio looked down to see Aravanis had lost consciousness. "Hang in there, 'Vanis. I'm not going to let that bitch take you."

PENELOPE ARAVANIS

"I was a kid. I guess. I never really found out my age. There were people who gave me food, shelter, cared enough about me to not hit me too hard when I rubbed them the wrong way. But they weren't mine, and didn't know enough about where I'd come from to give me a number. I was treated like a kid, even though I never felt like much of one. I was young enough that the woman who found me got to choose a name. Didn't much care for the first one, but her last name was fine enough, so I kept that.

She got sick, couldn't take care of me anymore, so I moved on. Found somewhere new to stay. Kept going like that for a few years. Sometimes I'd steal from the docks. Lots of crates full of good stuff that people barely paid any attention to. So I sat, I watched, I waited. People tend to move in patterns. You ever see a path beaten down in the grass, you know that much. So I could figure out when my target wasn't being watched.

I went after some fruits. They all looked so pretty sitting there, all orange and yellow and red. I started loading them into a bag, and someone clapped their hand down on my shoulder. I looked up and saw him smiling at me, and he said, 'Easier to just take the whole crate, little one.'

I yanked my arm away and made a run for it, but he caught up with me. Asked me if I wanted to earn some money. Not exactly honest work, but something perfect for a tiny little thief. I figured what the hell. I'd seen all kinds of lives on land. None of them really appealed. So why not find out what I could be out on the ocean?

His name was Laurens. His ship was called Emprendedor. His crew didn't like the idea of a child being onboard, but I learned how to earn my keep. Eventually they were angry that I'd grown too tall to be of use to them as a pickpocket. Some of them believed I was a man dressed as a woman, a rumor that started when I got strong enough to start beating them at their stupid games. I eventually left the ship before they could start thinking of other purposes I could serve.

I didn't go back to land. There were more than enough ships that needed someone reliable in a pinch. I learned how to steer so I'd be doubly useful. I learned how to read maps. It got to where I was more comfortable on water than on land, so I just stopped going ashore unless I could absolutely avoid it.

My last ship was wrecked off the coast of Spain, near San Cibrao. Most of the crew went with the captain, but I'd hated that asshole. I was in a bar. My feet were itchy. Too much dirt on them. I was impatient and waiting for a better offer. I only had to wait for a few weeks before a woman sat across from me.

She was small but I could tell how strong she was by the way she carried herself. There wasn't an ounce of fear in her, though she was maybe half the size of anyone else in the tavern. Her hair was bleached by the sun and her eyes, small and dark.

"I hear you're the person to see if I want a navigator."

"You're Clio Landau." I took a drink. "You have a whole crew of women."

She shrugged. Not even a little surprised I knew her name. "Not exclusively. But enough that I suppose it warrants commenting."

"So you mean I'm the woman to see."

"No. I asked around. Your name came up more than anyone else's. Sex didn't enter into it. Just like it didn't enter into it when I recruited anyone else on my ship. The men are happy to take second or third best, so long as the sailor is male. They don't even consider the sailors like you, who could probably read a map in the dark."

"What's your ship called?"

"The Banshee."

I finished my beer before I decided I would go with her.

It was a good name for a ship.

CHAPTER NINE

THE VILLAGE of La Llama remained silent until the storm passed. Ranzi kept the gunners and powder monkeys at the ready just in case, but they were never forced to follow through with their threat. Common returned to her perch and confirmed clear skies in all directions, so Clio called for them to pull up anchor and return to their original course.

Once they were underway, she went down to the infirmary to check on Aravanis. Delfina had spent most of the first day after the attack getting Aravanis stable, cleaning out her wounds and stitching her up. She'd been unconscious since, now into the second day. She was set up in the corner bed, both arms bandaged from wrist to elbow. Bruises had bloomed on her neck and face, and the swelling over her right eye implied she'd been struck several times by something much harder than a fist. Delfina speculated she might have actually hit her head on the bottom of the *Banshee*, but she obviously couldn't confirm until Aravanis woke up.

At the moment, Delfina was sitting on a stool at the foot of Aravanis' bed. Her hands were on her knees, elbows locked, and though she was upright, she seemed to be fast asleep. Clio approached as quietly as possible and lightly touched the doctor's shoulder. Delfina opened her eyes but betrayed no other signs of being woken suddenly.

"It's okay if you sleep," Clio said.

"I wasn't," Delfina insisted. "I was just trying to remember... it's not important." She looked at Clio. "I take it everything is peaceful with Aldoncia Reyes."

Clio shrugged. "So far. I don't think we'll ever be friends, and we'll probably have to go through this whole ridiculous dance again if we ever need another favor. But let us try to live our lives in a way that doesn't require her fucking assistance."

"Sounds like a viable goal." She stood up and tried to stretch in a way that Clio wouldn't notice. Clio pretended she didn't, just to be a friend. "Aravanis is making progress. That's something to be thankful for. No infections. She's only unconscious now because I gave her a sedative. I don't want her running around topside, trying to steer the ship, popping all my stitches."

"Probably wise," Clio said. "It's always good for the crew to know their limits. To lie down when they're tired. To *rest*."

Delfina sighed and pushed her hair out of her face. "I'm fine. I'm~"

"I don't know how you'd react to a patient saying what you're about to say. So just save us the trouble and give yourself the speech."

Delfina pursed her lips. "At least five hours of sleep."

Clio said, "My advice? Listen to yourself. I've tried arguing with this doctor, and it's a lost cause. We're not likely to have any excitement in the next few hours anyway. I'll have someone sit with Aravanis in case she wakes up."

"Aye, captain." Delfina already seemed more exhausted, as if her stubbornness had been the only thing keeping her upright. "Maybe I'll take six."

"You have my blessing, Doctor."

When Delfina was gone, Clio sat on the side of Delfina's bed and took her hand. There was no reaction from the unconscious woman. One of the deckhands had taken a circuit around the *Banshee* to make sure there was no damage from the attempted boarding. Other than a little cosmetic damage, they hadn't found anything worth worrying about... until they arrived at a spot on the hull where it looked like someone had gotten one or two good swings with a hatchet. The deckhand reported the damage seemed to match the shape of the wounds on Aravanis' arms, revealing why she'd made the choice to dive into the water during the attack.

"Thank you for saving my ship, Penelope," Clio said softly.

"We all owe you our lives. So come back so you can lord it over us."

Aravanis made a soft grunt, a clearly unconscious sound that nonetheless made Clio smile. She doubted she would have gotten much more of a reaction even if Aravanis had been awake.

She squeezed the other woman's hand, settled in, ready to stay there until Aravanis awoke unless someone else on the ship needed her.

Cariad was shaken. She didn't like admitting it, and there were very few people she would have told, but she had been shaking since she found out there were enemies on board. People armed with guns and knives with the intention of killing. She hadn't actually seen any of them, thank God, but she'd definitely heard the fighting. She heard ominous thuds against the hull that her mind translated to the fingers of a giant trying to get a grip on the *Banshee* to lift it up out of the water.

Even now that the threat had passed, she couldn't stop shaking. She kept thinking of that tree of a woman, the beast with the dark eyes and wavy brown hair. Someone said she'd intentionally thrown herself overboard, then came back with hatchet wounds in her arms. As if someone had actually mistaken her for a tree and tried chopping her down.

She planted herself in the mess hall. Not because of Estacia, although her presence was definitely a bonus, but because crewmembers flowed in and out of the room to get meals, snacks, to sit around and drink while regaling each other with tales of what they'd done during the boarding. Cariad ignored their stories. She just wanted to not be alone, and this was the safest and easiest place to achieve that. Even the sway of the ship was almost comforting down here.

During a lull when Cariad was the only person at any of the tables, Estacia brought over a plate with meat, potatoes, and sliced carrots. She put it down in front of Cariad with a nod.

"Eat, please."

"I can't eat. I feel like I'm going to scream if I open my mouth."

Estacia sat down across from her. "You're opening your mouth now. And your voice is a lovely, manageable volume."

Cariad gave a shaky laugh and wrapped her arms around herself.

"Hey." Estacia reached across the table. "I'm not teasing you right now. Are you okay?"

"I am. I'm fine. I'll be fine." She shuddered and stretched as much as she could without rising from her seat. "I just feel like I'm, I'm, like my body heard all that fighting and decided it should be helping even though I can't fight and I probably would have just gotten hurt, but it flooded me with all this adrenaline and no way to get rid of it."

Estacia raised her eyebrows and then looked away. She chuckled softly. "Ah. Well, that can be frustrating. I'm not a fighter, either. So I hide down here, but it happens to me from time to time. You learn how to deal with it."

"What do you do?"

"Me? Um." She wet her bottom lip with her tongue, still not looking at Cariad. "Sometimes I just get rid of the excess energy by going for a run on the deck. Once the all-clear has been given, of course. Mostly I cook. It helps me calm down, and the crew is almost always half-starved after a fight, as you just saw for yourself. Ah, what else..."

Cariad decided to stop hedging. "Fuck?"

Estacia grinned and finally looked at her again. Sparks danced in her eyes and she raised an eyebrow, resting her elbows on the table and leaning forward. "Well, sure, if there's a willing partner about." Her Spanish accent was much heavier now. "But in a pinch, even a little self-touch does the trick."

Cariad looked down the front of Estacia's blouse. The collar had fallen open to reveal her cleavage, which was no doubt the intention. She couldn't believe she was considering this, especially with someone she barely knew, someone who had drugged her immediately after they met. But she couldn't imagine getting up from this table without tasting the woman across from her.

"I bet you don't even know my last name."

Estacia narrowed her eyes. "Jessup."

"No," Cariad said, and closed the distance between them.

Estacia's lips were plump against hers, and Cariad lifted her eyebrows at how soft they felt. She immediately regretted the table between them. The wood dug into her waist. She tried to keep her focus on the kiss while also figuring out how to get to the other side of the table. Estacia grabbed the collar of her shirt with both fists and pulled her closer, and Cariad decided over was as good as around. She used her seat as a step and knelt on the table. Estacia stood as well, breaking the kiss and moving down to kiss Cariad's neck. Her hands also dropped and cupped Cariad's breasts through her shirt. Her nipples were hard and she sucked in a breath as Estacia discovered that fact for herself.

"I've wanted to fuck a woman for so long," Cariad said, closing her eyes, filling both hands with Estacia's thick hair.

Estacia kissed her chest, just above her collar. "I highly recommend it. And gladly volunteer to show you anything you need to know."

She kissed Cariad's nipple through her shirt, and Cariad arched her back. She opened her eyes and looked toward the door.

"Someone could come in here."

"You don't like it when people watch?" Estacia said. "I love people seeing me."

Cariad's cheeks burned. "N-no. I don't think so. At least not this time."

Estacia growled and wrapped an arm around Cariad's waist. "I like 'this time.' Come on."

Before Cariad could respond, Estacia had pulled her off the table and lowered her to the floor. Cariad leaned against her as she hurried her into the kitchen.

She was rushed past a stove, between two fragrant cabinets stuffed full of foodstuffs, and into a narrow pantry. There was barely enough room for her to turn around and, when she did, Estacia pressed against her for another kiss. Cariad moaned and surrendered to the soft lips. She ran her hands over Estacia's body, finally allowing herself to do what she'd always considered forbidden and off-limits. She had a woman's tongue in her mouth. She was running her hands over curves, there was a thigh between her legs... She trapped it there by squeezing her legs and rocked her hips forward.

"You've been waiting for this a long time, haven't ya?" Estacia whispered against the corner of Cariad's mouth.

"My whole life."

"You never...?"

"Not by a woman," Cariad said. "Not by anyone I actually wanted this badly. So no. Not really."

Her heart was pounding so hard she was legitimately afraid, and it felt like every inch of her body was shaking at a different speed. She didn't know how to make her hands do what she wanted, because they seemed to have their own opinion about where they should be. She wanted to run her fingers through

Estacia's hair, but her hands drifted to the small of Estacia's back, and she had to admit that curve felt very, very fine on her palm. When Estacia stretched, Cariad's hand moved with her, and she shuddered at the thought of them moving in concert.

"I'm going to take your clothes off now," Estacia said.

Cariad didn't say anything. She closed her eyes and tensed.

"Cariad Baillie, did you hear me?" Estacia said. "I'm going to take your clothes off."

Her voice was shaking. "I... I'm waiting."

"Well, I'm giving you the option of it." She kissed Cariad's jaw. "If you're not comfortable with that, I can just touch you through your clothes. Or put my hand inside your clothes." She nibbled on Cariad's earlobe. "Whatever you're comfortable with right now."

"Take my clothes off," Cariad said, not giving herself a chance to think or reconsider.

Estacia chuckled and the sound went straight to Cariad's core. "You wanna be naked with me, girlie?" Her fingers were already at Cariad's waistband, working the buttons of her pants. "Because I've wanted to see you since you came aboard. Tall Irish lass, probably got all kinds of freckles all over these curves. Anyone ever kissed your spots, Irish?"

"No," Cariad said on an exhale. Her pants were dragged down her hips and she shuddered as they brushed her calves on the way down. "Fuck. They're all yours, Estacia."

"Oo, I like how you say my name. Your accent is coming back."

"Yours is, too," Cariad swallowed hard. "Estacia Navarro..."

Estacia said, "Cariad Baillie. Listen to us, makin' a symphony." She pressed her lips to Cariad's again and her hand slipped up under Cariad's shirt, cupping her breast.

Cariad let herself be pushed back, bracing her hands on the shelf behind her as Estacia began kissing her way down her body.

"Legs apart," Estacia said sweetly.

"You... y-you... know my last name."

Estacia smiled, biting down on the tip of her tongue. "And I told you to spread your legs for me."

Cariad did as she was told, moving one foot and bending the other knee, and then...

She arched her back and lifted her hips, thrusting forward, her jaw dropping as she stared at the ceiling. Estacia used her lips. Then she used her tongue. Then her tongue and fingers. Then wicked combinations of them all, so many that Cariad couldn't keep track.

She knew she was making noises but she couldn't make herself stop.

After a second, or several minutes, Estacia stood up and pressed her body against Cariad's. Cariad dropped her chin to make up for the difference in their heights and Estacia kissed her hard. Her lips and tongue tasted different now, and Cariad moaned when she realized why. Estacia kept one hand between them and started moving it faster. Cariad flexed her toes, curled them, flexed, curled them, and thrust hard against the searching fingers.

Estacia murmured, "C'mere, gimme this," and used her free hand to guide Cariad's hand. Cariad realized what was wanted of her and slipped her fingers under the waistband of Estacia's pants.

"What do I...?"

"Just do what I'm doing to you, sweetness."

Cariad exhaled and closed her eyes. "You're wet."

"So are you."

"Kiss my neck," Cariad asked.

Estacia did, and Cariad's middle finger was suddenly inside of another woman, and something happened behind Cariad's eyes. She choked on her own voice and used her free hand to cling to Estacia like she'd suddenly been thrown over the side of the ship. She felt like she was suddenly made of wood and steel, but every muscle was vibrating on a different frequency.

"I think I just had an orgasm," she said when she was capable of speaking a full sentence.

"I've seen a few in my day," Estacia said with a breathless chuckle, kissing Cariad's jaw. "And trust me, girl, that was a good one. And if you'd like to see one for yourself, I suggest just watching me for the next few minutes."

Cariad pulled her head back. Estacia's face was very close to hers. Cariad usually hated being this close to other people, but she realized that was because of rules telling her there were lines she couldn't cross. Estacia had obliterated those lines. She could do whatever she wanted. She pressed a kiss to Estacia's cheek, then another, then one to the corner of her mouth.

"Don't stop, ahh, moving your fingers," Estacia gasped. "That's right, girl, keep that up..."

Estacia had one hand on the shelf behind Cariad, one leg hooked on her hip, and she was using her whole body to thrust against the hand between her legs. For once, Cariad was grateful she was a tall woman, with long slender fingers, and she uncurled a third one to see if it added anything. Estacia inhaled through her teeth and then let it out as a groan, and her head dropped onto Cariad's shoulder.

"That's it... yes, that's it... oh, girl... what a girl... yes... oh my lord, yes..." She lapsed into Spanish and turned her head, and her lips locked onto Cariad's neck. "Now, now, now," Estacia moaned. "What you're doing to me, oh... oh, Cariad."

Cariad closed her eyes and held tight as Estacia trembled in her arms. When she finally went still, she slumped against Cariad, dead weight that forced Cariad to pull her hand free just to hold her. She sat down on a bag of what felt like potatoes, and Estacia sat on her lap, straddling her, moving just enough to lift her head and kiss Cariad. There wasn't as much passion or energy behind the kiss, but somehow that made Cariad treasure it more.

Lazy, sleepy kisses, the smell of sweat and what they'd just done to each other. The sound of their breath trying to find a manageable rhythm. The ship swayed beneath them and it almost felt like it was trying to rock them to sleep.

"What do you think?" Estacia stroked Cariad's hair and tucked a lock behind her ear. The finger that trailed down over her cheek was wet, and she didn't know if it was from sweat or something else. "Burn off all that excess energy?"

Cariad nodded and slumped back against the shelves. "But now I'm starved."

Estacia chuckled. "Benefits of fucking the chef." She searched the area around them and stretched for something above Cariad's head. The move meant that she pushed her chest into Cariad's face, and Cariad took advantage by snapping and flicking her tongue at whatever she could reach. Estacia chuckled and thumped the top of Cariad's head. "Cut that out, you. Here. Open your mouth. Tongue out."

Cariad did as she was told. Estacia bit her bottom lip as she placed a green grape on the tip of Cariad's tongue. They never broke eye contact as Cariad drew it into her mouth, lips brushing over Estacia's fingers - the wetness wasn't sweat - before she could pull them away. Cariad chewed slowly and then swallowed.

"That may have been the finest grape I've ever tasted."

"I know of ways it can taste better."

Cariad raised an eyebrow. "Care to enlighten me?"

"First you need a little rest. In a real bed." She leaned back and offered her hand. "Shall I show you where officers sleep on this boat?"

Cariad placed her hand in Estacia's. "Only if you promise to show me what else they do there."

Estacia gave her a wild grin.

CHAPTER TEN

TWO OR three orgasms later, depending on which one was asked, Cariad ran her finger around Estacia's nipple. It was dark, and looked darker right next to her own pink breast. She had spent most of the last hour exploring them with her lips and now her fingers were taking a slower and more thorough survey. She was fascinated by the way the skin around it turned bumpy in the wake of her touch. And the nipple was so big, both thick and long, that she marveled that they weren't visible through her shirts.

She bent down and took it into her mouth again, and Estacia chuckled and pulled her hair.

"Haven't you had enough?"

"I've been denying myself too long. No more. If I want something, I'm going to take it." She put her hand between Estacia's legs.

Estacia gasped, stiffened. "I've created a monster."

Cariad bared her teeth and snapped at her. Estacia laughed and put her hand on Cariad's cheek to kiss her.

"So does this mean you forgive me for drugging you?"

"Yes, Estacia."

"Good." She bumped her nose against Cariad's. "We can't be too careful."

Cariad nodded. "I understand. Now that I've seen the crew in action, I know why you did it."

Estacia's eyes flicked across Cariad's face. "What are you doing here, girlie?" She asked it so softly, it could have been mistaken as a rhetorical question. But she brushed her finger over Cariad's jaw and then touched her lip as if prompting her to speak. "What puts a smart writer girl like you on a ship full of brigands and crooks?"

Cariad tensed and looked away.

"Oh. So you want us to tell our stories, but won't tell you own?"

"It's not that I won't..."

Estacia touched her lips again, this time silencing her. "No. I'm not judging. A person's story is their own thing. A gift. And I can tell that yours is maybe rougher than I'd expect. Yeah?"

Cariad nodded. "A lot of things led me here," she admitted. "Things I've never told anyone. But if I was going to tell, I'd tell you."

Estacia smiled. Then, seized by an idea, she rolled away and climbed out of the bed.

"Where are you going?"

"Relax, just here." Estacia stopped at the small chest of drawers next to the bed. She bent forward at the waist to get something out of the bottom drawer.

Cariad propped herself up on an elbow and admired Estacia's naked profile. Full breasts, wide hips, the curve of her back...

"Come back here," Cariad said, suddenly craving her again. "Please."

"*Calmantes montes*," Estacia murmured. She crawled back into bed and settled against Cariad's side. She was holding a folded piece of paper which she held out to Cariad. "Here."

"What is this?"

"It's something I'm not supposed to have. And if you were to tell Captain Landau I had it without explaining why, you could get me in very much trouble. I'm giving it to you as a sign of... trust. To show you that I won't lie to you again. And because I believe what you said, about a person's story being their own. This is someone's story. I shouldn't be the one holding it."

Cariad looked at the paper. "I don't know what to say. You don't have to do this."

"I want you to know you can trust me. The best way to do that is to trust you."

"So... what is it?"

"We don't have a library aboard, but there are a lot of books floating around the ship. Reading fills time. Not long after I came aboard, I found that in a book. It's a note from the former Captain Landau to the current one. I don't know when it was written or why. And I know I should have gone directly to Clio and given it to her. But I didn't know her well enough then. It didn't seem like my place. I kept it because I didn't want it to be passed around the ship for everyone to see. It's a private message. It was bad enough I had seen it. And then so much time passed that I didn't know if giving it to her would be opening old wounds... or how to explain I'd held onto it for so long."

Cariad unfolded the paper and skimmed the words. "...did I simply find you beautiful and know what a waste it would be losing you to the Atlantic?" The note became achingly romantic, personal and intimate, and she stopped before she read anything that she might consider compromising.

"I think I would want something like this from... a person I'd lost."

"You can do whatever you want with it," Estacia said. "I trust you."

Cariad looked at her. "But if I did something to harm you, I could never share your bed again."

Estacia shrugged. "I've fucked women I was mad at before. It can be fun."

Cariad twisted to drop the note on the nightstand, then rolled back and settled on top of Estacia.

"But why take the risk when playing it safe is so much more fun?"

Estacia laughed.

Ranzi found Clio on the quarterdeck. "Kitchen's still closed."

Clio raised an eyebrow, more impressed than irritated. "Little journalist is insatiable."

"So it would seem," Ranzi said. "Luckily I'm not exactly useless in front of a stove, so I made a little stew. Set some aside if you want to take a dinner break."

"Thank you, Ines."

"How's Aravanis?"

"Still unconscious, but Delfina is hopeful." She finally slipped the eyeglass from its spot on her belt and held it out to Ranzi. "Directly behind us, twenty degrees starboard."

Ranzi turned around and scanned the horizon. It took her a moment but eventually she spotted the sails. She made a soft noise of irritation, but there was no surprise in it.

"Flame queen?"

"Who else would it be? All the way out here in the middle of nowhere, churning toward a sea full of nothing. It hasn't drifted much more than a few degrees since Common first spotted it, but they're keeping behind the horizon as much as possible."

Ranzi said, "Sneaky beggars. What's the move?"

Clio shrugged. "We carry on to our destination. The coordinates are well known, if Cariad's story is true, so there's no reason to evade or try to deceive her. She knows where we're going. If it turns out to be something there worth fighting for, we'll reassess the situation."

"Seems reasonable enough." She looked again. The ship had fallen back. "Wouldn't mind a real confrontation with some of her people, though. I hate to slash and run."

"I'll hold out hope for you, Ranzi."

"Thank you, Captain. How long until we reach the end of this boondoggle?"

"We'll reach the coordinates by nightfall."

Clio didn't know if she should sound hopeful or resigned. She had no idea what to expect but, the longer they'd spent at sea, the more she believed there would be a whole lot of nothing. But if there really was nothing, it meant she'd risked her ship and her crew at La Llama for no reason. Harriet would never have taken this risk. She never would have come all this way and stuck her neck in a noose to follow a rumor.

"At least we'll have an answer soon," Ranzi said as if she could read Clio's thoughts. "Whatever happens, I think the crew understands."

"You think Aravanis will understand? If we get out there and it's all some big joke, and she discovers she was wounded so badly for no reason?"

Ranzi nodded. "She will. Do you know why she will? Because you're her captain. You're *our* captain. You brought us out here because there's a chance for all of us to come out on top. Same reason you do everything else. Trust us. To trust you. Or else it all falls apart. I know you're still worried about living up to Hattie's reputation. But you're looking at it the wrong way."

Clio raised an eyebrow. "Enlighten me."

"You really think Fausta and I would have let you stay in charge if we didn't think you deserved to be?"

Clio laughed and slapped the rail in front of her. "I suppose that's fair enough, Ines. Keep an eye on that ship. Let me know if it gets arrogant."

"Aye."

She slapped Ranzi on the shoulder and descended the stairs to the main deck. She was about to go below when she spotted Cariad hurrying toward her. The Irishwoman's hair was wild, untied but still holding the shape of its binding as the wind caught hold of it. She looked as if she had dressed hastily, and Clio couldn't help but smile as she thought about what had left their new passenger in such a state.

"Hello there, Miss Baillie," Clio said, stopping to face her. "It seems you finally found something in Estacia's kitchen worth eating."

Cariad came to a sharp stop, eyes widening. She brought a hand to her mouth as if to wipe away an invisible trace of what she'd been doing.

"P-pardon...?"

"Some crewmen saw you in the mess earlier. I assumed you were having quite a feast."

Cariad's cheeks burned pink. "Oh. Right." She cleared her throat and then shook her head. "Um. Forget about that. I-I wanted to give you this." She held out a folded piece of paper. "It was in a book. Tucked in tight. I thought you should have it."

Clio raised an eyebrow and took the paper. She unfolded it and her amused expression faded as soon as she recognized the handwriting. She felt suddenly cold as she skimmed the message, and she raised angry eyes on Cariad.

"What is this?"

"Like I said, it was found in a book."

Clio could barely think. She couldn't focus on forming words, or even paying attention to what was in front of her. She was desperate to read what her wife had written but the words refused to form.

"When you agreed to let me come on this journey," Cariad said, inching closer, "you were afraid of being exposed in the press. That letter made me realize that you were afraid of the wrong thing. What would have happened if Aldoncia Reyes killed you back on that island? Or if her men had succeeded in sinking this ship, or setting it on fire? What if your crew was pulled off the wreckage and hung in front of her palace? Who would remember Harriet then? Who would remember you, or Ranzi, or Fausta? Everything you've done, all your successes and accomplishments, would die at the end of a rope or on the edge of a blade."

Clio ran her finger over the pen markings.

"You deserve to be known, Captain Landau. Your wife and crew deserve to be known. Let me be the one who tells your stories."

Clio tightened her jaw. She inhaled sharply and looked past Cariad, then out to sea. The reflection of the sun on the waves forced her to squint. She finally folded the note and slipped it into the inner pocket of her vest.

"You don't talk to anyone who doesn't want to talk. You change their names if they ask. Everyone gets to read what you wrote about them before you do anything with it."

Cariad nodded. "I agree to your terms, Captain."

"Then get out of here and do whatever you need to do. And... thank you."

She turned away before Cariad could respond. The paper burned in her pocket, begging to be read. But how could she do that? It was the last new message she would ever receive from Harriet, her sweet Hattie, and once she read it, it would just be a memory. It could never be new again. This was a precious gift, and she wasn't going to squander it.

She had to wait for the right moment. And she knew that no matter what lay ahead of them, or whatever was coming up behind, this was as far from the right moment as she could imagine being.

"Land ho!"

Fausta arrived on the deck at the same time as Ranzi and Clio, and the three of them moved to the gunwale to sight their destination. Fausta had never claimed the best eyesight among the crew, but she was confused to see nothing but clear ocean ahead of them. She looked up to the crow's nest to see Common was pointing to the northwest, off their starboard, and she tried looking again. The water was clear and calm.

"I don't see a damn thing," Ranzi finally said, freeing Fausta and Clio to admit the same thing. Ranzi walked toward the mast and whistled. "Tis Common! What the blazes are you on about?"

The lookout's head appeared over the side of the basket. She looked ahead, then stuck her arm out straight. "Land!"

"What fucking land?"

The head disappeared. A moment later, Common's leg came over the side of the basket and she skittered down the pole as if she'd been born in a treetop. She sighed heavily, turned to face the bow, and started to jab her finger forward. The irritation faded from her face in an instant and she lifted her chin, furrowed her brow, and dropped her arm.

"The fuck did it go..."

"Over the horizon?" Cariad had joined them at some point and was searching for land as well.

Clio said, "Common knows not to alert us from that far away. Besides, at that angle, anything sizeable that she sees from up there should be visible from here."

Fausta went to the mast and climbed it herself. She was slower than Common, less practiced, but she managed to make it without slipping or losing her grip. Halfway up she stopped and looked over her shoulder. The sea was still empty. She climbed a few rungs higher, turned, and gaped at what she saw.

"I'll be a strumpet's knickers," she muttered. "Land!"

"Where?" Clio and Ranzi both replied.

Fausta extended her arm and pointed. She realized she was doing the same thing Common had been doing, so she looked down.

"Ines, get to the wheel. Just aim us where I'm pointing. It's there, Captain."

Clio nodded her approval of the orders to Ranzi, who wasted no time crossing the deck and taking up her position.

Fausta found a more secure position, one arm wrapped around the mast with her weight resting against the wood, and looked back at the island. There was no way they could have simply missed it, and it was far too close to blame on the curve of the horizon. They should have seen it. There was no possible way they *couldn't* have seen it. It covered a full quadrant of the sky and rose into a stony peak that should have been spotted at least an hour earlier. The island was covered with thick foliage, but she could see three, no four, inlets and two coves that looked large enough for the *Banshee*.

She guided Ranzi the best she could, and the ship slowly changed course. She was glad she had chosen to go up the mast because she had the easier job. She couldn't imagine how Ranzi was going to get them safely into a harbor she couldn't actually see. They just had to act like it was a thick fog or heavy snowfall, some normal low-visibility situation they could wrap their heads around.

When they were close enough that the island seemed to fill the entire world ahead of them, she started hearing shouts of surprise from below her. She looked down and saw the deckhands gazing around in wonder. Even Clio looked stunned. Whatever had been blocking their sight had fallen away and she knew they could see it as clearly as her now. She looked over her shoulder to confirm and Ranzi gave her a nod.

Relieved, Fausta climbed down and stretched out her sore arm. Clio came over to her, mouth still open in surprise as she looked around her.

"It doesn't make sense. Where did it come from?"

"Your guess is as good as mine," Fausta said. "But I believe Common when she said it was there before any of us could see it."

"And I have to take your word it was there before," Clio said. "The evidence is right in front of us now. But it doesn't make any sense whatsoever."

Cariad, who had lingered on the sidelines of the situation, said, "Surely you've seen and heard tell of stranger things out here at sea, Captain Landau."

"Hearing stories, sure," Clio said. "Fata morgana, without a doubt. And if you spend long enough at sea, you'll start imagining all kinds of things. But this is a completely different league of bizarre."

Fausta had a thought and went to the railing, looking behind them this time. "The ship Aldoncia sent after us is still there. She's trailing, but that's probably intentional to keep us from spooking. Do you reckon they can see us, or are we part of whatever this island is?"

"There's no way of knowing," Clio said, "so we might as well not waste time worrying." She turned to Common. "Keep an eye on that ship and let me know if it stays away or comes toward us."

"Aye, Captain."

She clambered up the mast and was soon out of sight in her basket again.

"What should I do?" Cariad said.

Clio started to answer, then hissed through her teeth and squeezed her eyes shut. She pressed her thumb against the bridge of her nose and slumped against the railing. Fausta was at her side in an instant but the captain held up her free hand. Her face was twisted in a grimace of pain like she'd been hit by a full hangover in the space of a few seconds. Fausta rested a hand on Clio's bicep as support.

"It's nothing," Clio said. "Just a..." She shook her head, gasped, and moved her fingers to her temples.

Fausta looked at Cariad. "Get the doctor."

"No," Clio said. "It's already fading. I was looking too damn hard for the island. The sun off the water... It just spiked my eyes a bit. Thank you for your concern."

"I'm not letting up on it just yet, if that's okay with you."

Clio smiled and clapped her hand on Fausta's shoulder. She looked at Cariad, paused to remember the woman's question, then nodded. "Stay on deck. We have ship's business to take care of, but this is where you led us. We might need you nearby."

"Whatever you say, Captain."

Fausta followed Clio up onto the elevated deck where Ranzi was steering them into position to drop anchor and berth.

"Looks like the Irish lass had good information after all," Ranzi said.

"All we know for certain is there's an island."

"That appeared from thin air," Fausta said. "Remember what the story promised? Safe harbor. I'd say invisible is about as safe as anyone could hope for."

Clio said, "If we can get all the way out here before whoever is chasing us catches up. Safe, sure, but not exactly convenient. I say we wait until we find out whose island this is before we call the trip a success."

"And Miss Baillie?" Fausta asked.

Clio looked down at the deck and locked eyes with the redhead.

"She's coming ashore with us. Whatever she led us to, it's only right that she faces it head-on with the rest of us."

CHAPTER ELEVEN

DELFINA DIDN'T like defying captain's orders, but she equally hated being useless when someone on the crew needed her. She'd slept for an hour, maybe two, and then her body woke up and refused to go back to sleep. She tossed and turned until she finally decided laziness was a bigger sin than insubordination. She stopped by the mess hall on her way to the infirmary and, finding it apparently abandoned, made a sandwich and took it back to watch over Aravanis.

She heard the calls of land from above, and she felt the ship change course and speed in anticipation of dropping anchor.

Aravanis sat up.

Delfina hurried to her side. "No. Absolutely not. Lie down. You need to heal."

"What happened?" Aravanis asked.

"You were in a fight. It was vicious. You were badly hurt. You nearly drowned and then... and..." She was distracted by the sight of Aravanis' hands. Earlier the fingers had been almost black with bruises. Nicks and cuts had left cougar-spots from knuckle to wrist. Now her hands looked absolutely without blemish. Delfina turned one hand over and examined the palm. The skin, previously burned away from her foolish climb up the chains, looked as fresh as a landlubber's.

"My hands are fine," Aravanis said.

"So it would seem," Delfina muttered. She eyed the gauze around Aravanis' forearms. "Hold on. I need to check this."

She went to her supplies, retrieved a pair of bandage shears and carefully cut away the wrappings. Dried blood peeled away from Aravanis' skin, but there was no pain associated with it because the arm underneath was completely undamaged. Some of the cuts had been bone-deep, but now there wasn't even a mark. She'd stitched the cuts and she couldn't find evidence of a single knot. She picked up a bottle of water and washed away the blood as if it could be concealing the grievous injuries that had nearly made the bosun a double amputee.

"This isn't possible."

"What is so shocking?"

"Do you not remember your injuries? What about the fight at La Llama?"

Aravanis' eyes narrowed. "What were we doing at La Llama?" Realization flared in her dark eyes. She lunged, trying to get out of bed again. "Captain Landau..."

Delfina put her hands on Aravanis' shoulders, forced her back. "Clio is *fine*. You were the only on who suffered any major injuries. I don't care what you look like, I want you to stay here until I have a chance to run a full examination."

"There is no reason~"

"I will strap you to the mattress if it becomes necessary."

Aravanis bared her teeth, then looked toward the ceiling. "We're slowing. Have we arrived at a destination?"

"Yes. But you're not going anywhere until we've figured out what's happening with you. Fausta and Ranzi can take care of anything dangerous."

"I'm not suffering any pain or~"

Delfina held up the bloody gauze. "I sewed you back together, Penelope. I had your goddamn blood on my hands. I sat right there and wondered if you were ever going to wake up. If you were going to die from infection, or blood loss, or a brain injury from hitting your damn head on the ship, or some other thing I hadn't even spotted. I don't know how or why you're suddenly back in one piece. I don't give a damn as long as it's authentic. But until we're sure it isn't just some kind of hallucination, you are going to stay in that bed. Am I understood, bo's'n?"

Aravanis took a deep breath. She didn't blink as she released it through her nose. Then she slumped back onto the pillow.

"Fine."

Delfina relaxed. "Thank you. As a reward, I will go topside and find out what news. If you are in dire need, and only if you are the only one who can do what they need done, I will take you up myself. But otherwise you are not to leave that bed. Am I clear?"

Aravanis grunted.

"Am I clear?"

"Yes, Doctor."

Delfina nodded. "Good. I'll be back as quickly as I can."

She waited until she was in the corridor before she released a shaky breath of relief. She put a hand on the wall and hung her head, closed her eyes, and took a moment to accept what had just happened. She'd been terrified of so many less-than-ideal outcomes. There had been a chance Aravanis would lose her right hand. The blow to her skull could have caused any number of issues that may not have presented until years down the road.

But now she was okay. She seemed to be okay. She was willing to accept the miracle for now and search for explanations later.

Clio didn't want to leave the ship undefended again, not in unknown waters and one of Aldoncia Reyes' ships circling like a vulture. Ranzi would stay behind in command while Fausta accompanied her to investigate the island. Cariad would join them since it was her mission and it was only fair that she share the risk. The journalist seemed more than willing when the landing party was announced, so Clio didn't feel any guilt about endangering her. She also chose three deckhands, two women and a man who were adept with both swords and pistols.

The man rowed them away from the *Banshee*. None of them spoke, all of them enraptured by the sight ahead of them. Clio watched a flock of birds rise from a thickly forested area toward the central peak. She wondered if their shadowing ship would see the birds appear as if from nowhere, or if they were equally invisible to outside observers. There were trees everywhere but no sign of civilization.

"You said the message came from a country," Clio said without turning around. "I'm not seeing much sign of any population at all."

"Maybe country isn't the right word. Kingdom? Realm...?" Cariad shook her head, gazing at the island with awe. "This is as far as anyone's reports ever go. Nobody talks about the specifics, just that they were rejected."

Clio didn't like that explanation, but she had to admit she felt a certain thrill at~

Harriet on the deck of a ship, deck swaying under her feet, rain pelting her face. Harriet, facing forward, windblown hair veiling her face. Clio walked toward her, finding her balance. She was still quite far away when she caught sight of motion from the corner of her eye and turned just in time to register the boom swinging directly at her~

She threw herself backward to avoid it, landing practically in the lap of one of the female deckhands. Fausta turned to check on her, and Clio bared her teeth as she regained her seat.

"What's wrong?" Cariad asked. "Headache again?"

"Don't you worry about it," Clio snapped, straightening the hat on her head. She squared her shoulders and planted her feet on the bottom of the boat. "Something about this place is strange."

Fausta faced forward again. "I can feel it too, Captain. It feels off somehow."

"Dangerous strange?"

Fausta scanned the shoreline, then looked up at the sky for nearly a full minute before she answered with a quick shake of her head.

"No. It doesn't feel dangerous."

"I concur," Clio admitted. "But let's everyone speak up if that changes at all."

There were murmurs of agreement all around.

When they reached the sandbar, Fausta took the oar and planted her foot on the side of the boat, stretching out with the blunt end to poke the ground.

"Seems solid enough," she reported.

"Let's take the risk," Clio said.

One of the deckhands volunteered to go first. Fausta held onto the woman's hand as she stepped over the edge of the boat and rested her weight on the sand. She bent her knee and pushed down, nodded, and took a few steps away from the boat. She hopped once, kicked the sand, and proclaimed, "It might have been invisible for a bit, but it's definitely solid, Cap'n."

"Good enough for me."

The male deckhand secured the boat once everyone was off. Fausta went further inland to examine the forest. She pointed at the trees when Clio joined her.

"This is the most obvious place to lay anchor. Assuming Miss Baillie is correct and we're just the latest in a long line of visitors, we'll probably be able to find some form of path through here. I'll go ahead and see what I can find from up close. The rest of you should stay back until I know there's nothing waiting to pounce on us."

"Be wary," Clio said.

As Fausta moved inland to search for a path, Clio turned and spotted Cariad bending forward so she could roll up the cuffs of her trousers. She hesitated and then walked over to the journalist, lightly thumping her on the shoulder. Cariad stood quickly, almost toppling, and swept her hair out of her face with the back of her hand.

"Hello. Sorry. Am I in the way..."

"No. I needed to tell you... to tell *someone*..." Clio checked to make sure they were alone, then lowered her voice. "I remembered something."

"Okay..."

"Something from before."

"Before..." Cariad's eyes widened. "Oh. I-I had heard about your injury. You remembered something from before that happened?"

Clio nodded. "I think so. I was on a ship, there was a storm. I saw Harriet across the deck. I walked toward her. And then the boom came swinging around and..." She tapped between her eyes with two fingers. "Right in the bean."

"Is this the first time you've had a memory like that?"

"I don't know. Maybe I've had glimpses and then they faded again. Maybe my memories from before just can't be held long-term. That's why I'm telling you."

Cariad said, "Why me?"

Clio shrugged. "You're the writer. Who else am I going to tell? Keep it to yourself for now."

"Of course."

Fausta was already walking back, and the rest of the group was converging around the captain to hear about their next steps. Clio was about to ask Fausta what she'd found when she spotted movement through the trees. She made a short, sharp whistle between her teeth and dropped her hand to the hilt of her sword. Fausta followed the captain's lead, drawing her pistol as she spun on her heel to face whatever had followed her from the tree line.

A woman dressed in a white gown emerged from the forest. She looked as if she had been sculpted from porcelain, with fine pale skin and dark eyebrows that cut wide arcs over shining green eyes. Clio couldn't help but compare her curves to those of figureheads she'd seen in the past. Her center-parted hair was midnight dark and fell over both shoulders in twin curtains. The woman smiled as she approached them and stopped a few feet away, hands folded casually in front of her.

"Hello. Welcome. May I have the pleasure of speaking to your captain?"

"That's me," Clio said.

The woman smiled condescendingly. "You are not the first to attempt this deception." She leaned her head to the side and raised her eyebrows at the male deckhand. "You avow you are not the captain of the ship I see behind you?"

Clio glanced over her shoulder at the only man in their party. He blinked in surprise and moved his lips a few times before he managed to form words. "No. I mean, yes, I vow... uh... what?"

Cariad spoke up, though the tremor in her voice indicated she was terrified to draw attention to herself. "It's true. Clio Landau is the captain. I sought her out specifically~"

The woman held up a hand to silence her. "It stands to reason that people are speculating about our intentions. It was only a matter of time before they realized we wanted to employ a female captain."

"I am the captain of that vessel. Captain Clio Landau, and the *Banshee* is under my command. This is my crew. You will speak to me, and you will not elevate a man whose name I don't even know simply due to his sex."

Fausta muttered, "I'm sure she meant no offense, Roger."

Clio kept her eyes on the mystery woman. "I could give two tosses if he's offended or not. Do you plan to mutiny, Roger?"

She heard him clear his throat. "No, captain. I served under your wife and-and I'm happy to serve under you as well. You treat us good and that's not nothing on a lot of ships."

The woman seemed intrigued. "Wife... you are Sapphic?"

"Not familiar with that term," Clio said. "But I had a wife, yes."

"I know the word," Fausta said, "and a fair number of the crew can be described as such. If not every night, then from time to time."

The woman's smile widened. "There is another word for that. If you are truly the captain…"

Fausta said, "This is my captain. You have my oath and my word. I sail under the flag of Captain Clio Landau, proud to tell anyone who inquires."

Clio felt a surge of emotion at those words but struggled not to let it show on her face as she watched the woman.

"Well, then! Perhaps an agreement can be made. My name is Boe. I shall escort you to my mistress. First, I must request that you leave your weapons here."

"That won't happen." Clio intended her tone to leave no room for debate.

Boe countered by saying, "The other option is returning to your ship and going home. This is a peaceful island. You will find no weapons here, and you will respect the residents by not brandishing yours in their face. I would have thought our gift would be enough to prove our benevolence."

"Gift?" Clio asked.

"The gift of wholeness." Boe's smile wavered as she registered their lack of understanding. "Your injuries were healed when you passed through the veil."

Clio looked down at her arms. She turned to see Fausta rolling up her sleeve and remembered her being cut during their escape from La Llama. She didn't remember exactly where the wound had been, but the skin seemed completely unblemished save for a few faint scars from previous encounters. Fausta looked up and met Clio's gaze with genuine wonder.

"Aravanis…?"

"I didn't think to check on her before we left the ship," Clio admitted. She faced Boe again. "Everyone on the ship has had their wounds healed?"

Boe nodded. "Recent, unhealed wounds have been mended. There is nothing to be done for the older injuries, but hopefully the imperfect gift is enough."

Clio considered the situation, drew her sword, and rested its blade on her weak hand. She started to lower it to the ground, then thought of another solution. She turned to the man Boe had presumed was the captain and held the sword out to him.

"Take our weapons back to the ship. Once there, check the infirmary. If Aravanis is healed, sound five bells."

"Aye," he said, then began gathering the weapons from the

women. He carried their arms back to the boat and pushed it away from the beach.

Boe said, "If you wish to remain here until you receive the signal—"

"That won't be necessary." Clio's hand instinctively went to her empty sheath. She covered the move by hooking her thumb in her belt. "You have to believe we're telling the truth about me being captain. We have to believe that this truly is a peaceful kingdom and we're in no danger. I would say that places us in the same position, don't you?"

"With more risk on your part," Boe said, smiling.

"So long as you acknowledge that."

Boe gestured behind her. "I will lead the way. Our destination is not far, but the forest has no clear path and it's easier if you follow."

Clio glanced back at Fausta, who shrugged and slipped her hands into her pockets as she started up the beach.

They'd come all this way, after all. And she had a feeling very few of the other people who had followed the same rumors Cariad brought to them had made it past these first two trials. No female captain, and certainly no disarmament. It only made sense to see what lay ahead.

ESTACIA NAVARRO

"I was barely more than a child back then, honestly. I've only ever been interested in cooking. I was good at it. I loved coming up with recipes and seeing people enjoy what I made. I had four brothers and two sisters, so I got a lot of practice. I was the youngest. And eventually they married, moved on, died... soon it was just me and my parents, and they were getting too old to work. So I found a tavern that needed a cook and I offered my services. I was too young and stupid to know how to ask for what I deserved. Payment or respect. So I just jumped in with both feet.

Tavern was owned by a man named Bastia. I think he only hired me because I was young and stupid enough not to know things. Things like, I could tell him to stop when he put his hand on my bottom. Or I didn't have to suffer his attempts to kiss me every time we were alone in the kitchen. He would pinch and poke and brush and I told myself it was nothing. It was harmless. He was just being a flirt. But I hated it. I hated every touch. I started to sweat at the sight of him. He thought it was cute. Or that it was part of a game.

He never went too far. But he might have if it wasn't for the night he stepped behind me and put his hands on the counter on either side of me. He was so much bigger than me, and I was completely trapped. He said he was just going to show me the proper way to prepare meat for casola de carn. I told him I already knew, but he said he had a special way. And he *put his hand around my wrist and he...*

He didn't have a chance to do anything else, thanks to Captain Landau. That's the first Captain Landau. Harriet. She stepped through the kitchen door with one of our bowls in her hand. She was a tall woman and she could intimidate someone like Bastard Bastia without saying a word. She looked at him, then she looked at me, and she strolled toward us with the bowl held out.

'I want to complain about the quality of your food, sir.'

Bastia's weight left my back, and I've never felt freer than I did at that moment. He blustered about how he only used the freshest and finest ingredients in his food. Which was true. For all his faults, Bastia knew that he had to spend money to be considered the best meal in town. He took pride in that, and Harriet... somehow she knew that was exactly where to jab him.

'Finest?' she said, sounding hysterical. 'Finest? Then how do you explain the mold on my bread?'

She held the bowl out and Bastia leaned closer to look. There was no bread, only very fresh stew, which she shoved up into his fat-nosed face. Bastia fell back in surprise more than anything, but oh that broth... I'd splashed some on my wrist before, and it was still steaming when it hit his cheeks. It had to sting like fire. And Harriet moved like a flash. She stepped around the table and grabbed the back of Bastia's collar and swung him down to crack his head on the counter. She did that three times! When she finally let him go, he fell flat on his fat ass, and she put her boot on his throat. Then she looked at me.

'I could kill him,' she said. 'Or I could just scare him bad enough that he never comes anywhere near you ever again.'

'You're one of them pirate bitches,' Bastia said, brave words from a man with a boot on his neck and stew in his eyes. 'You ain't gonna be 'round long enough to scare me. The second you leave, which I think is tomorr' mornin', I'll show her who really runs this kitchen.'

Harriet pressed her foot harder against his throat. She looked at me. 'You see, he makes a strong argument for killin'. But I leave it up to you.'

'Are you really a pirate?' I asked.

'Aye,' she said. 'And what he said about us leaving tomorrow is true. But between me and some of my mates in the other room, we can spend the rest of tonight putting enough scare into him that he'll never touch a woman again without having nightmares.'

I didn't want to tell a stranger to kill him. I didn't want a murder on my soul, you know? Even the murder of someone like Bastard Bastia. But my mind was really stuck on other thoughts.

'Does your ship have a kitchen...?'

And Harriet, she looked at me like I'd just become someone else. Someone maybe she knew.

'Yes it does,' she said. 'And we happen to be in need of a cook.'

'And it pays? I can send money home?'

'It pays very well, in fact,' Harriet said.

So I took off my apron and I threw it in Bastard Bastia's face, and I said, 'Then I don't give a fuck what you do with him. I'll be at the dock in an hour.'

'Our ship's called the Banshee. And by the way, I just needed to get him angry and away from you so I could hit him. Your stew truly was delicious.'

I smiled and I said thank you very much. And then I walked out of that kitchen and never looked back."

CHAPTER TWELVE

FAUSTA BELIEVED they had walked almost a mile when they heard the sound of five bells echoing across the water. They stopped and looked back, then Clio and Fausta looked at each other.

"That's not possible," Fausta said. "Some of those injuries would have taken months to fully heal. If they ever healed at all."

Clio said, "Do you believe Robert would deceive us?"

"Roger," Fausta corrected, but she was utterly perplexed. "And no. He would have no reason to lie. If the bells have sounded it means Aravanis is healed."

Boe said, "As I promised. I am glad your friend is no longer hurt."

"So are we," Clio said, sounding suspicious. "Please, let's continue."

"By all means." Boe turned her back and started walking again.

The girl seemed perfectly fine. Friendly, polite, nothing amiss. But Fausta hated being unarmed with anyone she didn't know. She wished she could have kept at least a small dagger. But the more time she spent on this island, the more she seemed certain Boe would have been able to detect its presence. Smarter, and probably safer, to be unarmed. At least for right now.

Clio was ahead of her, with Cariad and the two deckhands behind them. Fausta caught up with the captain. She kept her eyes on Boe, who continued her march through the underbrush as if she was unaware they were behind her. Even so, she leaned close to Clio and barely spoke above a whisper.

"Before we even hear what they're offering, I want to make sure you keep your mind on what we're being offered for this unknown mission."

"Safe harbor."

"Pretty far to run for a safe harbor," Fausta pointed out. "And to what end? To get protection from peaceful folk who nicely ask interlopers to disarm themselves. What do you think would happen if we'd insisted?"

"I wasn't inclined to find out," Clio said.

"We may learn soon enough if Aldoncia decides to swing this way."

Boe replied without turning to face them. "We will dissuade her, as we've done with others in the past." She chuckled and shook her head. "Our veil is a powerful defense, but it is far from the only thing keeping us safe."

Clio raised an eyebrow at Fausta.

"Right, right," Fausta muttered, then fell back. She checked to make sure Cariad was keeping up with them. The journalist was sweaty and out of breath but didn't seem in danger of collapse. She noticed Fausta watching her, gave a nod, and forced herself to stand up straighter. Fausta returned the nod and, saving Cariad from being forced to ask, said, "How much further to wherever you're taking us?"

"It's not far." Boe pointed. "There's a peak here, it's on the other side."

As promised, Fausta saw a clearing when they reached the top of the incline. A small stone structure stood in the center of the space. The northern side of the building had a sprawling wooden deck, where they could see a woman in a long white gown preparing a food on some sort of built-in oven. Boe picked up speed as she descended the hill, like a child eager to return home. The woman on the deck heard, or otherwise sensed, their approach and lowered a hood on the grill. She came down to the grass and held her arms out, gathering Boe into an embrace that turned into a passionate kiss.

Fausta raised her eyebrows and looked at Clio, who seemed more amused than surprised.

When the kiss ended, the woman gazed into Boe's eyes, then

stroked her cheek as she surveyed the new arrivals. She was clearly older than Boe, with silver streaks at her temples and interwoven through the rest of her long curls. Her face didn't give away anything about what she was thinking as she scanned the group.

"And who have you brought us, Boe?"

"Captain Clio Landau. My first mate, Fausta Gittens." Fausta dipped her chin, the slightest of acknowledgements. "Our... historian, Cariad Baillie. The others are Bethel and Jeffries."

The woman nodded to them all.

"They are Sapphic," Boe said, apparently unable to withhold the revelation any longer. Her fingers teased the placket of the older woman's shirt. "Like us."

"Well, not with each other," Fausta clarified. "But she had a wife. And I've been known to dabble. And I don't know about her..." She looked at Cariad.

"I lay with women, if that's what you're asking."

Fausta raised an eyebrow but refrained from comment.

"Wonderful!" The woman stepped out of her embrace with Boe. "My name is Leola Fairfax. I am the patron of this island and its inhabitants. Welcome. Captain, the name of your ship?"

"*Banshee.*"

"Ah!" Leola's eyes danced. "Irish spirit whose cry is a portent of death. A wonderful choice. I'm sure it has struck fear in a great many hearts." She said this last with a gruff, almost mocking, inflection that she tempered with a bright smile.

"We've won our share of battles."

Leola laughed. "I would be thrilled to hear them, I'm certain. Perhaps over our meal. You must be hungry after such a long journey." She smiled at a private thought, then held up a finger. "I should assure you, out of deference to the faerie origins of your ship's name, you have no fear from accepting an offer of food from us. We are not fae."

"Good to know," Clio said. "Very comforting."

Leola chuckled and motioned for them to follow her back to the deck. "I began preparing the meal as soon as you passed through the veil. It should be nearly ready by now. Have a seat, have a seat."

Boe led them to a table at the far end of the deck. It looked out over a stretch of tall wild grass that ended in a barrier of trees which seemed crowded too thick for anyone to pass between them.

Clio sat on one of the benches. Fausta sat across from her, still overly aware of her lack of weapons. She eyed the cutlery next to the plates and wondered how much damage she could do with them if push came to shove. Boe retrieved a pitcher from the house and returned to fill everyone's cups. Fausta perked up, hoping for something alcoholic, but a quick sip revealed it was merely some kind of fruit concoction. She slipped a flask from the pocket of her vest and added a tipple to her cup.

"Are there many other residents of this island?" Clio asked as Leola tended to their food.

"Oh, a great number. How many neighbors do we have, Boe?"

Boe raised her chin and proudly declared, "Seven hundred and eighty two at last count, but Toscana is with child. So it is soon to be seven hundred and eighty four."

"Your math is off," Leola scolded. "Try again."

"I am correct. Toscana is bearing twins."

"Ah!" Leola laughed and shook her head. "Always trying to trick me, love. I must watch you with both eyes."

Boe laughed and tossed her hair. "So long as you like what you see, Madam."

"Oh very much so, love. Very much indeed."

Boe ducked her chin and bit her lip, color rising in her cheeks.

Fausta and Clio looked at each other across the table. Fausta knew exactly what the captain was thinking. Seeing two women, especially committed lovers, was nothing strange aboard the *Banshee*. But even Clio and Harriet had muted their interactions when among strangers. Sure, they had declared themselves of like minds, but certainly they hadn't gained the trust of these women so easily.

Clio cleared her throat. "Boe explained the 'gift' you gave us when we passed through the veil. It would seem I may owe you for the life of my bo's'n."

"You owe us nothing," Leola said. "That is the nature of gifts. I am ready to begin serving, if you will bring me your plates."

They lined up next to the grill. Fausta saw thick slabs of meat, potatoes as big as her fist and carrots that made them look puny by comparison. Leola was generous, serving more than Fausta thought she could comfortably eat, but she nodded her thanks and carried the plate back to the table.

Clio waited until everyone had food and Leola had taken a seat before she spoke. "We might as well take this opportunity to discuss the mission you have for us."

"So quick to talk business," Leola said.

"Miss Baillie implied you had been looking for the right ship for quite a long time. I know that if our positions were reversed, I would be quite tired of waiting."

Leola accepted that logic with a dip of her chin. "You speak the truth. Very well. We may discuss while we eat." She began carving up her vegetables. "The source of the veil protecting our island is natural in origin. But like thunderstorms and hurricanes, its existence requires certain elements in just the right arrangement. For the past few years, one of those elements has been diminishing. In a few years' time, if nothing is done, it will vanish entirely and we will be left unprotected.

"Fortunately, the missing element can be restored, but it is only available on another island. We only lack the ability to travel there ourselves to acquire it. We have a home we love, a home that provides everything we need, and we are safe. There's never been a need for vessels to travel farther than the harbor so we can fish. That is why we need your help."

Clio said, "It sounds like a simple pick-up and delivery job."

"There will be hazards," Leola said. "I don't want you to be unprepared. And I fear that if word of your quest was to spread, you would be in danger of... well..."

"Other pirates," Fausta said.

"Quite so. Others would try to take what you had, or pursue you to the other island. You must not allow that to happen. We have gone to great pains to protect its location. To that end, you cannot be given a map to find its location. Boe will accompany you, showing you the way."

Boe beamed proudly, clearly eager for her part in the undertaking.

Cariad said, "You handed out the location of this island to anyone who showed the slightest interest." Everyone at the table looked at her. She cringed slightly at the weight of their attention. "Surely that was incredibly dangerous. You had no idea who would show up."

Leola smiled and tilted her head to the side. "You have implied several times, or directly said, that we are defenseless. That assumption is incorrect. Everyone who has answered our call returned unharmed, yes, but I assume they have kept our secrets. Is that true?"

Cariad nodded. "Yes."

"Think of the crews who followed the coordinates and then returned home empty-handed. Do they strike you as the kind who would happily turn around and go home simply because I asked them nicely?"

"I suppose not," Cariad allowed.

"Quite right. We have ways of ensuring that our island remains protected. The other island, the source, is not as fortunate. That is why it's imperative that we trust you before we make our contract."

Fausta braced herself. "How do you suggest we accomplish that?"

"One of your crew must spend an evening here, on the island," Leola said.

"Alone?" Clio said.

"And unarmed."

Clio was already shaking her head. "I can't ask~"

Fausta spoke at the same time. "I'll do it."

The captain looked at her. "Are you sure?"

Fausta shrugged. "I can count at least twenty more dangerous situations I've put myself in for much lesser rewards. I'm confident I'll be fine."

"No harm will come to her if she respects our land and our laws. I am, after all, entrusting you with the safety of my lovely Boe. We must establish our trust."

"Seems like a simple enough test," Fausta said.

Clio looked as if she wanted to argue, but Fausta knew she wouldn't want to have the discussion in front of the strangers. Asking to speak privately would be just as much of an issue. So she was trapped at the table, forced to debate herself internally. She finally reached a conclusion and nodded her head once.

"If Fausta is willing, then I won't stand in her way."

Boe clapped her hands together once and bounced on the bench, giggling quietly. "It's been so long since we had a guest! It's so exciting!"

Leola smiled and held up a hand to calm the younger girl. "Okay. Okay. If you're that excited, you can go begin preparing her rooms."

"Gladly." She rose, smoothed her hands over her clothes, and bowed to the group. "I will give her a space with a view of the water so she can see her ship. That way she will not be lonely."

"Very considerate," Leola said.

Fausta turned and watched Boe hurry away, then turned to Leola. "She's a very excitable thing."

"Hah, yes. Very much so. Even on days which are less

auspicious, she always finds something to be excited about. It can be as tiresome as it is endearing." She arched an eyebrow and shrugged as if dismissing her own complaint. "But I would not change her. She is my beloved."

Cariad cleared her throat. "I would love to sit with you and speak about~"

"No," Leola said without waiting for her to finish the question. "I appreciate your profession, and your goal to seek truths. I will answer your questions for your own enlightenment, but I cannot allow you to share those answers with the general public."

"With people who haven't earned it," Clio clarified.

Leola nodded. "Precisely. In the morning, we will meet again on the beach. Your crew member will be returned to you, and I will provide the coordinates of your destination. Boe will accompany you to aid in navigation. The other island is not as easy to find as we are, even if you're looking for it."

"You would trust us with Boe? Given how close the two of you are..."

"That is another reason for your friend to stay with us tonight. You will see that our intentions are honorable, and we expect the same to be extended to us aboard your vessel."

Fausta said, "A trust exercise, then."

"Just so," Leola said.

Clio raised her cup. "Then to a new and mutually beneficial friendship."

Leola raised her own cup in a toast, and they drank.

"About that," Fausta said. "Part of what you're offering is a safe harbor. It's certainly obvious that you can follow through with that. Assuming a ship is able to get here to take advantage of it."

"You are quite out of the way," Clio admitted. "And there's a ship waiting for us just beyond your veil. They may not know where we went, but they know we can't stay here forever. A sanctuary isn't particularly useful if your enemies can just lurk outside and wait for you to show your face."

Leola said, "Oh, you misunderstood. The 'harbor' is metaphorical. If you assist us in rejuvenating our veil, we will give you the ability to create the same effect on your ship."

Clio and Fausta both went still at that. They looked at each other, communicating silently.

"You mean our ship would be invisible?" Clio said.

"Or you could make it become invisible when necessary, yes."

Fausta sat up straighter. That was so much more valuable than just a safe place to run. If they could conceal themselves the same way the island was hidden, they could have avoided the entire mess at La Llama. All sorts of jobs that were otherwise impossible simply because they couldn't get close enough without drawing attention to themselves.

"And the healing aspect...?"

"It's an element of the veil's powers. It would be diminished, but given that it's only protecting one ship instead of a whole island... yes, it would be included."

"That's quite a reward," Fausta said.

"It is quite a valuable service you are providing," Leola said. "This is one reason I was adamant about finding a female captain. You have enough obstacles in your path simply due to your sex. I decided to help you even things up a little."

Clio took a drink and raised her eyebrows at Fausta over the rim. There was no need for them to say anything. If they could travel wherever they wanted without the risk of being seen, with no chance of being pursued...

The possibilities were endless.

CHAPTER THIRTEEN

CLIO THOUGHT she had successfully ignored the pain behind her eyes throughout dinner, at least to the point that no one noticed. But on the walk back to the beach, a sudden spike hit her so hard that she was briefly blinded. She stumbled and reached out for what she thought was a tree. She dug her fingers in and only realized it was Cariad's arm when the woman grunted in pain and put her other hand on top of Clio's. She tried to relax her grip but a second painful jab sent her to her knees. She put her other hand against her temple and hissed sharply through her teeth.

"Captain?" Somehow Cariad's arm was now free, and she put both hands on Clio's shoulders. "Should I go back and get Fausta?"

They'd left her behind at Leola's home, and there was nothing she could do about the pain even if she was with the group.

"It will pass. I just... need..."

—blood red velvet furniture. Exactly what she would have expected from a man like this. His liquor was top shelf, though. She was holding a tumbler of it in her right hand so that the weight of the ice rested against her palm. The sun shone through the quartet of windows in the western wall, so bright that she was grateful for her amber-tinted lenses. She was dressed in finery to match the office; a floor-length skirt, pinstripe suit jacket, and a high-collared shirt with a ruffled bow at the front.

"A simple enough assignment," the owner of the office said. She turned

toward the voice, but he was a blur. No face, not even a vague body shape. The person behind the desk was a smudge on reality, the memory of him still lost to her. "Is it within your wheelhouse?"

Clio walked closer to the desk, every step measured. "You said you had never heard of me before you asked for recommendations." She didn't recognize her own voice. What was this accent? She sounded posh, refined, arrogant. "My anonymity is my calling card. I have been doing this job for, mm, a number of years and my name has never been leaked to anyone who might wish me harm. My enemies don't know where to begin looking for me. I am a ghost. And I am very good at my job."

The man, she was fairly certain it was a man, made a noise she couldn't parse. "A salient point. Very well. We've discussed your payment…"

"~passed out."

"I swear if that fucking faerie put something in our food…"

"She said she wasn't a faerie."

"She said a lot of fucking things."

Clio opened her eyes. The worst of the pain had faded, but the throb was still there, testing the boundaries of her skull. She was on her knees, leaning against someone.

"She's awake." It was one of the female deckhands speaking, crouched in front of her, gazing into her eyes with concern. "Captain? Are you all right?"

"We weren't poisoned. I was having head pain before we even met the woman." Clio was alarmed at the sandpaper quality of her voice. She held out her hand, which Bethel took to help her stand. "I can get back to the ship. Once we're there, Delfina can check me out."

Jeffries, the other deckhand, snorted. "So much for the island healing all our injuries. Can't even knock down a soddin' migraine."

"We'll see what Delf has to say about that before we dismiss the claims, hm?" Clio slipped her arm around Cariad's waist. Cariad did the same to her, tacitly accepting the role of support. "Come on. We're almost to the beach. We don't want Miss Fairfax to think we've changed our minds. Onward."

Bethel and Jeffries looked at each other but then continued on. She would have to keep an eye on them. All it would take is the wrong rumor to get started. Whispers among the deckhands, spreading to the powder monkeys, eventually drifting up to the crew. It would only take a simple 'doesn't she look tired…?' before she ended up with a ship full of mutineers.

"It was another memory, wasn't it?" Cariad was close enough to Clio's ear that she didn't have to speak loudly for her voice to be heard. "You were saying something while you were unconscious. We couldn't make out any words, but you were definitely having a conversation."

Clio said, "Yes," because nodding would have been far too painful. "I don't think I can make much sense of it yet. But it was… new. It was something I know I've never remembered before."

"Leola implied old injuries wouldn't be affected by the veil," Cariad said. "If your memory loss was caused by an injury, that was more than thirty years ago, right? Why would it be healing?"

"No idea. And I also have no idea why I'm suffering such bastardly pain with the healing. Fausta's arm healed without her even realizing it."

"Perhaps the size of the injury has something to do with it. Losing half your life is a far larger wound than a cut on the arm."

"That is… very true." She grunted and tripped over her own feet.

Cariad kept her upright and forward-moving. "It's all right. I've got you, Captain."

"Thank you, Miss Baillie."

"Aye, aye," Cariad said.

They continued on. Clio hadn't been lying, the headache really was starting to abate. But now she was more worried about what unpleasant surprises might be left in its wake.

Ranzi paced along the starboard railing, taking one step for every heartbeat so the thump of her bootheel marked one second. She had been tracing this path for two hours, and Aldoncia's ship hadn't budged. Her arms were crossed over her chest and her eyes were locked on the ship which had hounded their trip here and now waited patiently just a few hundred leagues away. She felt like a fawn in the shadow of a lion. And she hated feeling like a fawn. She spun on the ball of her foot and continued in the other direction.

Aravanis stepped into her way. "I can make them leave."

"I have no doubt. But you won't." She stepped around the bosun and continued her march.

Aravanis fell into step behind her. "Let me take the launch and go have a talk with them."

"And how would you explain where you'd come from?" Ranzi

asked. "And how exactly do you plan to fight off an entire ship that's no doubt armed to the gills."

"I can handle myself."

"You absolutely can. But I'm not going to send you on a suicide mission just because you were miraculously healed from your last idiotic plan."

Aravanis grunted. "Maybe I recovered for a reason. They're still going to be out there when we leave this place. Do you think they'll allow us to simply brush by on our way to our next destination? What will be done then?"

"That will be Captain Landau's call, not yours and not mine. You may outrank me on a normal day, but the captain left me in charge. So for now, I am the captain of this vessel, and I am ordering you to remain here."

"Very well," Aravanis grunted.

"Hey." Ranzi stopped and turned to face her. "How are you feeling? Truthfully. I saw your wounds. Hell, I scrubbed your blood off those boards over there. It's astounding to me that you're walking around and talking right now."

Aravanis raised her hands, gazing at them as if they had just appeared. "I don't feel any different. But I saw my clothing in the infirmary. I saw the rips and tears, and the... blood. And yet I don't have a single new scar to account for the trials I went through. I can't even remember the fight. I suppose that makes it a null point."

"Don't be in a hurry to reclaim those injuries just for a bit of pride, aye?"

"Aye," Aravanis said.

Ranzi kept up her watch until dusk, when bright fireflies of lanterns began bursting to life on the deck of the distant ship. She'd ordered their own lamps to remain dark in case the light penetrated whatever was concealing them. She planned to continue her march for another hour, but she heard a whistle from the crow's nest: two sharps and a long, the prearranged signal that meant their people were on the way back from the island.

She returned to the port side of the ship and watched the dark shape cut through the harbor.

"I only counted four," Aravanis said. "There should be five."

"It's dark." Ranzi tried not to let worry creep into her voice. "Perhaps you were mistaken."

"Perhaps," Aravanis said, but she didn't sound convinced.

The boat was lifted out of the water and Ranzi reluctantly

confirmed the incorrect headcount. Bethel and Jeffries were the first over the railing, with Cariad behind them and Captain Landau bringing up the rear. Clio answered their question before it could be asked.

"Fausta stayed behind. Part of a trust exercise. It was her own choice, and I believe we have no reason to fear the inhabitants of this island."

"A lot of faith to put in folks you've known for a handful of hours."

Clio said, "A lot can happen in a few hours. Miracles, in fact." She put her hands on Aravanis' shoulders and leaned back to examine her. "This is uncanny. It's unbelievable. How do you feel?"

"Annoyed that people keep asking me the same question." She sighed. "I feel adequate. Mostly confused. But otherwise fine."

Clio smiled. "Wonderful news."

"Any idea how that's possible?" Ranzi asked.

"Yes, but it can wait until morning. It's quite a tale and I would prefer to have everyone well-rested before I try explaining it. Any report on Aldoncia?"

Ranzi nodded toward the ship. "It continued on a bit, then circled back. I think they know we vanished somewhere around this area but can't figure out where or how."

"They must have someone in their crow's nest," Clio said. "Why can't they see the island the way Common did?"

"They didn't have the coordinates."

Everyone in the group looked at Cariad. "Why would that matter?" Clio said.

"I don't know," Cariad admitted. "I don't know how any of this works. But maybe the fact we were coming here opened some kind of... passage. Aldoncia was just following us. The island isn't going to welcome her in just because she happens to be standing in the right place."

Ranzi narrowed her eyes. "So the coordinates are a key?"

Clio held her hands up. "Given what we've witnessed, I'm willing to accept that explanation. It makes as much sense as anything else going on with this island. We saw it because we were meant to, and Aldoncia can't see it because she's not pure of heart. Works for fairy tales, works for me. Right now I suggest we all get some sleep. If everything works out we may have a long journey ahead of us."

"Aye, Captain"

As Ranzi headed off to start dismissing crew and calling in the skeleton crew, she heard Clio ask for Cariad to accompany her to the infirmary.

Delfina recounted the situation with Aravanis while she examined Clio. "Not even a scar," she said. "I can't even find a trace of the stitches I gave her. You saw those wounds. I don't care what kind of magic these ladies claim that veil has, just passing through it shouldn't have had that kind of instantaneous benefits. Human bodies don't work that way."

"I saw her myself when I returned," Clio said. "She certainly looked completely restored."

"Looked is the operative word." Delfina stepped away from the bed so Clio could sit up. "I don't trust whatever this is. I don't want to risk her pushing too far and finding out the limits of how far this magic can go."

Clio sighed. "It makes sense."

"As for whatever is happening to you, I have no idea. You're in perfect health, which shouldn't surprise me given what I saw this afternoon, but you were also healthy before you left. I don't see anything that might be causing these headaches."

"Thanks for checking. I didn't really expect you to find anything, but I still wanted the confirmation."

Delfina looked at Cariad. "And what's wrong with you?"

"Nothing," Clio said at the same time Cariad did. Clio continued, "I just didn't want her wandering off somewhere while I was being checked out. Miss Baillie, if you please?"

She eased off the bed, nodded her thanks to Delfina, and then led the journalist out of the infirmary. Cariad started to say something but Clio silenced her with a raised finger.

They remained silent until they arrived at the captain's cabin. Clio went to the shelf above her bed, retrieved a folded piece of paper, and handed it to Cariad.

"That was my wife. The first Captain Landau. Harriet."

"She's gorgeous," Cariad said.

Clio nodded, also staring at the portrait. It wasn't the best likeness, and the artist hadn't even attempted to get the right color blue for her eyes. They were blue with flecks of green and gray, not this pedestrian shade of sky. The drawing had been made about ten years before Harriet died. Her hair was center-parted and windswept, pushing away from her face on both sides to highlight the shape of her cheekbones and the line of her jaw.

"She was the first thing I saw when I woke up. After the..." She tapped her forehead. "But I think I'm starting to remember more."

Cariad handed the portrait back. "And you're retaining the information?"

Clio nodded. "After learning about the veil, I have to assume it's the reason. Even though the injury is decades old, somehow coming to the island healed it."

"Maybe..." Cariad pondered for a moment before she spoke again. "Maybe it wasn't healed. Maybe whatever damage had been done was still considered a permanent wound. It's like... if... being hit in the head knocked your brain sideways a little. And in your case, healing meant putting it back the right way. That's why it's giving you headaches."

"I don't think that's how brains work."

"You know how brains work?"

Clio said, "Well... no. Not at all. But I don't think it's just rattling around up there like dice in a cup. And even if it was, I don't think you could just block a whole life of memories."

Cariad shrugged. "It doesn't matter why you're remembering. The veil is magic. That's enough of an explanation for me to accept it."

"Me too." Clio went to her desk, resting her hands on it to look out the window. It was pitch black outside, so she could no longer see the mysterious island. Invisible again, just because the light had gone away. She pressed her lips together and then knocked her knuckles on the desktop. "Have a seat. You're going to be doing some writing."

"Now?" Cariad said. "It's nearly midnight."

"Are you tired?"

Cariad shook her head. "No, actually. Quite energized, to be honest."

Clio nodded. "Me too. And on the off chance these memories aren't here when I wake in the morning, I want to take advantage of having a writer aboard." She pointed at the chair. "Sit."

Cariad crossed the room and sat down. She found a sheaf of papers, a pen, and arranged them in front of her. Clio looked down at the portrait of Harriet, holding her finger just above the page to trace the lines of her throat. She almost never touched the page. She was frightened of smudging something or erasing some small line that made her wife whole. She couldn't trust her memory to hold

Harriet's face, so this portrait was the only thing she had.

"I'm not sure where I should begin," Clio admitted quietly.

Cariad turned and saw what Clio was looking at. "Tell it like you're telling her."

"She knows what happened."

"I'm sure she would still like to hear your version of it."

Clio looked into the eyes of the drawing. "I was born in your arms, blood in my eyes, aboard a ship of mutineers. Your eyes were the first thing I saw in this world."

Cariad turned around and began writing.

Chapter Fourteen

Boe escorted Fausta away from the clearing to a cluster of small stone buildings similar to the one where they'd had dinner. Windows in the other buildings were shaded by heavy cloth curtains, which Fausta saw twitch as she passed by. Boe saw her watching them and laughed softly under her breath.

"Don't worry. They are not dangerous. Only curious. We don't get very many visitors who pass the tests, so outsiders rarely stay the night. They are shy."

"As long as they don't sneak up on me, they'll be fine."

Boe nodded and pointed ahead. "This is your space for the evening. Inside you will find comfortable clothes for sleeping, water, food, anything you may require in the night."

"Thank you." They stopped in front of the entrance. "And in the morning...?"

"We will escort you to the beach to reunite with your crew. We will give you the information so you can find the other island."

"And all I have to do is spend the night here. Just... sleep?"

"While surrounded by strangers. You are showing us trust, and honoring us by respecting our rules. It may not mean much to you~"

Fausta shook her head. "No, no. I understand. It just doesn't seem like a lot to ask."

Boe shrugged. "I admit, it's more symbolic than anything. But when one is dealing with pirates, one must be cautious. Even if the pirate is very... charming."

Fausta smiled at that. "You've been quite charming yourself, Boe."

"Thank you." Boe leaned in and pecked Fausta's cheek. "Dream of calm seas, sailor."

Fausta wished Boe a good night and watched her walk away, taking a moment to scan the rest of the village. None of the homes were lit, but there was enough moonlight for her to see the curtains were still twitching. To the south, she could see the harbor, and the *Banshee* sitting calmly. She saluted her crew, turned to offer a second salute to her new neighbors, and then went inside her temporary lodgings.

Inside was a single room. One bed against the far wall, a squat dresser, a desk, and a nook that included rudimentary bathroom facilities. It reminded her of nothing more than a jail cell, but far cozier than any prison she'd ever been a guest of. In the drawer she found a nightgown and a long shirt, but no trousers. The shirt was essentially the same thing as the gown, but she chose it for the principle of not wearing any kind of dress. It left her legs mostly exposed and the collar was cut to reveal a generous amount of cleavage, but she figured it would be comfortable enough to sleep in. Besides, it wasn't like anyone was going to see~

There was a light knock on the door. Fausta raised an eyebrow and searched the room for anything she might use as a weapon. Naturally there was nothing, so she decided to act on trust and opened the door.

Boe slipped inside and pressed her back to the wall. She motioned for Fausta to close the door quickly.

"Are you running from someone, Boe?"

"No, I..." She noticed Fausta had changed and slowly ran her eyes down her body. "Oh. You look l-lovely in that."

"Thank you. Why are you hiding here?"

"I just didn't want anyone to see," Boe whispered. "Gossips. They had to see me leave you here and then depart. I snuck back through the woods." She stepped forward suddenly and put her hands on Fausta's hips. "I wish to spend the evening with you, Fausta Gittens."

Fausta leaned away from her. "You... I thought you and Leola..."

"We are." Boe was staring distractedly at Fausta's lips. Her own lips were parted, as if she was finding it difficult to catch her breath. "She approves of my explorations. I learn things from other partners, things I can introduce to our bed." She grinded her hips against Fausta's. "I was so thrilled when you volunteered to be the one to stay. All your women were lovely, but you... are... gorgeous. I imagine you can teach me all sorts of new things, madam. And I can be a very eager student."

With a growl, her lip curled hungrily, Boe lunged and surprised Fausta with a kiss. Her hands slid around to cup Fausta's ass, pulling her close.

Fausta let the kiss happen for a few seconds, maybe a minute, perhaps two, but she eventually returned to her senses and rested her hands on Boe's shoulders to push her back.

"Test of trust and respect, hm?" Fausta said, raising an eyebrow. "I admit, this is far more tempting than I expected."

"This isn't a test. I assure you, Leola knows I'm here. She encouraged me to come. She saw how I was looking at you during dinner. She knows how badly I want you. And she knows that if we spend time together at sea, eventually I will give in to my desires. She would much rather have you take me for the first time here, on our island, where I can report to her immediately." She ran her hands up Fausta's back. "She is quite eager to hear what happened."

Fausta licked her lips and shifted away again. "I honestly don't know whether this is a test of trusting you or respecting her. I'm sort of damned if I do, and damned if I don't, really."

"Then why not just do it? At least then you'll have a wonderful night to look back on."

Boe kissed her again. And again, Fausta was a heartbeat away from just letting it happen. But she turned her head, and closed her eyes as Boe's lips trailed over her jaw, down her throat. Boe whimpered pleadingly and put her hands on Fausta's breasts, massaging them through her borrowed nightshirt.

"With my most sincere apologies... you have no idea how sincere... and utmost respect, I have to decline your invitation. I accept it's possible Miss Fairfax approved of this little dalliance. But I can't take that on faith. And this bell cannot be unrung."

She stepped out of Boe's embrace and tried to ignore the signals from her body. Boe dropped her hands to her sides and smiled sadly, inclining her head.

"I suppose that is a reasonable decision to make in this situation. I am sorry to have put you in an uncomfortable situation,

Madam Gittens."

"It's–it's fine. And please. My name is Fausta."

Boe nodded and went to the door. She opened it but didn't leave, instead stepping aside to let Leola come in. The leader of the island had changed into a sheer robe which did nothing to conceal the leather bodice underneath, nor the effect the new addition had on her curves.

Fausta raised an eyebrow and lifted her chin in surprise. "Ah. So I was indeed being set up."

"In a way," Leola admitted. Boe went to her, clinging to her side and resting her head on Leola's chest. Leola brought a hand up and lazily stroked her hair. "There was no correct response to the test. Either you respected our relationship as you saw it, or you trusted Boe's word that I had granted permission for her to give herself to you. I was curious which route you would take."

"Well, knowing that, I mightily regret my decision."

Leola chuckled and kissed the top of Boe's head. "There's no reason you can't change your mind. Would you like to take my love to your bed?"

"Very much," Fausta admitted.

"And would you like that, Boe?"

Boe looked at Fausta. "Yes, ma'am."

Leola smiled. "Do you object to me staying? I've come all this way, and I quite enjoy watching."

"By all means," Fausta said, wrapping her arms around Boe's waist and pulling her to the bed. "The more the merrier..."

Estacia was almost asleep, and the knock on her door was very quiet, but she still heard it and got out of bed before the second knock began. Cariad was standing in the hall looking ragged, eyelids half-mast, swaying on her feet. Estacia cooed comforting noises and pulled the poor girl inside, pausing just long enough to close the door before she started undressing her.

"You look like you've had a day," Estacia said.

"I think I've had a week since I last sleep," Cariad said. "Sleeped. Slept."

Estacia smiled and kissed the corner of Cariad's mouth. "My writer... come on. Get into bed."

"I wasn't... I didn't..." She pushed both hands through her hair. "I wasn't thinking. I just want to sleep, and I came here because your bed..."

"Sh, I know, it's okay. I want you to sleep here." She guided Cariad to the bed and laid her down. "I hate the thought of you being down there with the rest of the roustabouts. As far as I'm concerned you can sleep here every night. Now settle in. That's a good girl. Scoot back and give me a little room." She slipped under the blankets and arranged her body so Cariad could cuddle up against her. "Cozy?"

Cariad nodded. "Thank you."

"Sh, go to sleep." She kissed Cariad's forehead. "Go to sleep. We can talk more in the morning."

Cariad gave a deep sigh and seemed to be asleep in a matter of seconds. Estacia closed her eyes and followed her quickly thereafter.

She didn't know how long she'd slept before she woke up aware of attention on her. She turned and looked up at the dark shape of Cariad above her. There was moonlight coming in through the porthole, enough to see the writer's skin but not so much that it revealed her eyes. They were just dark coins framed by her hair falling on either side of her face.

"What's wrong?" Estacia whispered.

"Nothing. I don't know. Maybe a lot of things. I talked to the captain tonight when we got back. She told me the story about waking up. Her first memory. She said I can talk to other members of the crew. Get their stories, if they're willing to tell 'em. And I thought I would really like to hear your story."

"Do I have a story?"

"You must. Everyone has a story. The only reason you don't know it's amazing is because you were inside it when it happened."

Estacia considered that. "I guess I could tell you what happened. Then you could decide if it counts as a story."

"We can do it in the morning, if you'd prefer."

"No, no." Estacia pushed herself up. "You had a much harder day than me. And if you're willing to do it now, then why not."

They got out of bed. Estacia lit a lamp and set it on the table, where Cariad straightened a pile of loose papers and found a pencil. The light of the flames was gold and orange, and it illuminated Cariad's pale skin, freckles, and hair in a very striking way. It made her hair look supernaturally red, almost glowing, and she could resist reaching out to touch it. Cariad looked up at the caress.

"I'm proud to have been your first, Cariad."

"Oh." Cariad lowered her eyes, suddenly bashful. "Well... I'm just honored to have been chosen by you, no matter which number

I happen to be."

Estacia blushed. "It's not a terrifically high number, to be clear."

Cariad smiled, fiddling with the pencil. Finally she cleared her throat and tapped the paper. "Right. Um. I suppose start wherever you believe would be best."

"Okay." Cariad pressed her lips together and thought back to her younger days. "I was barely more than a child back then, honestly. I've only ever been interested in cooking..."

She told her story, remembering the disgusting heat of Bastard Bastia's breath on her neck and the fear when he finally had her pinned against the table. Later on, Harriet admitted she'd come to the kitchen to compliment her on the food. Instead, she had saved Estacia for the first time. The first of many, as it would turn out.

"What are you going to do with the stories?" Estacia asked when she reached the end.

"I haven't the foggiest idea," Cariad said. "I can't exactly publish them in the newspaper with your names plastered everywhere for the whole world to see. And I don't want to put new names on the stories you lived. It would be as bad as stealing them."

Estacia reached out and put her hand on top of Cariad's.

"Even if no one else ever reads it, I'm glad you know my story. It feels good to have it written down. Only me and Harriet were there that night. Well, and Bastia, but who knows how he's telling the story. It feels safer now. Thank you."

She leaned across the table, aiming her lips at Cariad's cheek. Cariad allowed that kiss to land, then turned her head to offer her own lips. Estacia took the invitation gladly, then stepped around the table so she could settle herself in Cariad's lap. She still had Cariad's hand in hers and broke the kiss to look down at it. The thumb and forefinger were smudged and smeared with graphite. She brought the hand up and slipped the finger into her mouth, sucking the dark marks away. It tasted oddly metallic, but not entirely bad.

"Your fingers must ache terribly after all the writing you've done tonight."

"Terribly," Cariad said, adding an extra touch of whimper to her voice. "Do you have any ideas what could be done...?"

"Oh yes," Estacia said, rising to pull Cariad back to bed. "Quite a few exercises spring to mind. Let me show them to you..."

Clio cupped her hands under the water in her wash basin and brought them up, splashing the water against her cheeks. She could feel the tremor in her fingers as she rested them against her face. The shaking had started while she was talking to Cariad, but she was almost certain the girl hadn't noticed them. She thought she would be safe recounting things that happened after she woke up. The first days of confusion and fear, clinging tightly to Harriet as a lifeline, the slow realization that her memory wasn't going to come back when she recovered...

But the more she shared, the more of the past started seeping through the cracks. She'd spent decades trying to knock down that wall, and now it felt like it was collapsing all around her, burying her in stone and choking her with its dust.

She sat down on her bunk and pushed her hands through her hair, then leaned forward with her elbows on her knees.

"You didn't ask for this. You've done enough for me. You don't need some stray pup following you around. Go. Go back to your ship. I'll be fine."

Harriet brushing the hair away from her temple. The bandage had already been removed, but there was an angry red wound at her hairline.

"Maybe I like having someone to take care of."

Clio exhaled. She needed to focus on that. Focus on how it felt to walk beside Harriet, at her shoulder. Harriet was only taller than her by a few inches, but she held herself like a queen as she returned to her ship. Clio had been hunched over, folded in on herself, hands in her pockets. Avoiding eye contact. Then she felt a hand on her shoulder and looked up. Harriet smiled reassuringly at her.

"It's okay. You're welcome here. Whoever you are."

But now that Clio had a better idea of what had preceded the accident, now that those lost days were starting to come into focus, she felt only terror at what might have happened. She saw herself in her fine clothes, her hair slicked back, and she saw herself counting money.

"She'll be away from her ship," the man said as Clio sorted the bills. "Away from her crew and any kind of support. It should be easy enough for you to accomplish your mission."

Clio folded the money and stood, slipping the payment into her coat pocket. She retrieved her hat from the side table and settled it in her head.

"Don't worry, sir," she said as she walked out of the room. "You've hired the best pirate hunter in the business. Harriet Landau isn't leaving that boat alive."

Chapter Fifteen

Fausta wasn't sure when she slept. She'd made love to Boe, then pleasured Leola, and touched herself while she watched them with each other. At some point she closed her eyes long enough for the sun to rise and her overnight companions to vanish. She sat up and planted her feet on the floor. Her flask was on the bedside table, and she uncapped it. There was barely more than a single swallow inside, but she tipped it back gratefully.

Boe and Leola may have vanished, but they left treasures behind: a fresh outfit, a bag for the clothes Fausta had worn to the island, and a plate with some kind of meat and egg dish. The food was delicious, and the clothes fit perfectly. She packed away her clothes and slung the bag over her shoulder before stepping outside the lodging.

Boe sat waiting a few yards away on a stone bench. She smiled when she saw Fausta and rose to meet her on the path.

"I hope last night was as wonderful for you as it was for us," Boe said.

"It's definitely top level," Fausta said, leaning in to kiss Boe on the cheek. It felt like the right choice, given the absence of Leola. "Will she be escorting us to the dock?"

Boe slipped her hand into Fausta's and motioned for her to start walking. "She's not as young and resilient as we are. She's sleeping now, but I have all the information we require."

"Feels strange to leave without saying goodbye."

"She won't be offended. Besides, your friends are probably eager to get you back."

Fausta smiled. "I'm sure they're all beside themselves with worry for me. Are you..." She scanned the area around the beach. "Do you have any bags? Clothing or belongings...?"

"I have everything I need," Boe said.

"If you insist," Fausta said. She doubted the girl had ever been away from home for longer than a night. If push came to shove, she could borrow clothes and toiletries from the crew as needed.

While they were in the cluster of houses, and for the entire walk through the forest to the beach, Fausta kept an eye out for any of the other seven hundred-plus inhabitants of the island. She didn't see a hint of anyone, not even a tremble of underbrush as someone slipped away just before she spotted them. If she hadn't seen the curtains twitching the night before she would have easily believed Boe and Leola were the only residents. At the moment she wasn't entirely convinced Leola was still there.

"Boe, how many people did you say lived here?"

"Seven hundred and eighty-two. Seven-hundred~"

"~and eighty-four when Toscana has her twins," Fausta said. "That's right. I remember."

Boe smiled proudly.

They could see the launch rowing away from the *Banshee* well before the reached the shore. Fausta raised her hand in greeting and the rower, Aravanis, paused just long enough to return the greeting.

"Who is that?" Boe asked, sounding like a child at the circus. "She wasn't with your party."

"That's Aravanis. Last I saw her, she was torn to shreds. Your veil may have saved her life."

Boe gasped and gripped Fausta's arm. "How amazing. It's wonderful when the veil helps good people. I'm glad it helped your friend."

"Me too."

They reached the dock and waited until the boat reached them. Fausta smiled at Aravanis and climbed down first, then reached up to put her hands on Boe's waist to lift her down. Once they were settled, Fausta clapped Aravanis on the shoulder.

"Good to see you up and around." She picked up the other woman's hand before she could start rowing. "Not even a scar. Not even a seam or stitch. That's amazing."

Aravanis eyed Boe warily. "Captain says it was magic."

"Hard to deny now that we've seen the results."

"Everyone's acting like I'm made of glass now. I had to beg them to let me do this much. Hopefully now they'll see my arms won't snap like twigs and they'll stop babying me."

Fausta laughed. "Hard to imagine anyone babying you, Penelope."

Aravanis glared at her and started rowing back. "We might not be able to leave immediately. Aldoncia's ship is still lurking around. Ranzi spent the night watching the other ship and trying to think of a way we could sneak past."

"I guess that's what we get for disappearing right in front of her," Fausta said.

Boe said, "Aldoncia is an enemy...?"

Fausta sighed. "She, uh, doesn't like our captain very much."

"Oh I see." Boe looked over the side of the boat and reached down, letting the water pass across her fingers. She chuckled softly. "I've never been off the island."

Fausta and Aravanis both looked at her. "Never?"

"I never had reason enough to leave. I was born here and it's given me everything I need. I'm excited for the adventure."

"Wow." Fausta put her hand on Boe's knee. "Now I wish we'd taken the time for you to say goodbye to Leola."

"We said our goodbyes," Boe said with a dreamy smile. Fausta decided not to press for details.

When they reached the boat, Boe watched with wonder as the ropes were hooked and they were hauled up the curved hull. Ranzi was waiting when they stepped off onto the deck.

"Is Aldoncia still there?"

Ranzi nodded. "Still there. Glad to see you survived your harrowing night on land. Do you need some time to get your sea legs back?"

"I think I can manage. Where's the captain?"

"Haven't seen her since she got back from the island. I think she was up late talking to Cariad about something. But we~"

Aravanis interrupted by pointing. "Captain on deck."

They turned to see Clio walking toward them, determination in her eyes. She was still wearing the clothes she'd worn the night before, and her hair was more of a tangled mess than usual.

"Do we have everyone we need aboard?" she asked, looking at

Boe.

"Aye, captain," Fausta said. "We're ready to go once we figure out a way to get past Aldoncia without being seen."

Clio brushed past them. "We're not waiting. We're going. Now."

"All due respect, Captain," Fausta said, following her up to the quarterdeck, "we can't give her the chance to shadow us all the way to the island. Leola and Boe have gone to great lengths to conceal its location."

"We're not going to sneak past that bitch," Clio said, then raised her voice to shout to the deckhands. "Heave round and secure the anchor!"

Ranzi joined them at the wheel. "What exactly is the plan here, Captain?"

Clio stared straight ahead. "We're going to send Aldoncia a message. We don't wait, we don't sneak, and we absolutely do not run from her. We're going to punch her right between the damned eyes."

Ranzi looked at Fausta and raised an eyebrow. Fausta shrugged.

"Aye, Captain," they said together. Ranzi gave the captain one final worried look before she descended the stairs to take her position.

Fausta put her hands behind her back and watched as Clio turned the ship starboard. Their enemy's ship was soon positioned right ahead of them. The sight made her skin crawl; it was like standing in front of a lion and being unsure of when or if its eyes would open. She scanned the deck to see where Boe had wandered away to. The girl was staring fascinated at the deckhands as they brought the ship about, eyes wide and unblinking as she watched them scale the rigging and shout orders to catch the wind. Fausta went to her.

"How long will the veil keep us out of sight?"

It took Boe a moment to realize Fausta was speaking to her, and another few seconds to consider her answer. She looked out at the water, then at the island.

"The boundaries aren't exact," she finally said. She pointed at Aldoncia's ship. "If they came closer, the veil would shift so they wouldn't breach it or see through it."

Ranzi spoke up, having drifted over to eavesdrop on their conversation. "Yes, why exactly is that? We could see the island once we got close enough."

"You were coming here with intent," Boe explained. "An invitation, however broadly delivered, affords you passage. It's the same reason I will be able to see it when we return from our quest."

"Okay." Fausta rubbed her thumb across her bottom lip, thinking. "If the veil is clever enough to prevent people from passing through without an invitation, shouldn't it also have a way to make sure that ship won't see us appear from out of thin air?"

"I truly don't know. I assume that makes sense."

Clio said, "What are you thinking?"

"I think..." She spoke slowly and gave her brain time to form the thought. "I think if an enemy vessel is lurking, the veil would be useless if it just let them see a ship come barreling through. I think there will be a veil drawn over us so the island's secret remains safe."

Boe said, "But even if they don't see the island, they would eventually run aground if they approached at the right angle. It has happened in the past. Shipwrecks, crews who insisted the island simply appeared out of nowhere. We always blamed fog and fata morgana."

"I know you said no creeping, Captain, but it might be our best shot of making it out of this situation without suffering too much damage. I think we can assume they won't see us until we make our presence known."

Clio nodded, already moving. "We can work with that."

They would have to move slowly, so she ordered the crew to cut their speed by half. "Work as silently as possible," she told them. "Hand signals if you can, no shouting, and by god, no singing. They're blind until we give them a reason to look at us. Be a mouse!"

The ship creaked and groaned at being forced to creep. Clio paced to the bow and withdrew her spyglass. Aldoncia's ship remained still and quiet, just a vessel with its anchor dropped in the middle of nowhere. She could see vague, blurry shapes of the crew moving on the deck. She could imagine the debates being held. Remain here and wait for the *Banshee* to return and raid their hold, or consider the pursuit lost and return home. Clio knew Aldoncia would never turn tail and run, so she was there for the long haul.

"Steady," she said with just as much volume as she dared. "Bring us up alongside."

She heard whispers from her crew as they relayed her orders. When they were close enough that she could make out the faces of the crew, she returned to the quarterdeck and took over steering.

She wanted to get them as close as humanly possible before they announced themselves.

She brought them up alongside Aldoncia's ship, close enough that a strong breeze might have knocked their hulls together. And still no one aboard the other ship seemed aware of the *Banshee*'s presence. If this mission was a success, they could handle every skirmish just like this. No danger for her crew, the element of surprise on every engagement... it was a hugely attractive idea. The crew looked to her for orders.

"Howl, banshees!" she shouted.

Every woman and man on the deck howled. A chorus of voices melted into a single ungodly wail. Fausta, Ranzi, and Clio added their own cries to the cacophony, Fausta raising her sword in the air and waving it so the sunlight caught the blade.

Aldoncia's crew howled as well, but their cries were clearly from fright. Clio could imagine what it must have looked like; open sea suddenly darkening to become a ship's hull, the clouds flattening to become sails. The *Banshee* had simply faded into being beside them, the space between them so narrow that her men could simply step across and start taking prisoners.

"Miss Gittens, you have the helm."

"Aye," Fausta said.

Clio stepped away and marched down the stairs to the main deck, straightening her blouse and drawing her cutlass. She kept the blade at her side as she walked to the railing.

"Aldoncia Reyes! Show yourself!"

The crew of the other ship exchanged worried glances. One man lifted his chin and spoke in a voice that aimed for defiant but trembled with fear.

"She has no reason to speak to you."

"I beg to differ, sire. She has five minutes before we begin firing. Unless she wants to make her final stand here, she will step forward for parlay."

A fraction of the time had passed before Aldoncia appeared on deck. She wore a red velvet coat lined with gold, her hair pinned at the sides but flowing freely down her back. When she arrived at the gunwale, two sailors on either side of her brought up shotguns and aimed them at Clio. Aldoncia ran her eyes along the *Banshee*'s railing, taking in the sight of this surprising ship and its crew. When her gaze finally landed on Clio, she raised an eyebrow and betrayed a hint of respect.

"Interesting trick, Landau. I'd love to know how you pulled it off."

"I've cowered from you for too long, Aldoncia. Your daughter was a thief, and a poor one at that. She tried to betray us, and you, and I know you're fully aware of that fact. If you're looking for someone to blame for her behavior, look to the person who raised her."

Aldoncia lowered her chin. Her brows knit together, and her shoulders rose as she drew in a deep breath. The ships creaked as the ocean tried to push them into each other, and both crews were silent as their captains faced each other across the breach.

"Do not let this will be the end of your glorious kingdom. We have the advantage here, and you are well aware of that fact. I can cripple your vessel with a single order. You will drown here in a shattered ship in the name of a daughter who intended to betray and dethrone you. Don't let a traitor define your legacy. Let her go."

After what seemed like ages, Aldoncia made a slight gesture with her right hand. The sailors looked at her, then at each other, and lowered their weapons. Aldoncia turned on the ball of her foot, sweeping the tail of her coat behind her. Clio took a deep breath and let it out slowly. She waited until Aldoncia had left the deck before she turned her back and looked up at Fausta. She crossed to the stairs and ascended just enough to be heard without raising her voice.

"Hold steady until she's well away. Don't give her a chance to circle around and latch onto our hind end again. As soon as you can't see that fucking ship, set out. Boe will give you a heading."

"Aye, Captain," Fausta said.

Clio stepped down, head lowered, and ducked out of sight. Once she was in the darkness, she rested her shoulder against the wall and allowed herself a deep, calming breath. Her hands were shaking now, the adrenaline fading. Yes, Aldoncia had been in their crosshairs, but the *Banshee* had been just as vulnerable. The past five minutes could have ended very, very tragically.

"What the hell just happened?" she heard Aravanis ask.

"I don't have the faintest fucking idea," was Fausta's response. "But I think the captain just bluffed Aldoncia using all our lives as a bargaining chip."

"Lucky it worked out," Aravanis said.

"Yes. Very lucky..."

Fausta sounded skeptical. Clio didn't blame her, she just prayed she wasn't coming to an end of the first mate's trust.

FAUSTA GITTENS

"People have all kinds of ideas about how to survive in this life. Sword and sailing skills, of course. Knowing your way around a ship. All that is vital but that's shit you can learn. What you really need is trust and loyalty. That's something that's incredibly hard to get and really fucking easy to lose. Captain Landau, the first one... Harriet. I trusted her with my life. I was just a kid when I first set foot on this ship. My parents gave up everything to leave Persia and come to London. We had been there ten weeks when they died in a house fire. I had nothing, no ties to the community, no inheritance, no family. I was on my way to an orphanage, if I was lucky. But I wasn't exactly the sort of kid who counted on 'lucky.' So I gathered what I could carry and looked for a ship that needed another body on board.

I was just a powder monkey at first. Puny little kid with no real skills, best place for me. I spent a few years running around cannons and stinking of gunpowder and matches. Real sickening stick, you can probably imagine. When I was too tall for the gun deck, I asked to be moved somewhere else. Anywhere. So I joined the carpenter, learned his trade. If the ship was damaged in battle, I helped repair it. If we needed a barrel, I built it. Got damn good at it. Captain came and said there was a chance I could move higher. Possibly become a gunner, what with my experience with the cannons. I jumped at the chance, and he invited me to his cabin to talk it over.

It quickly became very clear what was required for me to get the promotion. I was prepared to go through with it. Sex wasn't part of my life. I never even thought about it. So I figured it was just part of being a pirate. Hell, it probably is on a lot of boats.

He was on top of me when Harriet knocked down the door. Nothing had happened but some awkward and painful groping, something I'll always be grateful about. Harriet had heard that the captain took 'that young desert rat' to his cabin. She grabbed him off me, threw him to the ground. He drew a gun, she kicked it away, and after that it was just fists, knees, and boots. He tried to run, and that's how the fight ended up on the deck with the whole crew watching.

I think we all knew that fight was going to change everything on the ship forever. She was his bo's'n, and– what? Hell, I don't know, spell it how it sounds, you're the writer. Fuck. If he beat her, then that would be it. He would be a dictator. He probably would've dragged me back to his cabin to finish what he'd started. If she won...

Well. We know what happened because she won. Captain got tossed overboard, and Harriet became our new captain. She checked to make sure I was okay, then told everyone else that they were welcome to keep sailing with her or be dropped off at the next port to find another vessel to join. Those what left, Harriet made a point of replacing with women.

I served under her for a long time. Long time. She made me her first mate. We trusted each other to the ends of the earth. And when she died, the choice for captain was between me and Clio. It didn't seem like a choice to me. Clio deserved it, it's what Harriet wanted. Besides, I know myself well enough to be terrified of the job. I wouldn't make a good captain. But I'm a damn good second.

I've served under Clio for near a decade now. And I can say without hesitation, that woman is a damn good captain.

Chapter Sixteen

IT HAD taken Clio nearly ten minutes to get from the quarterdeck to her cabin. Her stomach pains had only gotten worse, and her head was killing her. More memories rushing in, too many for her to itemize or investigate what they meant. She prayed she'd already learned the most damning truth, but who knew what other sins were waiting to be uncovered? She was terrified at the thought of what else lurked in the pits of her brain. She needed to lie down and give her body a chance to catch up with her head.

She closed her eyes against another spike of pain and, when she opened them, she saw Cariad standing in front of her cabin. She sneered and carefully shook her head.

"Fuck off, Miss Baillie."

"No."

"I'm not interested in your little fucking stories right now." She put her hand on Cariad's shoulder to physically move her. Cariad surprised her by reaching up, grabbing Clio's wrist tight enough to get her attention. Clio stared daggers. "You'll lose that hand."

"Maybe." There was fear in Cariad's eyes, maybe even terror. But there was determination in the set of her jaw. "I may be new to the ship, but even I know that was unusual. I saw the faces of your crew. Fausta had no idea who she was watching. It was a bit of a relief, to be honest, because I thought you were always like that and you'd just been hiding it until now. Good to know it's a switch from the norm."

Clio jerked her hand away. "I'm not feeling well."

"And I know why better than anyone."

"Let go of me." When Cariad didn't reply, Clio tugged her closer. "We will not have this discussion in the hall. Release me so I can open the door."

Cariad dropped her hand. Clio considered jabbing her fist into the other woman's side, just to send a message, but decided against it.

She thrust open the door to her cabin, letting it bang into the wall as she entered. It almost hit Cariad as it swung back, but she stopped it with her hand. Clio stalked to her window and stared out at the wide expanse of apparent emptiness. Even though she knew Leola's island was there, she couldn't see a hint of it. Her brain rebelled at the idea she had just stood on a beach there, that she'd seen a dock and a small stone home, when all her eyes could see was open ocean.

"Fog and darkness," Clio muttered.

"What was that?"

"In fog and in darkness," Clio said. "Something can be two inches in front of your face and you can't see it. Unsettling as all hell. It shouldn't be possible in sunlight. It shouldn't be possible in a fucking brain. Memories should be there."

Cariad said, "That's not how it works for anyone. We all forget things..."

"Not thirty damn years."

"No. Not usually."

Clio closed her eyes. More memories were flooding in, but there was no narrative, no connecting tissue. They reemerged like any old memory drifting to the surface. Once she had waded through waist-deep water with a sword in her hand. Once she'd screamed in pain as her shoulder was yanked back into its socket. She remembered lovers... *male* lovers, though something in her felt that even before losing her memory, she'd known that wasn't where her true interest was. Harriet was the first woman she'd ever bedded, she knew that for a fact now, but she wasn't the first one she'd ever had the thought about.

"What are you remembering?" Cariad's voice was kind.

"Everything," Clio said, her voice trembling with pain. "All at once."

She heard Cariad move closer. "It may help to talk through them."

Clio looked over her shoulder. She and Cariad were separated by a desk.

"I'm a pirate hunter. I tracked down pirates, people like Fausta and Ranzi, people like Harriet, and I turned them in for bounties. I attended their hangings. I celebrated their deaths and bought rounds of drink with the coin I earned from turning them in. Human beings, dangling from the end of a rope, because of me."

Cariad's eyes widened. Her posture straightened. But she nodded slowly and spoke carefully. "That's who you were. It doesn't matter now. It doesn't matter to the life you've built in the years since you woke up in Harriet's arms."

Clio rubbed her hands over her face.

"Is it that you don't believe a person can change? That we're doomed to be the same person we were as children?"

"I wasn't a child. I was in my thirties. I was an adult, I had made my choice."

Cariad took a deep breath. Clio wanted the girl gone, didn't want anyone to see her at the moment. But when she started to speak, Cariad beat her to the punch and spoke first.

"I spent ten years in an asylum."

Clio closed her mouth and stared. "Why?"

"Reading and overtaxing my mind were what they wrote on the form." Cariad flipped her hand dismissively. "But the shorter version is because my father asked them to lock me up. He hated that I learned to read and write before he could stop me. And when slapping me, yelling at me, and locking me in my bedroom for twenty-three hours of the day didn't work, he decided to let the professionals have a crack at it.

"I was sixteen and a group of men put me in a coat with sleeves that wrapped all the way around my body and locked, like this..." She hugged herself tightly. "They cut off all my hair. They dumped me in ice baths. My entire body would go numb and they held me under. Not so long that I would pass out, but they made my lungs burn. They gave me pills that made me go to sleep while I was still awake. I would just... stare. And drool. And... and soil myself."

Clio took a seat. "I've heard of places like that. I'm amazed you were able to get out."

"Oh, it's easy enough to get out." She straightened her posture, put her hands in her lap, and lowered her chin to her chest. She fixed her eyes on the floor. "Yes, sir. No, sir. Whatever you say, sir. Silence helped, too. If you don't speak, men won't find reasons to shut you up. I was eventually declared fit for society and they released me back to my parents."

"I assume you found a way to get out of there as quickly as possible."

"It was quite easy once I killed them."

She said it so casually that Clio was, at first, certain she'd misheard. "I'm sorry?"

Cariad furrowed her brow. "Certainly you don't have any qualms about that. Given what they did. Given who you are."

"No, of course not. No one on this ship will hold that against you. I just never would have pegged you as the type."

"They never would have let me go. My father would have tracked me down. By then I was twenty-four, but he still would have taken me over his lap and swatted me until I couldn't sit down. I know because he did it to my mother. Right in front of me." She pressed her lips together. She breathed in so deeply that her cheeks briefly caved in. "She didn't just allow it to happen. She encouraged it. If I fought, she would hold my arms, or she would put something in my mouth so I wouldn't 'bother the neighbors.' Must keep up the image of propriety, understand."

Clio swallowed hard and looked away.

Cariad sighed. "They had quite a bit of cash stashed away... sometimes I wonder if the chief physician paid them to keep me insane for as long as they did. If that was the case, the money was rightfully mine. At least that was my logic."

"Works for me," Clio said.

"I took the cash, along with whatever I could carry from the house. Sold the shit and spent the money getting as far away from them as possible. I found work at a newspaper... not the kind of work I wanted to be doing, of course, but my ability to read got me farther than I otherwise might have gone. I had access. I was inside the walls."

Clio said, "And now you just need a story they can't say no to, regardless of who is bringing it to them."

"Rumors of that island we just left are spreading like wildfire. Another year, it will be a myth as big as Atlantis. I want to be the one who tells the world what was really waiting out here."

"I'm not sure that fits with Leola Fairfax's plans."

"I'm not terribly concerned about that. I may have to fudge the details, leave out identifying facts. The story is the story. Besides, maybe my story will satisfy the curiosity of all the sailors wasting their time chasing this treasure. They deserve to know if it's been claimed by Captain Landau and the intrepid crew of the *Banshee*."

Clio considered all the information that had just been dropped into her lap. "How exactly does this relate to my situation?"

"You seem convinced that your past must define you, just because you can remember it. I refuse to be known as a meek daughter, or an insane girl, or a murderess. We have the opportunity to decide how we are seen, regardless of who we once were."

"But I didn't decide to change. I didn't repent, I didn't~"

"That doesn't matter," Cariad said. "You've spent just as long building this life for yourself. You've changed the lives of every woman aboard this ship. Don't throw it away for someone who died three decades ago."

Clio raised an eyebrow. She had to admit that was a solid point.

"Have you slept since we returned from the island?" Cariad asked.

Clio grunted and squeezed her eyes shut. She held up a hand next to her temple and waved it, indicating the turmoil within. "No. These goddamned memories are bad enough when I'm conscious. I shudder to think of what would happen if I gave up control."

"I think that's exactly what you need to do. Sleep is the brain's way of sorting itself out. And if anything bad happens, trust your crew. They're capable."

"I'll do that," Clio said. "Thank you."

Cariad nodded and went to the door.

"You know," Clio said, "considering the mood I was in when I came down here, if you were a member of my crew, I probably would have had you clapped in irons."

"Good thing I'm not a member of your crew, then." She smiled and stepped out into the corridor. "Sleep well, Captain."

The door closed and Clio was alone. She sighed and used her foot to push her chair around so she was facing the window again.

"Sleep," she muttered, rubbing a spot just above her eyebrow. "Sure... like it's that easy..."

When the deck had grown calm again, Fausta handed the helm over to Aravanis and went seeking for Boe.

She found their newest passenger at the bow of the ship with her hands on the gunwale. She had her stomach against the rail, leaning forward to look down at the water. As she approached, Fausta remembered her experience with the girl the night before. She and Leola had both been magnificent in their own ways. Leola, older and experienced, generous and patient. Boe was young, naïve, eager to explore a new lover's body. Between them, they had utterly exhausted her by the time she finally passed out. She wondered if there would be a chance for more experiences during the trip.

She cleared her throat to get the younger woman's attention. "Careful you don't fall in."

Boe stepped down carefully, but said, "I'm sure you would rescue me like the valiant hero."

"Not if you fell from here," Fausta said, she held out her hand for Boe to take. "As soon as you hit the water, you'd go right under the boat. You might could be fished out on the other side after a trip down the keel, but pulling you out of the water at that point might not be a mercy."

Boe shuddered, resting her weight against Fausta's body. "Terrifying. I admit at first I was just watching that other ship as it departed. It was amazing to just see it get smaller and smaller. But then this ship began to move and I was distracted by how the water was slapping up against the side here. It was like the whole world was moving." She twisted to look over her shoulder. "Will the other ship eventually just vanish? Bloop, gone...?"

"Eventually," Fausta said. "The world curves and we can't see around corners. And to them, it will look as if we've vanished."

"Amazing." Boe faced her again. "I am very excited for our journey."

"Hopefully it will be very dull, and you can look at the water to your heart's content."

Boe grinned. "I hope to see all kinds of amazing things on this journey, not just the water. This ship is miraculous and wonderful."

"Just be careful. Miraculous and wonderful can turn deadly in the wink of an eye."

Boe put on a serious face and nodded. "I understand. I will be very cautious and only travel with guardians to tell me when I am in danger."

"If you're looking for volunteer guardians..."

Boe giggled and leaned in, kissing Fausta's lips. "You will be an excellent protectors, Miss Gittens."

Behind them, Fausta heard someone shout a command to the quarterdeck. She looked and saw that Aldoncia Reyes' ship had indeed vanished over the horizon. She felt the lurch as Aravanis followed Clio's orders and got them underway.

"You're going to be needed at the helm. To point us in the right direction."

Boe nodded and they started walking there together. Halfway there, Fausta spotted Cariad using the gunwale as a desk, writing something on a sheet of paper. She told Boe to continue to the quarterdeck without her and changed direction, whistling to get the writer's attention. Cariad looked up, finished what she had been writing, and then folded the paper in half. She was tucking it into a pocket when Fausta reached her.

"I saw you go after the captain. Everything okay with her?"

"I don't know. Hopefully. I think talking to her did some good."

"Any idea *why* she's acting like this?"

Cariad opened her mouth, then closed it without saying anything. After a moment she said, "Not rightly sure it's my place to say."

"Fair enough." She looked out at the water. "So you've been hunting this story for a long time. And you finally got a big piece of the puzzle back there."

"I did." Cariad tapped the paper with her pen. "I'm writing down as much as I can while it's all fresh in my head. I've got everything I've seen and done, and things I've been told by Estacia and Captain Landau, and I'm just worried it's all going to start pushing stuff out before too long."

Fausta hmphed and nodded. "Any theories about what we'll find out there?"

Cariad looked at the horizon. "We've already found an invisible island that can apparently heal any wounds in the blink of an eye. Whatever this other island is, it's the source of that veil. It's bound to be something more incredible than we can imagine."

"Be careful. One thing I've learned out here at sea? Sometimes the incredible is just a trick to draw in prey so something awful can grab them."

Cariad considered the warning. "How can you tell the difference between something truly amazing and something that's just a trap?"

"Sometimes you can't. At least not before you're already

trapped."

"What can you do then?"

Fausta shrugged and answered as she walked away.

"The only thing you can do, Miss Baillie. You fight like hell."

CHAPTER SEVENTEEN

CLIO HAD *never sounded right. It didn't look right. She tried writing it down on a piece of paper and stared at it, but her hand didn't seem familiar with the shape of the letters, and she didn't recognize the mark. With everything else she'd lost, shouldn't she at least get to keep her damn name. She spent the first few days after "waking" in Hattie's rented room above a pub. Hattie tried to prompt her memory using games, tricks, showing her newspapers or looking at maps to see if anything looked familiar. They carefully examined everything that had been in Clio's cabin on the ship, but nothing struck a memory or even seemed the slightest bit familiar.*

(Because it was all lies, Clio knew now. Her name, her luggage, her reason for being on the ship... She had even altered her looks in case she ran across other pirates who might recognize her. She had made herself a new person before she lost everything that tied her to her true self.)

The ship on which Hattie served as first officer, the Banshee, arrived after a frustrating and fruitless week. Every morning, Clio had woken expecting her memory to have miraculously recovered. She slept on the couch in Hattie's room, a sagging monstrosity that threatened to swallow her every time she rested her weight on its cushions. She would open her eyes and stare at the cracks in the ceiling and try to remember more than three days earlier, four days earlier, five. But no matter how she tried, she could never get past that bloody storm.

The cracks in the ceiling were the first thing she saw every morning. The second thing was when she rolled over to see Hattie watching her, hope in her eyes turning to disappointment when Clio shook her head negatively.

"At least I always seem to remember you," Clio said one morning.

"As touching as that is, I doubt it's much comfort to you."

Clio shrugged and stood up off the couch, stretching her back carefully. "At this point, I consider recognizing anything to be a win."

Hattie was sitting up in bed. She wore a lightweight cotton shirt to bed, and the sunlight hit her just so to reveal the curves of her naked body underneath. Clio tried not to stare and instead glared at the window providing the lecherous light.

"My ship is due this afternoon," Hattie said. "I won't abandon you. I'll convince my captain to bring you aboard."

"I may not remember much, but I know most captains don't like dead weight on their ships."

"You can be useful."

"How?" Clio demanded to know.

Hattie shrugged. "We'll figure it out."

In time, Clio would learn that when Hattie said things like that, when she used that confident and optimistic tone, it was hard to disagree with her. But that morning she had felt too defeated to find much hope in the other woman's words.

In the past, recalling these days had given her comfort. The terror of being lost in a strange world, with very little money to her name and no safe harbor, panic could have overtaken her. She considered herself fortunate to have found someone as caring and warm as Hattie to take guardianship of her. And just as she had predicted, they found work for her aboard the ship. Nothing overly taxing, just something that required a human with a bit of muscle to work with. She worked the rigging, loaded and unloaded cargo, supervised the upkeep of various equipment and ship gear. She became a trusted member of the crew, someone the officers knew they could trust with more responsibility.

And the entire time she'd been a snake in the grass. Had there ever been moments when the old her slipped through? Moments when she felt an irrational violence toward Hattie? No... no, there couldn't have been. Sure, they had argued and fought. All couples had angry moments. But not murderous, not based in hatred. Feelings like that would have seemed alien among all the other feelings. Gratitude at first, soon growing to friendship, eventually... eventually...

But those memories were no longer where her story began. She could see past them. She saw a dark woman in dapper clothes, a woman called

Alice Malyns who put up her collar and pulled down the brim of her hat when she walked the streets of London. She wore glasses tinted green to hide the shape of her eyes so a passing glance might not identify her as female.

She felt Alice's hatred for pirates. It burned like a hot coal in the center of her chest. A hatred born with the pirates who targeted the coastal town where she was born. Pirates who raided her parents' shop, left them with nothing, nearly destroyed everything her father had built for them. As a girl Alice had loved the sea, but that changed the day that dark ship rolled into their harbor. They ransacked every shop, every tavern, even smashed in the doors to a few homes.

Alice saw the effects of that day erode her father for the rest of his life. He was ruined, and he nearly took Alice and her mother with him when he fell. It was only through her mother's determination and strength that they were able to stumble along until Alice was old enough to be married off. But her father refused to "sell his daughter" just to fill his coffers. She and her mother both pleaded with him, but he wouldn't budge.

So he turned to gambling. Every penny he got went to cards. And then came the debts. And then came the bullet in an alley. The people he ran with insisted it was suicide, but he owed money to every last one of them, and Alice couldn't make herself believe their version of events. She decided her mother would be better off supporting herself and headed to London.

She didn't know if pirate hunting was a job. If it wasn't, she would invent it. She would find a way to make money at it. Whether there was a market for the profession or not, she figured London was the best place to get started. She couldn't think of any better purpose for her life than hunting down every last pirate on the seas and watching them hang from the neck until dead.

Clio opened her eyes. The sun was setting outside her window, and she initially panicked at the thought of an entire lost day. She sat up quickly, but a quick stab of pain behind her eyes made her freeze. She grunted and pressed the heel of her hand against her temple. She waited until the throbbing died down and then resumed getting up with more care.

Alice Malyns. Her name was Alice. It didn't sound right, but this time it was because she was fighting against thirty years of being Clio Landau. Deep down, she knew it was her true name. She remembered the scared girl. She could feel the first time she tracked down a pirate and slapped his wrists in irons. It had taken all her willpower to take him to prison instead of just slitting his throat.

She went to her wash basin and slipped her hands into the water. She rubbed her palms together, linked her fingers, and then brought her hands up to her face to pat her cheeks.

"You're a pirate?" Clio asked.

Harriet had finished taking a sip of her water, ran her tongue over her lips, and then tilted her head to look at her. "I am. If that's going to be an issue..."

"I can't judge," Clio said. "A woman without a past can't very well sit in judgment of someone else's choices, right? Who knows what I've done. Maybe I'm just as bad as you."

Harriet laughed. "Well, I don't think I'm particularly bad."

"You just said you were a pirate."

"That doesn't mean I'll rob every tavern I see, or kill anyone who looks at me cross-eyed. It means I live on a ship with a crew of folks who don't care about unjust rules or laws. The law wouldn't let me be a first officer. It would never let me captain a ship, which is my plan in due course."

"There are laws against women captaining ships?"

"Hell, I don't know if they come out and say as much. But there are barriers and 'traditions'. There are restrictions in place that make sure it can't happen. So it might as well be a written law. And I have no trouble breaking those laws. And of course, a woman has to eat and drink and be merry. That costs coin. I've no problem stealing from the right people."

"Who are the right people to rob?"

"Those what can afford it," Harriet said, slipping into a lower accent. "Them as think we're too far beneath 'em to care what happens to us. Those are the people we rob from. And we take in lost lambs who would otherwise lead terrible lives and give them a chance at something better."

"Lost lambs," Clio repeated.

Harriet held out her cup of water. "Baa."

Clio shook off the memory. "Baa, Harriet..."

She sighed and dried her hands on her shirt. Fausta and Ranzi would have woken her if there were any pressing updates on their destination, but she wanted to know sooner rather than later. She left her cabin and went out for some fresh air.

She heard the crew before she saw them, their voices echoing from the open hatches on the gun deck. Clio went down, sticking to the shadows as she descended the stairs.

The gun deck felt to her like the bowels of the ship, low-ceilinged and claustrophobic, full of heavy cannons and the scrawny young men called powder monkeys who were tasked with delivering bags of gunpowder to the weapons. At the moment, however, by the light of lanterns swinging from the joists, she spotted most of her command crew gathered around a young man doing a dance to the rhythm of the song the crowd sang.

> *"So watch her, twig her,*
> *She's a proper ju-ber-ju*
> *Give her the sheet, let 'er rip!*
> *We're the gals to pull her through*
> *You should see us rally*
> *The wind a-blowin' free*
> *On the passage from Dogger Bank*
> *To Great Grimsby!"*

Clio saw Miss Baillie and Estacia sitting together in the crowd. The chef was sitting in the V of the writer's legs, and one of Cariad's arms rested in what looked like a very comfortable drape across Estacia's shoulder. Delfina had a stein in her hand, though judging by how much she swung it without drenching her neighbors, it was bone dry. Her shirt was untucked and unbuttoned to reveal much of her upper chest, though her hair was long enough to preserve her modesty when the two halves fell too far apart.

Ranzi had taken the lead, her hand-claps and stamping boots guiding the others to keep them on the same beat. She spotted Clio on the stairs and winked, her smile widening. She raised her voice to begin the next verse.

> *"So watch her, twig her,*
> *The powerful way she goes*
> *With high heels and painted toes*
> *She is on the show*
> *She is one of them flash girls,*
> *Ain't she cut to shine?*
> *She can do the double shuffle*
> *On the Knickerbocker line!"*

Clio rested her shoulder against the wall of the stairwell. Alice Malyns' memories still swirled in her head, the image of pirates as cruel and bloodthirsty thieves, crooks and criminals who would rob you blind and slit your throat as soon as look at you. Maybe that was one reason she was still, after all these years, worried the crew hadn't accepted her as their captain. Maybe that contempt had always been inside her somewhere, and she feared they could sense it.

Ranzi picked up her voice to sing louder, stomping harder, raising her arms above her head. The rest of the group yawped in response.

Clio pushed away from the wall and raised her voice loud enough to be heard above the group. Every eye turned to her as she slowly strolled to join their mob.

"Now we're the lasses who make a splash
When we come home from sea
We get right drunk and full of beer..."

The whole company shouted, "And *cause a jubilee!*" and Clio raised a fist to punctuate the sentiment before she continued.

"We roam the town from pub to pub
We stagger door to door
And when our money's all been spent,
We go to sea once more!"

The song ended with a cheer and much backslapping from those who had participated. Clio took the opportunity to wave Delfina over, and the medic extracted herself from the crowd to join her. Clio guided her away from the group so she could be heard without raising her voice.

"There's something I need to ask you. How drunk are you?"

"Sixes or sevens," Delfina said, "but steady enough. Unless you need me to do an operation."

Clio shook her head. "I just need your memory." Delfina nodded that she was capable of that, but her eyes were closed, and the nod made her wince. "Do you remember if Harriet was scared of something right before I came into her life?"

"Fuck, that was thirty years ago." Delfina furrowed her brow. "I have a hard time remembering shit that happened back then when I'm sober. Why?"

"I don't want to say just yet. I just... I need to know if she was acting unusual at all."

Delfina sighed and pressed her back against the curved wall. "I don't know. She asked for some time away from the ship. I guess that was a little unusual, but we all need to take a break once and again." She pushed her hand through her hair and looked hard at Clio. "Seriously. Why are you asking?"

Clio looked back to make sure no one was paying attention to them. "I'm starting to remember things." She immediately raised her hand, clapping it across Delfina's mouth before she could make a sound. Delfina's eyes widened at the shock of what she'd just heard. "Sh. I'm not ready to confess it to the whole ship. The only ones who know about it are you and Miss Baillie. It started when we went through the veil."

Delfina's expression changed to confusion. When Clio dropped her hand, she said, "That implies it was a fresh wound."

"I can't explain it. But I'm remembering things I've never had access to before."

"Like what? Do you remember your surname? Or where you came from, why you were on~"

Clio cut her off by slicing a hand through the air between them. "I'm not ready to go into all of that. But yes. Details, truths... things I'm not sure I'm better off knowing."

Delfina put a hand on Clio's bicep. The doctor looked almost completely sober now. "That sounds difficult. Do you want to spend the night with me?"

Clio tensed. She and Delfina had shared a bed on a handful of nights since Harriet died, events that weren't always sexual but also weren't strictly platonic. Clio knew Harriet would have approved. She loved them both, and absolutely would be happy to know they'd found solace with each other. But knowing what she knew now... knowing about Alice... She couldn't bring herself to think it would be okay.

"I'll pass tonight." She leaned in and kissed Delfina's cheek. "But another time."

"I'll hold you to that, Captain."

Clio smiled and stepped aside to let Delfina rejoin the crew. Until she had a better idea of who she was and what Alice Malyns may have done to these people in the past, she would feel like she was lying to them in any kind of intimate setting.

She wasn't going to risk crossing the line with any of them until she knew for certain just how many sins she had to atone for.

CHAPTER EIGHTEEN

THE TRIP to the next island would take them six days. Cariad took advantage of having no duties related to sailing the ship to try enjoying the fact she was at sea. She spent as much time as she could on writing deck. Several people had told her looking at the horizon would help the queasiness she still occasionally suffered. They were right and, in addition, the breezes could be invigorating and the sights were breathtaking. She always imagined vast expanses of empty ocean to be dull. But there were creatures out there, giant fish that would occasionally breach like creatures from a fantasy book. They saw tiny islands carpeted with trees and she couldn't help but speculate about what those forests might conceal.

She also spent the time enjoying her new relationship with Estacia. The night after the revelry on the gun deck, they'd drunkenly made their way back to the chef's cabin. While they were undressing each other, Estacia nipped Cariad's earlobe and whispered, "All those things you've been ashamed of wanting your whole life... I want you to do them to me."

Cariad was still hesitant. The following night, however, encouraged by Estacia's passionate response, she got a little bolder. And bolder still on the night after that. They had done things she probably wouldn't want to do again, now that they were out of her system, but the act of exploring still made her feel freer than she ever had. She knew she could ask Estacia for anything, to do anything, with no shame. And she knew that would extend to less lustful areas of her life.

Sometime during the journey, she had also acquired her sea legs. She could cross the deck as easily as Ranzi, her hands instinctively knowing when to reach out or grab something for balance. The only downside was that the sun burned her but Delfina, who was also very fair, shared a plant-based concoction which not only protected her from burns but also gave her skin a nice even tanned color. Delfina also gifted her a wide-brimmed hat which came with a veil that also provided relief.

She filled her days interviewing the crew, discovering all the paths they'd taken to get aboard the *Banshee*. Some had served under the original Captain Landau, others were recruited by Clio, but they all reported the same draw: the promise of a place they could feel safe to be themselves. Maybe that was what she needed more than the story. She was still writing and, even though she had no idea where she would eventually publish it, she was building quite the archive of biographies for her newfound friends. And if whatever she had with Estacia didn't settle into something permanent, it had at least set her on the path to understanding what and who she wanted. That path would be much easier to follow aboard the *Banshee* than if she tried returning to shore when this quest ended.

She became aware of someone standing at the gunwale near her and turned to see Boe was also staring out to sea. She hadn't seen much of the mysterious girl since they set out, even though the revelry the other night had partially been to welcome her aboard. But since then she seemed to keep to herself. Cariad moved closer and caught her attention. Boe smiled and turned toward her.

"It's lovely on the sea," Boe said. "You must be used to it."

"Actually this is my first time, too," Cariad admitted. "But I don't think you ever get used to it."

Boe looked at the crew hurrying around the deck. "They seem to be."

"They have a job to do. They're focused. But when they have a chance, I know they can still appreciate a sunset."

"Oh!" Boe's face brightened. "I saw the one last night. It was splendid! So many colors. I thought they were lovely on the island, but nothing compares. It looked as if it was sinking into the water."

Cariad laughed. "It did." She sighed and rested her arms on

the rail. "Yeah. It probably never gets old. But I wouldn't mind testing that theory over the next couple of years."

Boe laughed and nodded.

Fausta joined them on Cariad's other side. "You ladies seem to be having a lovely time."

"This is a fun ship," Cariad said.

"Give it time. You might find all sorts of unsavory things about it. But enjoy the quiet while you can." She nodded to Boe. "We'll be arriving at the coordinates early tomorrow. Will you be ready for whatever you need to do when we get there?"

Boe said, "I don't know exactly what will be required, but I know I can handle it. Leola would not have sent me otherwise."

Fausta nodded. "We're counting on it. Cariad. Captain said you're cleared to come ashore with us. I don't like it, but..." She shrugged. "Just try not to trip or break your ankle. I'm definitely not carrying you back to the ship."

"I think I can handle myself."

"See that you do." Fausta saluted them and headed off.

Cariad said, "I assumed you had done this before. Leola implied it was something that needed to be done on a fairly regular basis."

"It is, but not for many years. I was just a child the last time it happened so I would have been a poor choice. I campaigned for the opportunity to go this time. I've always wanted to see what was outside the veil."

"The people who went before you probably had all kinds of stories."

Boe shrugged. "I know you market in stories, but we're not really like that."

"No stories?" Cariad said, shocked. "I can't imagine surviving there. No wonder you were eager to get out." She gestured. "There's a million stories out there right now. I hope you get one worth taking back to your people."

"Or..." Boe drew the word out, hunching her shoulders. "Some of those who left have chosen to remain out in the world. Perhaps I could be one of those."

Cariad smiled. "I'm sure Captain Landau would be happy to have you. And... if you'd like to practice telling stories, I've been interviewing some members of the crew." She slipped a paper out of her pocket and held it up enticingly. "I would love to hear about your island, Leola, everything."

Boe looked at the paper warily. "We're not really supposed to talk about the island with outsiders. But I... will... consider it."

"Okay. That's enough." Cariad returned the paper to her pocket and faced the water again. "For now we can just enjoy the view together. No stories, just a lot of really beautiful ocean to appreciate."

Boe's smile returned in full force and she rested her arms on the railing as well. "That sounds like a lovely way to spend the day."

Cariad couldn't deny the woman had a point.

Their destination wasn't veiled like Leola's island. Common shouted a sighting when they were still a fair distance away, and Ranzi confirmed she could see it from the deck. She decided maybe it didn't require much defense since it was quite possibly the least hospitable place she'd ever seen. The central peak was mostly bare gray stone with a scattering of vegetation that only served to highlight how sickly the rest of the plant life looked. The beach was skirted by what looked like a thick forest, but as they got closer it became clear that the trees were sickly and strangled by vines. The greenery was lush but it would have been a lie to call it any kind of thriving.

"I guess that's where we're heading," she said as she handed the spyglass to Clio. "Doesn't exactly look like the Garden of Eden."

"It could just be a mirage," Clio suggested. "Leola's island was hidden behind a veil. Maybe this is just another illusion to protect them from drawing in every ship that passes by."

Aravanis, at the helm, said, "It's working."

Clio couldn't help but smile and clapped the big woman on the shoulder. "Well, that's where the coordinates have aimed us, so that's where we're going. Wonderful things have been found in far worse places, remember. Have you ever seen where pearls come from? Disgusting."

Ranzi didn't have an argument for that. And no matter what the island looked like, she was itching for a chance to get off the ship and stretch her legs.

When they were close enough to launch a ship, Clio announced the landing party: Ranzi, Delfina, Cariad, and Boe would accompany her to the island. Ranzi knew the doctor's purpose was to keep her eye out for anything that looked interesting. If this place produced something as miraculous as the veil, there was no telling what other wonders it might conceal.

Although, she thought as she cast a look back at the desolate beach, she couldn't imagine what it might be hiding behind such a rough exterior.

Fausta was left in command of the *Banshee*. Ranzi rowed, keeping her eye on the captain. Something had happened when they went through the veil, but she couldn't figure out what it could be. There were no physical changes, but there had been a definite change to her mental state. It was almost like she was spooked, expecting a ghost to pop out from around every corner. She wasn't going to ask if anyone else noticed, at the risk of causing rumors to spread, and she wasn't going to disrespect the captain by bluntly asking her if she was okay.

But she could keep an eye on her. She could make sure she was there if and when the ghosts finally did make themselves known.

Cariad had sat facing the stern, but now she was twisted to get her first good look at the island. "I don't want to be rude," she said, "but I think Leola's island definitely has the upper hand on this place. Boe, what do you exchange for the source of the veil?"

"Nothing."

Everyone in the launch looked at her then. It was Delfina who asked what they were all asking. "I thought you were bringing something to swap. Your island gets something to refresh the veil, and this island gets... gets nothing?"

Ranzi scanned the shore again. "It certainly looks plausible," she said under her breath.

Clio said, "But why would anyone part with something so powerful without asking for something in return? They could at least ask for food, or... or..."

Boe seemed unconcerned. "This is the way it has always been. Leola and the inhabitant of this island made an agreement long ago and both sides have upheld it for decades."

Ranzi leaned forward. "Sorry. Did you say 'inhabitant'? Singular? There's only one person living on this island?"

"Aye," Boe said, smiling proudly to have used a 'pirate' word. "Her name is Uralde. She cultivates the source of the veil. She provides replenishment when it is required. This has been the arrangement since long before I was born."

Ranzi glanced to Clio and saw the captain was already looking at her. Ranzi gave a short shake of her head: she did not have a good feeling about any of this. Leola had given them just enough information that she wasn't lying directly, but they definitely didn't have the full story here.

Cariad also looked concerned. "Boe, you mentioned that sometimes the people who come to retrieve the source decided to stay in the outside world instead of coming home."

"That's right."

"How many of them actually came back?"

Boe shrugged. "I don't know. Not many. Why would they?"

"Boe, I need you to think about this question very carefully," Cariad said. "Can you think of a single person who came on this journey and then came back?"

"Why does it matter?"

"Because I think we know what the offering is," Delfina said. "Captain, we can't allow this."

Clio's lips were pressed together in a tight line. She was looking at the island the way she'd looked at Aldoncia's ship just before she gave the order to charge at them head-on.

Boe was watching them all carefully, her head pivoting from one to the next.

Ranzi slowed rowing. "What are your orders, Captain?"

Clio chewed her bottom lip and shook her head. "We don't know for certain, so we continue on. But be on your guard, and keep yourselves between Boe and this... what was her name?"

"Uralde," Boe said, sounding confused and more than a little frightened now. "I don't understand. What do you believe is happening?"

Cariad looked at Clio, and Ranzi saw her give a slight nod. Cariad put a hand on Boe's shoulder. "We think Leola is trading people for the source of the veil."

"What?" Boe laughed. "That's preposterous."

"It makes more sense than giving away something so precious for free," Delfina said. "She has to be getting something in exchange. And you just said no one ever comes back."

Boe sputtered, "Not that I remember! But I don't remember every..." She shook her head. "I've only been alive for two of the exchanges! W-we don't talk about the, the, the exchange..."

"It makes sense to keep that part close to the vest," Clio said. "Especially if they want people to keep volunteering."

Ranzi said, "And Leola might think it's worth losing one person to keep everyone else safe."

"Leola wouldn't do that." Boe's voice was quiet, and her eyes were focused on the floor of the boat. "She wouldn't sacrifice me like that."

"Didn't you volunteer?" Cariad said.

Boe's face fell.

"We're going to act in good faith." Clio sat up straighter, still staring down the island. "We're going to give her the benefit of the doubt. But the second she gives us a reason to doubt her intentions, we will protect you."

Boe looked over her shoulder at Ranzi, who nodded. Boe looked at Delfina, at Cariad, and saw that they were all in agreement.

"All right," she said. "But you will be proven wrong. I am certain of it."

"I hope we are," Clio said. "I'm not in the mood for a fight. But I'm damn sure going to prepare in case one is waiting for us on this island."

Ranzi continued rowing, this time with the knowledge they could be forced to fight their way off the island when the time came to leave.

She would be ready.

INES RANZI

"I fight. I like to fight, and I'm good at it, and I usually win. There aren't a lot of opportunities for that sort of thing on land.

Why did I choose... I don't know. I like water.

Okay, okay, fine. If everyone else is talking about it. I don't have a story, okay? I joined because I always dreamed of being a sailor. I built model ships, I read books about sailing, I knew my way around a ship better than any man. But they wouldn't let me join the Royal Navy. Too many rules, anyway. So if I wanted to live the life I wanted, there was really only one option.

I heard Harriet Landau was trying to make an all-female crew. Or at least a majority. I said there's not much opportunity for my interests on land? I can't think of any career where I could guarantee working with women, for women. The fewer men around, the better. I'm sure you've found that to be the case. And it works for us. We get along as well as any other crew. We don't judge each other, and we don't waste time with 'traditional' nonsense that would keep a lot of the women onboard lonely in their beds. Everyone's happy.

Is that enough? I honestly don't know what the hell everyone else is being so talkative about. We're pirates. We have a ship. It's a life. It's a damn good life."

CHAPTER NINETEEN

CARIAD STEPPED off the launch and didn't stop moving, taking long loping steps away from the tide across the sand. Estacia had given her the advice about how to recover from her sea legs and, despite a bit of lingering queasiness, it kept her steady and helped her avoid tripping over her feet. She didn't fall, but the trees and rocks did appear to rock from side to side in a manner her brain found utterly unsettling.

She moved along the tree line, head tilted back to examine the island. It wasn't large enough to conceal any kind of true settlement, but it was large enough that one woman could definitely reside there without being seen by passing ships.

Ranzi and Clio pulled the launch higher onto the beach. Boe stood near Delfina, her face sill pale from what they'd suggested. Cariad wasn't sure the girl believed it, but the doubt in her eyes had grown stronger throughout the last part of their journey.

Cariad turned back to the sea. The *Banshee* was the only thing visible against the horizon, tall and majestic even with its sails furled. She'd seen many ships in her time haunting the docks in search of someone to take her on this mission but she'd never taken the time to fully appreciate them. They were more than mere boats, more than transportation. What she saw now was a home. It was a life, and a living creature kept alive by the family who occupied it.

Ranzi snapped her fingers next to Cariad's head and she

blinked in surprise. She hadn't even seen her approach.

"You okay?"

"I'm fine. Just lost in my head."

Ranzi grabbed Cariad's arm and lifted it, slapping the leather hilt of a knife into her palm. "Captain said to be on your guard. Not really doing that if you're unarmed. Let alone daydreaming with your back to the trees."

Cariad nodded, sheepish. "It won't happen again."

Ranzi grunted and moved away from her. Clio had drawn her sword, a curved cutlass which reached just past her knee when she held it to her side. Ranzi had a similar sword with a blade so gray it almost seemed black, along with two pistols hanging from belts slung low on her hips. The wind off the water caught the sleeves of her shirt and whipped them wildly, which only served to highlight her stillness as she examined the area ahead of them.

Now that *is a pirate*, Cariad thought.

Clio motioned for them to get into formation, as they had agreed on the boat. Ranzi would take the lead, with Cariad and Clio behind her and Delfina bringing up the rear. Boe would be in the center of the diamond, protected from all sides in case this Uralde decided on a sneak attack. Cariad was grateful for her borrowed weapon but doubtful of her ability to actually use it against a living being. Hopefully she would be less conflicted when it came to protecting Boe.

Ranzi proceeded across the beach, and the others followed.

They were almost to the trees when a woman appeared. Cariad didn't know where she could have come from; there was nowhere near enough cover for her to have snuck up on them. But she was suddenly there, rushing toward them, face twisted into a mask of angry irritation. She was dressed in gray trousers that ended just below the knee in ragged shreds, her blouse little more than a rag draped over her shoulders. Her hair was too thin to tell its color, the remaining strands doing little to conceal her spotted scalp.

Ranzi assumed a defensive posture, sword out, and held her hand behind her to indicate the rest of the party should hold back. The crone, obviously Uralde, stopped short when the blade was aimed at her. She hissed and cowered away from the weapon.

"You waste time! You took so long. Look at me! Look at home!" She snarled at them. "Nearly killed us all, you did. Lazy. Lazy!"

"We came as soon as we were given the job." Clio stepped

forward. She kept her sword at her side. "I'm Clio Landau, captain of the *Banshee*. We~"

Uralde hissed and spit on the sand between them. "Show me! Show me the girl!"

Ranzi looked at Clio, who kept her eyes on the old woman. "Why? We were told her purpose was to show us the way and get the source."

"Is no matter to you. The girl!" Uralde leaned to one side to see past Ranzi. "Is her? That the girl? Girl, Leola Fairfax sent you?"

Ranzi said, "Don't answer her. Not until we get some answers from her first."

Boe ignored the advice. "Yes. I'm the one she sent."

Cariad put a hand on Boe's arm. "You don't have to do... wh-whatever this is about to be. You can make your own decision."

"I am." Bo stepped around Ranzi and face the crone. "They believe I was brought here to be sacrificed. To give my life for whatever you provide to Leola. Is that true?"

Uralde eyed Clio and Ranzi suspiciously. "Truth, truth... many have come before you. Life gives life to island, island creates source. Source goes to Leola, creates barrier. Protects them."

Bo nodded and then looked at Clio. "It's all right. I choose to go."

Clio's face went ashen. "You can't mean that. You can't be willing to die for..."

"For my home. For my people." Boe shrugged. "You stood in front of an enemy who was threatening your ship, your crew. If you knew you could have saved them by dying, wouldn't you have made that agreement? I'm sacrificing myself to save Leola. And to save your crew as well. You'll all benefit from the renewed source. Your ship will be protected from future enemies."

Delfina said, "For how long? A few years? And then we have to pick someone to throw to this wolf so it can be renewed. Right? It's not a permanent solution."

Boe said, "You ask your crewmembers to die every time they fight to protect the ship."

"That's self-preservation," Clio said.

Boe shrugged. "So is this. I'm sorry, Captain Landau."

Uralde reached out and grabbed Boe's wrist. "The girl has made her choice!"

Cariad said, "No. If you need a life, take mine."

Everyone looked at her. She was terrified, part of her uncertain of when she'd made this decision, but she knew she didn't regret it. She didn't want to take it back. She dropped the dagger Ranzi had given her and held her hands out to either side as she moved closer.

"Let Boe live, let her go back to her island. Take me."

Uralde sneered. "You? Old. Too old, not enough."

"Then take me as well," Clio said. "The years I have left should make up the difference between Cariad's age and Boe's."

Delfina stepped forward. "And if it doesn't, take mine."

Ranzi raised an eyebrow and shrugged. "Hell, why not. Hope the girl knows how to row her way back to the ship after we get done sacrificing ourselves for her."

"Not the way it works," Uralde sneered. "One. One sacrifice, one life, one young and healthy. Not... not old, not halves. One!"

Boe had tears in her eyes. "Please, Captain. How else can I protect my island, my home? And the wonderful people I've met aboard your ship? If I can do that..."

"At the cost of your own life?" Cariad said. "What about seeing the world? I saw the look in your eye when you looked at the horizon. There's so much more out there waiting to be seen."

"I won't see it from our island."

Clio said, "Then stay on the *Banshee*. That's the lie you've been told, right? That the other sacrifices chose to stay outside and see the world. It could be the truth this time."

"But without the source... the island will die."

Ranzi said, "Then let it die. Or they can fight and defend themselves like everyone else on the planet. Just like we will, without the source." She spoke to Clio without turning to face her. "Sorry, Captain. I was never too keen on the idea of us skulking around invisible."

"I've soured on the idea myself over the past while," Clio said. "Especially once I figured out what it was going to cost."

Uralde made a sound of derision. "Your people will die bloody, rather than allowing this girl to give her life now, peacefully. What a foolish choice."

"We'll die on our feet. Boe... do you want to die?"

"I-I'm..."

Uralde yanked on Boe's arm. "She has made her choice!"

Clio brought her sword up. "And I am giving her a chance to reconsider! Boe. Please. Don't think about Leola or the others on your island who decided your life was worth less than theirs. Don't think about my crew, who I fight alongside rather than sending them to a slaughter. Do you want your life to end right here, right now, on this decrepit island?"

Tears rolled down Boe's face. Quietly, she said, "No."

It was apparently all Clio needed to hear.

She brought her sword up and closed the distance between herself and the girl with two long strides. Uralde pulled Boe to her and twisted to one side in order to use her as a shield. It might have worked if Clio had intended on a body shot; instead she brought her sword down on the crone's forearm with enough strength that it drew a sharp cry from her lips. The blade cut into Uralde's papery skin and blood splattered out as she instinctively released Boe.

Ranzi swooped in like a bird of prey, using her free arm to pull Boe away from her captor. It was almost like a dance move, the way the pirate used her movement to direct Boe's, spinning them both so Ranzi was closer to Uralde. Cariad took the opportunity to reach out her hand to Boe.

"Come on! I'll take you back to the launch."

Boe took Cariad's hand. "I'm sorry..."

"Don't be sorry," Delfina said, joining them. "Just hurry."

They had only taken a few running steps when Uralde shouted, "No!" and stamped her foot down on the sand. The move only appeared petulant, as it released a wave powerful enough to knock Clio and Ranzi off their feet. Cariad looped her arm around one of Boe's, while Delfina did the same with the other, and they kept each other upright as they continued running. It wasn't far to the launch. They could make it, get back to the ship, return with~

Another wave of energy hit them from behind, a gale force wind that was almost too powerful to brace against, and continued down to the beach. The sand kicked up like a wave and threw their launch from where they'd secured it, sending it tumbling end over end back into the harbor. She was certain that even if the boat survived the impact, one or both of the oars would be completely lost to them.

Cariad looked back to see Ranzi grappling with Uralde. Going back to the *Banshee* was no longer an option, now they could only hope to put as much distance between them and the witch as possible.

"Along the shore," Delfina said, pointing.

Cariad saw a stone and a group of dead trees which would theoretically provide cover for them. But if Uralde was able to create an explosion of sand from two hundred paces, where on this island would they ever be safe?

There was no way to know for sure, but she had no doubt the beach was the most dangerous place to stand at the moment. She and Delfina cut to their left and pulled Boe along with them as they ran along the tideline.

Ranzi was stymied by how wily the witch turned out to be. Every thrust of her sword was deflected by a gnarled hand, sometimes leaving a bloody gash in its wake but never slowing the hag down. She was also somehow keeping Clio at bay, retreating a step at a time while never missing a beat or allowing a single attack through. Ranzi dropped back and took a moment to regroup, leaving Clio to hack and slash at the unarmed woman.

At one point Uralde grabbed Clio's sword, used it to pull the captain forward, and punched her hard enough that Clio was thrown back several feet. That was when she turned her back on them and ran.

Ranzi pulled her firearms and shot at the withered woman's back, but none of the bullets hit their mark.

Clio grunted in pain as she got back to her feet. "You're usually a better shot than that, Ines..."

"She's probably got some kind of wards set up to protect her." Ranzi sneered. "Fuckin' hate witches. Never a fair fight. Probably healing all her wounds right now."

"Most likely." Clio looked toward the water. "Miss Baillie and Delfina seem to have gotten the girl away, at least."

Ranzi started forward in pursuit of Uralde. "For now, anyway. We're running around blind while she knows every inch of this island. She can't hunt if she's too busy running from us."

Clio grinned, her face twisting into a predatory mask. She gestured with her sword and nodded her head.

"Then let the chase commence."

Ranzi returned the feral smile and then set off into the dying stand of trees.

CHAPTER TWENTY

FAUSTA LOWERED the binoculars and handed them to Aravanis. They were far enough away that she couldn't quite make out any small gestures of the landing party, but she certainly saw when things went to hell. The sun glinted off swords as Clio and Ranzi attacked. She watched as Delfina and Cariad, recognizable by their clothing, ran down the beach. And even from this distance it would have been impossible to miss a portion of the beach erupting upward as if an explosion had gone off under the sand. The launch flipped in the air and then came down hard enough to split its hull.

"Orders?" Aravanis said, because Fausta actually had to say the words before they could be put into action.

"Bring us in closer and bring us around broadside. Tell the gun crew to be at the ready to blow this rock out of the ocean."

Aravanis grinned and smacked Fausta's shoulder as she moved to comply. "Aye, ma'am."

Once she was gone, her shouted orders echoing over the deck, Fausta heard another echo coming from farther away. Gunfire. She brought the binoculars back up and scanned the beach, but everyone had vanished from sight. She clenched her jaw and braced herself as the ship began moving closer.

She could only hope that they could help without catching one of their crew in the crossfire.

The forest became denser beyond their landing site. They moved into single file as they entered the tightly-packed trees, Delfina in the lead and Boe still in the center for whatever protection that might offer. The ground was uneven, twisted roots and swampy ground that threatened to swallow their feet with every step, so they had to move carefully. Cariad braced her hand against trees and their dry bark cut and scraped her palm.

"Were you telling the truth?" Boe asked, breathless from running. "Would you really have sacrificed yourself to protect my life?"

"You were offering to sacrifice your life for us." Cariad was also finding it hard to breathe; a lifetime pursuit of writing hadn't prepared her for this level of exertion. "It seemed only fair."

Boe said, "Your lives are worth so much more than mine."

"You're wrong," Delfina said without looking back. "I know you may believe that. Leola Fairfax may have pounded that into your head to prepare you for this moment. But every life is precious."

"But you ask your crew to fight to protect the ship," Boe said. "Is that not the same thing?"

"They're not fighting for me," Delfina said, "or the captain. Not specifically. They're fighting for the ship. It's their home. They fight because the prize is worth defending."

Cariad said, "They fight because they share in the reward. They aren't fodder."

"And your island isn't under attack. It's hiding. They're sacrificing you because they're cowards and that is not a good enough reason for a beautiful young woman to die. Not in my book."

Boe looked back and met Cariad's eye, then looked away with something like shame.

"Thank you for protecting me."

"Don't thank us yet," Cariad said. "We're still trapped on that harridan's island with no way back to the ship."

"Fausta will have seen something went wrong. She'll bring the forces to bear. We just have to stay alive long enough for it to matter."

Cariad turned to look out at the waiting ship, but the forest had closed behind her so densely that she couldn't even see the water. Fear prickled her skin as she wondered if it was just the natural state of the forest or if this was more of Uralde's magic at work. What if they had just willingly entered a maze where they would scurry about like mice until the witch came to deal with them at her leisure?

"Cariad!" Delfina shouted. "Keep up, please."

Cariad nodded an apology and hurried to catch up. At the moment it didn't matter if the forest was natural or a trap. Their only possible tactic was to keep running until the moment they couldn't run any further. She whispered a prayer for Fausta to hurry with the rescue, because she had a feeling that wall was fast approaching for her.

Clio couldn't help noting that the old woman was fucking fast. She hopped twisted roots as easily as a frog, her arms now streaked with bright red blood that also stained her raggedy clothing. Ranzi tripped and slipped and cursed as she stumbled after Uralde, falling this way and that, unable to move in a straight line on this path, but they couldn't take another route or they would risk losing sight of their prey.

They arrived at a clearing, but Clio's relief was short-lived. Uralde was running for a hole in the ground ahead filled with an unnatural white glow. She sped up when she got close, then bent her knees and dived in. The light washed over her body and flared brightly enough that Clio and Ranzi both skidded to a stop and lifted their hands to cover their eyes.

When they looked again, the light had dimmed to the point where it could barely be seen in sunlight. Clio doubted it would provide much of a glow even after dark.

"Captain," Ranzi said, gesturing above them with her sword.

When Clio looked up, she saw leaves tumbling from the few trees around them that still looked alive. A moment ago they might not have been thriving, but at least they'd been green. In an instant, they'd curled and browned into husks. One landed at Clio's feet and she stepped to one side, crunching it under the toe of her boot.

"The source?" Ranzi said.

"Life has to come from somewhere, I suppose."

"It's no matter," Uralde said as she crawled from the hole.

Her voice was smoother now, rich and vibrant like a much younger woman. It quickly became clear why: she looked at least sixty years younger than when she made the dive. Her clothing was still in tatters, but the wounds their swords had inflicted were gone without even the hint of a scar. Her hair, once thin and brittle, was now a thick chestnut wave. She grinned, green eyes flashing.

"It took a lot of what I had left, but it will be replenished soon enough. With the lives of you four, and that ignorant girl, the island will be more vital than ever before. Especially since I won't have to share with Leola. She's gotten the sweeter end of the deal for too long anyway." She aimed one dangerously sharp fingernail at Clio. "I believe you should be first to fall."

Clio spread her feet apart and lowered her head, hunching her shoulders with her sword at the ready. "You're more than welcome to try."

Uralde hissed and launched herself forward, going for a straightforward attack. Clio remained motionless until she could see the red veins in the whites of the witch's eyes. She dropped to her knees, hunched her shoulders, and thrust her sword arm forward to drag its blade along Uralde's torso. She felt the resistance as it cut through the threadbare material of her blouse and the sturdier skin underneath, and blood rained down on her as her opponent twisted and fell to the side, clutching the wound in her chest with both hands.

"Disappointing," Ranzi said, approaching to deliver the final blow. "I thought she'd put up more of a fight than~"

One of Uralde's hands struck like a snake, grabbing Ranzi by the ankle. Ranzi jerked her leg back, but the hag's grip was too strong. Clio stepped forward but, before she could finish what she started, a white light flashed between Uralde's fingers and Ranzi's leg. Ranzi screamed in pain and fell backward, dropping her weapons to grab at her thigh as if she planned to physically yank it from the woman's grip.

"Release her!" Clio demanded.

Uralde did as requested, but Clio could see the damage had already been done. Every inch of exposed skin below Ranzi's pant leg was a charred ruin. She lay sprawled on her back, arms limp to either side. The wound Clio had just inflicted on the witch, however, was completely healed. Clio cursed under her breath and jumped back before Uralde could touch her as well.

"Benefit of a dive into the source," the witch said as she got onto her feet. "The effects tend to linger for a while. Just long enough to make sure the entire body is healed."

"Who was the child you sacrificed for that, hm?" Clio asked. "Do you remember her name? Or was it so long ago, did it matter so little, that you can't even remember?"

"She went gladly into the light," Uralde said. "Just as all the sacrifices before her did. Just as this one would have, if you hadn't filled her head with lies and confusion."

The witch was slowly advancing on her. Clio backed away, keeping the bloodied sword between them as she maintained their distance from each other.

Clio said, "How many have their been? How long have you and Leola been feeding young women to keep yourselves alive?"

Uralde laughed. "It's been hundreds of years."

"For what? This life? An old crone hiding out alone, watching the island die around her? Killing others so you can stay alive and merely survive? Boe has a chance to actually live. She wants to see the world, learn things, explore. You think it's worth throwing her away just so you can add a few more meaningless digits to your calendar?"

"You would do the same," Uralde said. "To extend your life. To continue living. To push back death just one more day."

Clio shook her head. "No. That's where you're wrong." Tears burned her eyes. "I've got someone waiting for me on the other side, and I cannot wait to see her again."

Uralde growled. "Allow me to end your separation!"

The witch threw herself forward again, once again flying across the space between them as if she'd grown wings when she went into the light. Clio prepared to swing her sword in a high upward arc, this time aiming for her opponent's throat. She didn't get the chance.

While Uralde was in mid-leap, when Clio reared back for what she hoped would be the killing blow, Boe stepped between them with a blunderbuss held in both hands. She brought up the weapon's flared barrel in a single smooth movement. Clio watched over the girl's shoulder as Uralde's ferocious snarl turned into a confused grimace. Then the gun exploded in a blinding explosion and the stench of gunpowder washed over them.

When the smoke cleared, Uralde's body was crumpled in a heap at Boe's feet. Her head was a smoking, cratered ruin of muscles, blood, and shattered bone.

Clio put a hand on Boe's shoulder. The girl recoiled, but relaxed when she saw who it was.

Delfina and Cariad emerged from the woods and stared, shocked, at the body in front of Boe.

"She got away from us," Delfina said, breathless. "We were lost... turned around. And suddenly she just grabbed the gun from my belt and ran off."

"I heard her voice," Boe muttered. "I couldn't let the captain and Miss Ranzi risk themselves to protect me."

Clio remembered. "Shit. Ranzi..."

Her friend's leg looked like charcoal. She knelt next to her, feeling for a pulse or any sign of life, but Ranzi was completely still.

"The source."

She looked at Boe, then at the pool of light. There was still a glow. Barely, but it was there. She could only hope it would be enough.

Cariad and Delfina helped her lift Ranzi, the three of them carrying her to the hole in the ground. Just before the edge of the pit, the ground was actively crumbling away. Delfina leaned forward to look down, then cast a worried look at Clio. The glow was still too bright to see the bottom.

"Uralde jumped in, then climbed out easily. We have to assume it's not that deep."

Cariad said, "It's not like we're going to hurt her any more than she already is."

"I have qualms about dumping a member of my crew down a hole, magic or not." Clio sighed and shook her head. "But here we go."

They lifted Ranzi over the lip and lowered her carefully. When they couldn't go any lower without the risk of tumbling in alongside her, Delfina nodded to Cariad and they let her go. Ranzi dropped and vanished into the light. It flared with renewed brightness, like a flame that had just been fed new kindling. Clio grabbed the back of Cariad's belt and pulled her back, doing the same with the collar of Delfina's blouse. The three of them stumbled away from the pit, watching as a beam of seemingly solid light erupted upward and then flickered and faded out of sight.

"How long do we wait?" Cariad asked, her voice hushed.

"It seemed almost instant when~"

A hand appeared on the edge of the pit. When she tried to pull herself up, the ground crumbled and the hand fell away again.

Clio and Delfina both rushed forward and bent down, reaching to take Ranzi's hands. She braced her feet against the side of the pit, using it to walk her way up even as it crumbled and collapsed underneath her boots. They managed to get her out of the hole, but the entire area felt alarmingly unstable now. The ground, solid as stone just a moment ago, now felt more unstable than the most windswept deck she'd ever tried walking across.

Ranzi dropped to her knees and coughed so hard her entire body shook with it. She was the same age, it seemed, and a glance at her leg showed no evidence of the damage Uralde had done.

"Ines?" Clio asked. "Can you stand?"

Ranzi nodded. "I just need a second."

Clio said, "I don't think we have a second, love. We need to get back to shore."

"The launch is a lost cause," Delfina said.

"Then we have to hope Fausta has a brilliant rescue planned. Now go before we..." She paused, frowned at the trees across from the pit. "Those are the trees we came through. But they should be behind us." She turned to look but didn't recognize the forest.

Cariad said, "This happened to us when we tried to get away from the witch." She stumbled as the ground beneath her right foot collapsed, and she jumped back to a more solid position. "It's like the island was trying to lead us back here."

"In that case," Clio said, "I suggest we just run and pray."

Boe hesitated. "Do I...?"

"You just saved our lives," Clio said, urging the girl to join the others. "Come on. You bleed for my crew, you're a member of my crew.

"But I didn't bleed, I just~"

Delfina grabbed Boe and dragged her along as she ran for the trees. "It's a figure of speech, love. Just *run*."

Clio got under one of Ranzi's arms, prepared to help her back to shore alone, but Cariad ducked under the other arm to take half the weight. They gave Ranzi a second to acclimate and then started after Delfina and Boe. The sand was falling away at blinding speed, and soon the only solid ground they could find were the twisted roots of trees which suddenly swayed and started toppling as their support gave way. She glanced down to see water flooding around their feet. Even more alarming was that there was a distinct current to its flow.

"The island is collapsing into the pit," she shouted to Delfina.

"What does that mean?" Cariad asked.

"It means it doesn't matter how fast we run," Ranzi grunted, "we're going to take a swim."

Ahead of them, as if foretold, Clio saw Delfina fall and go

underwater. Boe reached to help her and tumbled, joining her in the rising tide.

And then the trees were falling on them, Clio's next step came down on nothing solid, and her arm fell away from Ranzi's waist as the three of them fell into the depths.

CHAPTER TWENTY-ONE

FAUSTA LOWERED the spyglass. "Aravanis," she said, struggling to keep her voice calm, "is that island disappearing?"

Aravanis nodded, keeping one hand on the railing. "Aye, it seems to be."

"No," Fausta said. "I need you to confirm that the fucking island on which our captain and two of our crew members were last seen is *fucking sinking* right in front of us."

"Can confirm. The tides have changed as well. Looks to be a maelstrom forming yonder."

"Fuck." Fausta thrust the spyglass to Aravanis and half-ran back to the helm. "Brace up your yards!" she shouted to the crew as she took over the wheel.

She felt the familiar thrill of facing down an enemy, even if this time the enemy was the weather. She gripped the handles and planted her foot hard against the pedestal. The ship became part of her in an instant, her fingers digging hard into the wooden pegs until the entire helm felt like an extension of her body. She threw her back into the turn and felt the *Banshee* move through the water away from the pull of the sudden current.

The sails filled with wind and pulled them away from the whirlpool's grasp, every woman and man on the deck fighting to keep them from succumbing. Fausta heard the wood groan and protest but the *Banshee* held firm. It was half a century old. It had weathered hurricanes, squalls, running aground, and so many attacks she didn't even know the total number. The sea didn't have a single trick this ship hadn't seen and survived and left in its wake.

"Walk away, girl," Fausta growled. "Just walk away from it..."

She didn't relax until they had gained enough distance that the ship stopped fighting her. They were back in calm seas. Aravanis ascended to the quarterdeck.

"The island is gone. Just some scattered debris left."

"What kind of debris?"

"Lots of timber," Aravanis said. "It looks like a forest exploded out there."

Fausta raised an eyebrow at her. "It sort of did, 'Vanis. We just saw it happen."

Aravanis shrugged.

"Any sign of–"

"Persons overboard on the starboard side!" Tis Common shouted from the crowd's nest.

Fausta's pulse quickened as Aravanis lifted the glass to look. "There," she said when she spotted movement. "Amid the island's flotsam. Definitely signs of life."

Her shoulders burned as she brought the ship about, returning to the position she had just worked so hard to flee. Aravanis rang the bell to let their lost crewmembers know they had been spotted. Deckhands gathered at the gunwales and shouted out bearings, keeping their eyes on the floating survivors of the island. Fausta could see them now as well, a handful of people clinging to the bobbing trees. It was hard to tell at such a distance, but she was fairly certain she could see the captain's short blonde hair. The others were dark-haired, assuming Cariad's hair turned from red to black when it was wet, but it seemed like the number matched how many they were missing.

Fausta had to navigate carefully through the uprooted trees, moving slowly but still wincing every time she heard the hollow thud of another piece of driftwood against their bow. The launch Captain Landau and the others had taken to the island was almost definitely destroyed, either when it went airborne or after the whirlpool appeared, but they had another that was already being prepared.

Aravanis went down to the deck so she could get a closer look. The crew cleared a path for her and fell silent as she leaned over the rail, then lifted a hand in greeting.

"How do they look?" Fausta shouted.

Aravanis shouted over her shoulder. "Wet and miserable!"

Fausta grinned. "Then let's bring them up and get them more comfortable, aye?"

Clio remained in the water until everyone else was safely aboard. By the time she finally allowed herself to be pulled up into the launch, she was shivering so badly that she felt like she could feel her organs vibrate. The deckhands immediately wrapped her in a warm towel. Delfina, Cariad, Ranzi, and Boe were all sitting in a row along the gunwale similarly wrapped up and looking like drowned rabbits.

"What a sorry lot you are," Fausta said, strolling up to them with a flask in her hand. She smiled and held out the alcohol as an offering. "Need to warm up?"

Ranzi sneered at her and snatched the flask away. "We'll see how good you look when the ground opens up under your feet and dumps you in the middle of the ocean."

Clio said, "And don't forget, she was dead moments before she had to swim for her life. She looks quite spectacular, considering."

Fausta smirked and lightly tapped her boot against the side of Ranzi's. "Glad to see you cheated the reaper twice today, Ines. I'd have missed your face."

Ranzi nodded to her, then pulled the towel tighter around her shoulders.

Fausta watched the captain carefully to make sure she wasn't in shock or otherwise damaged before she spoke again.

"I get the feeling things didn't exactly go to plan."

"No, it definitely did not," Clio replied, carefully and deliberately getting to her feet. She swayed and Aravanis reached out to steady her, but Clio held up a hand. Once she had gotten her knees locked, she rested her hand on the bosun's shoulder both as gratitude and for support. "We didn't get what we came for, so Leola Fairfax is likely going to be highly irate with us. So we need to decide what our next step will be."

Cariad cleared her throat. "Leola said she needed to renew the source because it was losing strength. If it dies completely, there's a chance the same thing will happen to her island as happened here. Boe, how many people live on your island?"

"Seven hundred and eighty two," Boe and Clio said at the

same time. Clio finished, "Plus the woman who is pregnant with twins. We have to warn her the source isn't being renewed."

Ranzi said, "We barely escaped this time with our lives. Some of us more 'barely' than others. Fairfax is bound to be miffed we scuttled her plans. And if that means her whole island is about to go the way of Atlantis, I'd rather be as far away as possible when it happens."

Cariad said, "But seven hundred people..."

"People who were willing to sacrifice Boe for their own survival," Clio reminded them. "Even if we offered to evacuate them, we couldn't possibly fit that many refugees on our ship."

Delfina cleared her throat. "I think we should ask Boe what she thinks."

Everyone turned to the younger woman. She looked utterly shellshocked, hugging herself and dripping on the deck. Clio faced her fully.

"You have the most information here. What do you suggest we do? Should we warn Leola we won't be coming back with the source?"

Boe licked her lips and furrowed her brow. "I don't know. I-I think that she would be furious. I think you would be forced to fight her, and the rest of the island residents. They might try to take the ship if the island is at risk. If it's my decision, which I do not believe it should be, I would say we run. We... they don't have the means to pursue or chase you down. She would more likely assume your ship had met with some doom or another and you'd sunk before you could return."

"And leave all those people to die?" Delfina asked.

"To potentially die," Ranzi corrected.

Fausta said, "If there's a risk of this happening there, we have to assume Fairfax has a backup plan. It took her so long to find us that she had to know she was pushing the deadline. And if she didn't plan for failure, then it's not our responsibility to put ourselves in danger to warn her."

Everyone looked to Clio for her verdict. She didn't like it. Hell, she despised the idea of just limping away and ignoring what might happen to Boe's people. But they were willing to sacrifice her for their own safety. And there was no way to know how many other young girls had been killed so Leola and her cabal could go on living.

"It's not our responsibility," she said at last. "And it isn't worth the threat to the ship or the crew. We set sail for home."

Fausta said, "And we gain nothing from the entire endeavor?"

Clio shook her head and looked at Boe. "We saved a girl's life. And we prevented those people from killing anyone else in the name of security. And we gained a crewmate. Things would be very different if we hadn't been able to recover Ranzi, mind. If our gambit with the source hadn't worked, we'd be taking the fight to Leola and making her pay in blood."

Ranzi smiled weakly. "Thanks, Captain. Always nice to know I'm worth starting a war over."

Clio winked at her. "But we got her back. The ship is in one piece. Other than a few bumps and bruises and some lost weeks, we've not really lost anything we can't get back."

Fausta shrugged. "Works for me. I'll set a heading back to Spain."

"Wait," Clio said, the thought forming even as she spoke. "No. We need to make a stop first. Set a course for La Llama."

That caught everyone's attention. "I thought you opted against starting a war," Ranzi said.

"No war," Clio said. "A peace offering. Maybe." She shrugged and headed for her cabin. "We can at least put the ball in Aldoncia's court and see what happens."

She wasn't certain what she planned to do once they arrived at the island. She'd recklessly called the Flame Queen's bluff and sent her away with her tail between her legs. There was a chance the next time they met, Aldoncia would try to settle the score. Unless Clio had something to offer her. Like coordinates to an island with a failing security system and no means to wage naval warfare. She didn't know what outcome was most likely - Aldoncia triumphant, the feud between them calmed? Both sides destroying each other in battle? Aldoncia and Leola teaming up and coming after the *Banshee* as a united front? - but whatever happened, it was better than doing nothing.

She stopped before going below deck and looked back at her crew. Delfina had gotten to her feet and was helping the others stand as well. Other crew scurried to their posts, preparing to set sail once more. The sails wafted gently in the breeze as if awaiting orders, and the rigging swayed in time with it. The ship rocked under her feet as if it was taking deep and rhythmic breaths.

Aravanis saw her watching them and gave her a nod.

Clio returned the nod with a smile.

She wasn't concerned about setting Aldoncia and the La Llama forces loose on Leola's island. No matter what the aftermath might be, she was certain these women would be prepared for whatever happened.

Cariad couldn't get the taste of saltwater out of her mouth. She ran her tongue over her lips as she moved down the narrow corridor to the mess, resting her fingers lightly against the wall to keep herself steady. She'd gotten a mouthful of the sea when the island finally collapsed underneath them. Somehow she had managed not to swallow it, but her shoulder and chest were slammed roughly against the suddenly-loose trees that were bobbing on the surface. She grabbed hold of one, pushed her head above the surface, and spit out the water like a geyser.

The salt still coated her tongue, though, and her whole mouth felt like a desert. She wanted a cup of real water, but she could have gotten that anywhere. She wasn't going to lie to herself about her real reason for going to the mess.

Estacia was at the cutting board, halfway through a tomato, when Cariad came through the door. Estacia glanced up, saw who the new arrival was, and dropped the knife. She let the tomato fall as she hurried across the room and cupped Cariad's face in her hands.

"Are you all right? I saw the island vanish..."

"I'm okay," Cariad said.

Estacia breathed out in relief and kissed her. Cariad wrapped her arms around Estacia's waist, leaning into the kiss before the cook pulled away.

"Your mouth is very dry."

"Salt water. One reason I came here was so I could—"

Estacia stepped out of the embrace and retrieved a canteen. She shook it to make sure it was full, flicked open the cap, and took a long swig. Her cheeks ballooned out as she returned to Cariad, touched her cheek again, and angled her face up for a kiss. Cariad smiled and put her lips against Estacia's, almost choking with relief when her lips were parted with the tip of Estacia's tongue. Water trickled down both their chins, but enough got into Cariad's mouth to start the rejuvenation process.

"Delicious," Cariad said when the water was gone.

She pressed her lips to Estacia's again for a proper kiss.

"So I don't know much of what happened," Estacia said

eventually. "But I get the feeling the mission is over."

"Captain Landau wants to make a stop on our way home, but yeah. I think this one is done."

Estacia's finger traced a seam of Cariad's jacket, which was still sopping wet from her time in the water. "And I think it was implied you would... be... leaving the ship... after this mission."

"I can't quite remember the exact details of my arrangement with the captain at the moment," Cariad admitted. "But that sounds like what we settled on."

"I don't know if I have the right to say this, or if it's fair to you, considering it wasn't entirely your decision to leave. But I want you to know that I wish you were staying."

Cariad curled her forefinger and brushed it over Estacia's cheek. She'd spent her entire life on land. She wanted to be a writer. She dreamed of a desk stacked high with papers, dusty old pages. Sitting alone in dark rooms full of shelves brimming with books. She'd pictured articles with her name on them framed on the walls. None of that fit on a ship. Nothing in that room belonged to a pirate, to a woman who lived on a ship. And yet... she had always pictured herself alone, even in her wildest fantasies. It never occurred to her to conjure a perfect husband.

A perfect wife, on the other hand...

She traced the shell of Estacia's ear and surprised herself.

"I wish I was staying, too."

Estacia rested her head on Cariad's chest. "We still have the rest of the trip back home to Spain," she said. "We'll just have to make the most of it."

Cariad kissed the top of Estacia's head and smiled sadly. "I already have quite a few ideas."

CHAPTER TWENTY-TWO

ALDONCIA DIDN'T stir until Ranzi put a hand on her shoulder. The Flame Queen started to rise, but Ranzi pushed her back down onto the pillow.

"Ah ah." She tapped the underside of Aldoncia's jaw with the flat of her blade. "Wouldn't want you to cut yourself on this."

Aldoncia went stiff and pressed herself back against the pillows. There was enough light coming in through the window that it was clear there were at least two other people in the room, but they were just dark silhouettes flanking the other sides of the bed. Aldoncia clearly decided there was no point in trying to fight and relaxed. Ranzi kept the blade exactly where it was, just in case it was a ruse.

"That's the problem with a heavily secured fortress," Clio said from her concealed spot in the corner. "Makes you so certain that you're safe, you get complacent. Lazy. You're so certain your guards are reliable, that any approaching ship will get flagged, that no one could possibly get this far into your home without raising an alarm."

Aldoncia sneered into the darkness. "Captain Landau. I thought we had come to an agreement the last time we met."

"We did, but I couldn't be certain you'd stick to it. I risked my ship and my crew during that confrontation so I thought I'd be more subtle this time."

"How many of my men did you kill?"

"None," Clio said. "A few of them are going to wake with headaches, but they're all intact. We came here with an olive branch."

One of the dark shapes dropped a folded piece of paper on the sheets. Aldoncia moved her eyes to look but didn't reach for it. The shape spoke, revealing her identity as Fausta Gittens. "You wanted to know where all those ships were going. This is your chance to find out."

"These coordinates aren't exactly a secret," Clio said, "but you saw for yourself how it can be difficult to find what they're pointing to. There is an island at this location. It's protected by a veil, but has no ships of its own. We don't know how fiercely they'll fight a landing party, but I believe you can hold your own in a fight."

"Why should I invade this island? Are you using me to fight your battles, Landau?"

"No. Well... I suppose you could look at it that way. But I very much dislike the way she operates. So I thought you might appreciate the opportunity. But you might want to hurry. I can't explain and you wouldn't believe me if I tried, but trust that you have a very limited window to act."

"And what would be my reward for doing this errand for you?"

"We had the opportunity to ask a resident... well, a former resident now... if the island had stockpiles of riches or gold or anything like that. She said there wasn't much. But the problem with an invisible island is that, even with a big wide ocean, people still run aground there from time to time. And the residents took it upon themselves to liberate the cargo of those shipwrecks. Apparently the island was on a very specific shipping route."

Ranzi took a pouch from her pocket with her free hand. She placed it in Aldoncia's hand, loosened the string that held it shut, and took out a few of the contents. She held them up in front of Aldoncia's face. When she recognized the scent, her eyes widened.

"Cacao. Chocolate?"

"Whole storehouses of the stuff, apparently," Clio said. "They have an entire industry dedicated to keeping pests from getting at it. There's more than enough to sell for a lovely little profit, and still keep some for your own people."

Aldoncia breathed in again and sighed at the rich smell. Ranzi was even a little tempted to pop one of the beans into her mouth and start chewing.

"Very well," Aldoncia finally said.

"And that will make us square," Clio said. "No retribution, no revenge, no lingering anger. The next time the *Banshee* is in these waters, we can consider La Llama and its people allies, not enemies. Do we have an accord?"

Aldoncia glanced down, though the angle was wrong for her to see Ranzi's sword. She squared her jaw and nodded. Carefully.

"The animosity between our two groups is at an end."

"That's good enough for me," Clio said.

Ranzi removed her sword and sheathed it.

"Good luck with your raid, La Reina de Llama."

"And to you in your future endeavors, Captain Landau. Now if you please, and I swear that I would use the same tone with my dearest friends... get the fuck out of my bedroom."

Ranzi waited until the others were in the hall before she left Aldoncia's bedside. Fausta, Clio, and Aravanis waited for her to close the door behind her before they started walking away. Ranzi thought she was hiding her limp, but Fausta fell into step beside her and looked pointedly at her leg.

"The foot is still bothering you?"

"It's not so bad," Ranzi said. "Considering the alternative. Captain said that it looked like a piece of burnt firewood before they dumped me in that hole. Either it will get better or I'll learn to live with it. I'm not concerned. It didn't stop me from keeping up with you lot on the way here."

Fausta nodded. "Let me know if you need me to pick up any slack while you're recovering."

"I think I'll be fine. But thanks."

"Sure thing."

When they reached the exit, Clio held the door for the others. They had gotten to the fortress by taking the long ship to the far side of the island, then trekking through thick underbrush. It had also required them to descend a steep stone wall. It wasn't exactly climbing, but they hadn't exactly been moving horizontally, either. Going back was going to be a rough go even for the most able-bodied of them. Clio put a hand on Ranzi's elbow.

"You're sure you're up for it?"

"I'll let you know when I'm not. But for now, I am."

Clio nodded. "I can live with that. After you, Ines."

Ranzi stepped out into the night. She'd gotten a taste of the other side, of nothingness. There was an incredible amount of pain, the definition of blinding agony. And then she'd felt herself go somewhere else. And then she felt the warm pull of something else calling her back. The pain came with it, but that was so much better than the numbness she'd just experienced. She had no doubt she'd been dead and now she was alive. If the cost of that was a little foot pain, she could quite literally live with that.

On the fourth night they were at sea, the night after leaving La Llama, Clio went to Delfina's cabin. They sat together on her bed and Clio revealed what she had remembered about herself. She'd remembered so much more once the wall came down. She remembered specific pirates she had doomed, knew the ships she had watched sink with a sense of pride and accomplishment. Her tears burned as she recounted them all for Delfina.

When she finished, she bowed her head and looked down at her legs folded in front of her, waiting for the doctor to kick her out, to call her any variety of names, to raise the alarm so the crew could work out an appropriate punishment for her. Instead, Delfina reached out and slipped her hand over Clio's. Her fingers were calloused and rough, though Clio's were in worse shape, but her palm was cool and smooth. She squeezed and bent forward to kiss the knuckles.

"What are you doing?" Clio asked, her voice rough due to the tears she was holding back.

"I'm making my captain feel better."

Clio pulled her hand away. "Didn't you hear what I just said? I'm responsible for the deaths of countless pirates. People you may have known. And if it hadn't been for a storm and a loose piece of timber, I would have killed Harriet."

Delfina said, "Clio Landau didn't do any of that."

"My name doesn't matter."

"No, it doesn't," Delfina admitted. "But your choices do matter. I was raised to be Lady Pendergast, the pride of the society pages. I was raised to be happy in a corset and I knew the proper placement of silverware for every place setting. And I was supposed to happily marry some dreadfully boring man and raise his children while he had a career. Instead, I'm a medic on a pirate ship and I fuck any woman who strikes my fancy."

Clio laughed softly. "That was a choice you made. It was a decision."

"You made choices, too. You stayed with Harriet. You chose to learn how to live on a ship. That means this Alice Malyns person wasn't who you really were. It meant you were capable of being more. And when the opportunity arose, in the form of your memory being lost, you became the person I learned to trust and respect. You became the woman Harriet loved."

Clio shook her head. "Harriet didn't even know who I was."

"Sure she did. Of course she did. You showed her every day you knew her. You've given everyone on this ship a chance to forget who they were *supposed* to be and discover their true selves. The only difference is that you're a little late at the moment of truth because you didn't have to choose. So do it now. Who do you want to be? Do you want—"

"Clio Landau," Clio whispered. "Widow. Captain of the *Banshee*."

Delfina smiled. "Well, isn't that a shock." She leaned in and lightly kissed Clio's lips. "Harriet knew enough when she took you to her bed. And she certainly knew enough when she asked you to be her bride, to give you her name. We've never had reason to doubt that woman's wisdom, so why start now?" She brushed her thumb over Clio's cheek. "Alice Malyns died a long time ago, before you and I ever met. And good riddance to her. You've saved more than enough lives to make up for her sins. I absolve you, Clio."

"Thank you."

Clio leaned in and kissed Delfina. The kiss lingered, then slowly became more passionate. Clio allowed herself to be pushed down onto the pillows, stretching her legs out as Delfina straddled her right thigh. Clio tugged at Delfina's clothes while Delfina slipped a hand between their bodies, methodically working the catches and buttons of Clio's clothes. When she got the trousers loose enough to fit her hand in, she sighed triumphantly and hunched her shoulders, her palm skimming over Clio's stomach on the way down.

Delfina sat up so she could brace her free hand on the wall above Clio's head. This put Clio in the perfect position to notice Delfina's blouse had been unbuttoned far enough to reveal her cleavage during their entire conversation. Now the material sagged open enough for her to see the swaying movement of her breasts as Delfina began thrusting against her, her hand between Clio's legs and then two fingers inside her.

Clio bit her lip, then pressed her face between Delfina's breasts, grabbing Delfina by the belt loops and making her thrust harder, faster. Delfina obliged and used her whole body to guide her hand, grunting as Clio kissed her way to one nipple and took it into her mouth. It had been so long since she'd been with anyone that it didn't take much for her to finish. She dragged her tongue up over the curve of Delfina's breast, kissed her collarbone, and then began to kiss and lick her throat as she lifted her hips against the questing fingers in her pants.

"Oh god," Delfina grunted, grinding down on the leg she was holding captive. "You know what that does to me..."

"Mm-hmm," Clio said, redoubling her efforts.

Delfina whimpered and twisted her wrist, also moving faster, clearly determined not to be the first one over the edge.

"You're not even... gods," Delfina growled and then added a third finger. "You're... not... fair."

"Come for your captain, Dr. Pendergast."

Delfina cried out and clamped her legs closed around Clio's thigh. When she was able to relax, she sank down and playfully bit the tip of Clio's nose.

"That was a gross misuse of authority, captain."

"I'm a pirate, Delf. Now hush and take me over the edge."

"Aye, Captain." Delfina kissed her lips, then slid down her body. She kissed Clio's breasts through her blouse as she tugged the trousers down and out of her way. Clio put her hands behind her head and closed her eyes, letting one foot fall off the side of the bed as she pressed the other against the wall. Delfina kissed, bit, licked, and nibbled the soft skin inside Clio's thigh before she put her head down and started using her mouth to finish Clio off.

Clio settled in a more comfortable position on the thin mattress and wet her lips, enjoying the sensation of Delfina's gentle but confident attention. As she gave herself over to the sensation, she could almost imagine another hand on her body, gently cupping her breast and teasing her nipple. She could all but feel the warmth of a body curled up next to her, the warm breath on her ear.

"You know this is what I wanted," she imagined Harriet saying, "since I can't be here for you. But seeing the two of you together... you should feel very guilty for never suggesting we play with Delf when I was still alive."

Clio chuckled and ran a hand over her face.

Delfina lifted her eyes, then sat up. "Harriet's ghost?"

"Harriet's ghost."

"Enjoy the show, Hattie," Delfina said, and then did

something with her tongue that made Clio cry out with pleasure. Her toes curled, and she grabbed a handful of Delfina's thick hair, bucking her hips up as she orgasmed.

She relaxed with a sigh and pulled Delfina up her body. They kissed and Clio wrapped her legs around Delfina's waist.

"The ghost still here?"

Clio knew without looking. "No. She only shows up when I'm close to an out-of-body experience." She kissed the spot right next to Delfina's mouth. "Thank you for letting me see her again."

"Any time. And if you need me to draw it out next time..."

"I bet you would."

Delfina settled more comfortably on top of Clio. "Do you want to sleep here tonight?" She sounded like she was already falling asleep.

"I would. Thank you, Delf."

"You're welcome, Captain."

She didn't know if she was thanking her for the bed, the orgasm, or for accepting her true identity. But in the end, she supposed it didn't matter. Gratitude was big enough to cover the whole range. She breathed in deep, let it out slowly, and let the rhythm of the ship and Delfina's breathing lull her into a hopefully dreamless sleep.

At the cry that land was sighted, Cariad and Estacia went up on deck to see if for themselves. Land meant Spain and, as they had decided during several conversations over the course of their trip, it was the end of Cariad's time on the *Banshee*. Estacia rested her hands on the railing and Cariad embraced her from behind. She liked the weight of the cook, the way she leaned back against her, the smell of her hair. She liked that she was taller than Estacia, and how she would rest her head on Cariad's shoulder like that was where it was always meant to be.

"Are you sure you're sure about this?" Estacia said. "I'd be more than happy to let you share my cabin for as long as you need."

"I'm sure." Cariad kissed Estacia's hair. "I need time to process everything that's happened. Not just what I've done on the ship, but everything that's happened with you. I've never had a relationship like this. Or any real relationship, if I'm entirely honest. I need to make sure I'm not just swept up in all these changes."

Estacia sighed and nodded. "I suppose that's smart."

Cariad kissed her hair again. "Besides, I need to actually sit down and write this blasted book of mine. It's incredibly difficult to write on a ship at sea."

"I understand." She turned around in Cariad's arms and straightened her collar. "And I'll understand if you need to explore with other lovers while you're back on land. And I may have a dalliance or two of my own. But know that I will miss you terribly. And I will be here when you're ready to come back, hm?"

"That seems reasonable." She brushed her thumb over Estacia's cheek. "I'm already jealous of whoever you choose."

"I feel very much the same."

They kissed. Cariad pressed Estacia against the gunwale. Estacia hooked her leg on Cariad's hip, and Cariad let her hands drift and roam. She opened her eyes during the kiss and looked in the distance, trying to gauge how far away land was.

"How long will it be before we're actually anchored and going ashore?"

"Long enough," Estacia said, already pulling Cariad toward the stairs.

Cariad grinned and let herself be dragged to a proper farewell.

EPILOGUE

Three Months Later

CARIAD WAS waiting at the docks when the *Banshee* rolled back into the harbor. She'd meant to remain stoic, but her rebellious face broke into a smile as soon as she saw its sails. She could see people moving on the deck and told herself she recognized a few. The woman at the helm was almost certainly Ranzi, and that mountain of a woman watching from the gunwale was undoubtably Aravanis. When the ship was closer she could hear Fausta's voice echoing over the water as she shouted to the crew.

She was itching to get back aboard. If she thought she could clear the distance, she would have tried swimming out to meet them. But she was still rational and was willing to wait the long, agonizing seconds until it was berthed. The solid ground hadn't felt right under her feet, but she still believed time away had been necessary. Not just for her book, but so she could know without question what she wanted and where she wanted to be.

When she was finally allowed to board, she found Fausta waiting for her with a knowing smirk. "Welcome back," she said. "I hate to be the bearer of bad news, but your lady is currently entertaining ten or twelve insatiable sailors at the moment."

"And what *is* today's lunch, Fausta?"

The first mate's smile widened. She smacked Cariad's arm and nodded toward the stern. "Captain wanted to see you as soon as you came aboard anyway. Your gal can wait until business proper has been dealt with."

"Sounds fair," Cariad agreed. "It's good to see you again, Fausta."

"I suppose it won't be much of a hindrance to have you back aboard. So long as you keep Estacia happy. A happy cook means a fat crew."

Cariad grinned. "I'll do my best."

She opened her pack and withdrew the bound packet of papers which made up her book. Her hands shook as she straightened the pages, tapping the edges so they lined up nicely. She took a steadying breath and rapped her knuckles on the captain's door.

"Come in, Miss Baillie."

She smiled and stepped inside. "Nice to know I was expected."

Clio smiled without looking up from what she was writing. "Fausta told me you were spotted on the deck looking like a lost pup."

"I won't be ashamed of my eagerness," Cariad said. "I've been waiting weeks for you to return."

"We were delayed. Nothing of concern, but things at sea can get... unpredictable." She finally signed the page and put down her pen. "Glad to have you back. Is this a visit or a true return?"

Cariad tilted her head to one side. "That may depend on how this conversation goes."

Clio leaned back in her seat. "I'm intrigued."

"I finished it." She placed the bound pages on the desk in front of Clio. "My book."

She reached forward and thumbed through the stack. "I hope you don't expect me to read this entire thing before we leave again."

"No, you can take your time. Because whether I stay aboard or not, I intend to leave that with you."

"You went to the trouble of making me my own copy?"

"No. That's the only copy. And if you decide it should be burned, the entire thing will be lost. I hope you don't do that, obviously, but I leave it in your hands."

Clio narrowed her eyes. "Why?"

"Because I don't care if I gain fame or fortune from it. I'm not important. The book is. The women whose stories I tell are important. People need to know who they are, as themselves, with their own names. Fausta Gittens and Ines Ranzi and Aravanis...

uh..."

"Penelope."

"Really?"

Clio smiled and picked up the book. She chose a page at random and skimmed it.

"You can decide when the book is released. Even if it's years from now, after every woman named in the pages is dead. The world will know who they are."

"That's admirable. I'm sure they'll all appreciate it."

Cariad stepped forward, hesitated, then continued forward. "There's a story that isn't in there. Something no one brought up, and I felt awkward asking about. Harriet's death."

Clio's hand froze in the process of turning a page.

"I'd like to include her. She brought a lot of this crew together. She's a huge part of the *Banshee*'s history. It didn't feel right leaving her out, but I couldn't exactly ask her for an interview."

"Mm." Clio put the book down and rested her hand on top of it. "There's a reason no one brought it up. It's not something we discuss with passengers. The crew knows."

Cariad nodded solemnly. "I understand. I won't~"

"She sacrificed herself for us." Clio looked up and met Cariad's eyes. "Specifically it was for Ranzi and Aravanis. They were all three captured, scheduled to hang by the neck until dead. I took Fausta to rescue them. We came very close to failing. We made it out of the stronghold but the jailors forced us to run further inland rather than toward our ship. We were cut off. Doomed without question. But Harriet knew her worth. She knew..."

Her voice broke and she looked away. After a moment she stood up and walked to the window.

"She cupped my face. She kissed me. She told me that she had always loved me, would always love me. And she... ran. She shot one of the bastards, and she ran. They chased her. Obviously. Captain Harriet Landau of the *Banshee* was worth more than the rest of us combined. It gave us a chance to escape, get back to the ship."

Cariad held her breath throughout the story, letting it out slowly when Clio stopped talking. "That was incredibly brave of her."

Clio wiped at her cheeks. "We got everyone. Everyone. We went back. But they hadn't bothered with a trial or a public execution. By the time we got back to the town, Harriet was already ha~" She cut herself off mid-word as if her throat refused to say the words. Finally, after almost a minute, she said, "We killed the ones we could. Cut her down. Brought her home."

"I'm sorry," Cariad said.

"As am I. The hazards of our profession." She sniffed, gave her eyes another sweep with the back of her hand, then finally turned to face her again. "If you want me to give you an official, ah, book-worthy version, I'll need some time to prepare."

"No, it can wait. I actually, um... I actually have a story to tell you now."

Clio raised an eyebrow. "Is that so?"

"I spent my time away from the ship writing, obviously, but I also did research to match up some of the stories I was told with actual documented events. I feel like a great many readers will find it difficult to believe I didn't just make you all up. I wanted to be sure no one was embellishing their story, but also anchor what I was told in historical fact."

"Okay," Clio said warily, lowering herself back into her seat. "Was someone lying?"

"No. Well, not a lie so much as an omission. See, one thing about your recovered memories I found curious was the man who hired you to kill Harriet in the first place. Have you remembered anything else about him, by chance?"

Clio shook her head. "Not a clue. But I think that's likely a product of a degraded memory from thirty years ago than any lingering amnesia. There was no reason for his name to stick in my mind."

"Actually there was. His name was William Landau. Harriet was his sister."

Clio flinched. Then she became very still. "I didn't know that."

"I didn't think you did. I don't think you *ever* knew Harriet had a brother. There was an inheritance. He claimed it all, and if Harriet discovered what she was owed, well... He figured it was better to eliminate the possibility of her coming back to collect."

"If you're implying I knew that—"

"I'm not. You aren't the one who lied. You see, it bothered me that he just gave up. He sent you after Harriet and then you vanished. No report, no dead body of his sister. It made me wonder why he never sent anyone else to complete the job you failed to do. My first assumption was that he sent someone else who finally caught up with her seven years ago. But even before you told me the story of how she died, I knew that wasn't the case."

Clio said, "Well, please. Don't leave me in suspense."

Cariad took a deep breath. "The reason he didn't send anyone else is because he thought Alice Malyns had been murdered. He received a note saying she had been killed and, if any other pirate hunters went after Harriet, they would meet the same fate. And the local authorities would receive evidence that implicated him in the deaths."

"Who would send him a note like that?"

"Harriet."

Clio stared at her. "What?"

"I saw the actual letter. It was in the archives of his estate. He died years ago. Money plus alcoholism, never good for the liver." She cleared her throat. "Um, yes. Anyway. Harriet sent him the note. She claimed she had 'killed the bitch you sent after me,' and promised to do the same with anyone else employed to cause her harm."

Clio was breathing hard. "No. She couldn't possibly have... that..." She closed her eyes. "She couldn't have sent a letter saying that, because it would imply..."

"It would imply that she knew exactly who Alice Malyns was, and why she was on the ship that day." She gave Clio a moment to process that information before she dropped the next lead weight. "The letter was postmarked six months after you lost your memories."

Clio pushed away from the desk and stood up. "You're wrong."

"I'm not. I triple checked. She sent the letter twenty-eight years ago."

Clio's eyes filled with tears. "But she didn't know. She never knew..." She put a hand on the back of her head and turned around. Cariad winced when she heard a broken sob. "She couldn't have known."

Cariad stood. "But she did. For practically the entire time she knew you, she... she *knew* you. She knew who you were."

"Why didn't she tell me?"

"Would you have wanted her to?"

Clio's entire body was shaking. "I... I don't... know..."

Cariad stood. "I believe you should have been given the option. But I also can't be angry at Harriet for what she did. I like the woman I met on this ship, and I think she's done a lot of good. She helped a lot of people who might have died without her in charge. If you had been told who you were that early in your new life, I don't think you would have ever become this version of yourself. And frankly, Alice sounds like an utter shrew."

Clio laughed softly at that. "She does indeed."

"You're forgetting the most important part of the story, Captain. If Harriet knew your true identity that early, it means she did everything else with her eyes wide open. She knew who you had been and what you'd done. And she still trusted you. She loved you. There was no deception, no dark secret. Harriet knew and loved the real you. And she gave you her name. And she gave you her ship."

Clio turned to face her. "She didn't say my name before she... The last time we saw each other. Part of me always wondered about that."

"Because she was saying it to you. Your name didn't matter, she was saying it to you. Darkness and all."

The room was silent except for the creaking of the ship and the muffled sounds of the crew outside. Clio wrapped her arms around herself and went to the window.

"Thank you, Miss Baillie."

"You're welcome." She rubbed her hands together, unsure what else to do. "I think I'll give you some time to process everything I've just told you."

Clio nodded. "Estacia has been looking forward to your return with great fervor." Her voice was smaller, weaker than Cariad was used to hearing, but she could sense a spark of her normal strength lingering under the surface. "I think she will be most pleased to welcome you back aboard."

"I think I shall drop in and say hello."

She was at the door before she heard Clio say something else, very quietly. "Ships and storms..."

"I'm sorry?"

Clio breathed in and then let it out. "Something Harriet wrote. We were talking one night about how ships and hurricanes are called 'she.' Men belittle us and dismiss our strength, but then give our gender to their warships and set off to do battle. They give our names to the most destructive forces a ship can face. She found it amusing. She wrote a... a poem of sorts, I suppose."

"I'd love to hear it."

Clio chuckled and then began to recite.

"The fairer sex, we'll never be
When every threat upon the sea

Bears marks of femininity
Beware, my boys, and stay alee
Of all your storms and ships called she."

Cariad smiled. "I like that very much."
"I thought you would. You can have it for your book."
"My thanks."
Clio turned. "Miss Baillie. Will you be staying aboard when the ship sets sail again?"
Cariad thought for a moment and then nodded. "Yes, Captain Landau. I believe I will be. There are far too many stories out there waiting to be told."
"I'm glad to hear it. Don't keep my cook busy too long, Miss Baillie. I get prickly when my dinner is late."
Cariad opened the door and stepped out. "With all due respect, Captain, I would suggest having some saltines to tide yourself over."
Clio laughed and shook her head. "Enjoy yourself, Miss Baillie."
"Aye, Captain."
Cariad left Clio and went back up onto the deck. She easily avoided the deckhands as she crossed to the gunwale. Her legs automatically adjusted for the gentle sway of the wood beneath her feet. She rested her arms on the railing and looked toward the entrance to the harbor. Beyond, she could see an endless stretch of blue water that ended at a hazy horizon, the ocean and sky blending together in a blur of white and gray. She breathed deep and smiled.
She had never given much thought to the ocean. Ships were just a means to an end, and sailors were just potential stories waiting to be told. She never expected to miss the water. She never thought she would call a cramped bed home. But the only word to describe her feelings since leaving the *Banshee* was 'homesick.' And now she was back. Even before reuniting with Estacia - and she had to confess her feelings for that sneaky and sly cook had only deepened in their separation - she felt like she was back where she belonged.
"Ahoy, Cariad." She turned and saw Delfina crossing the deck, clearly in a hurry but it didn't seem to be a medical emergency. She smiled and gave Cariad a wink. "Come back to join us, have ya?"
"Indeed I have, Dr. Pendergast."
"Fantastic news. Welcome back aboard the *Banshee*."
Cariad smiled and touched her brow, tossing a salute to

Delfina. When she was gone, Cariad looked out at the water again. She didn't know what she would find on the ship, but she'd already found more than she'd ever had on shore. A home. A family. Someone to love without judgment. She was excited to find out what other treasures awaited her.

But first, she was going to grab something to eat. And she would hope against hope that something grabbed her back in return.

www.ingramcontent.com/pod-product-compliance
Lightning Source LLC
Chambersburg PA
CBHW061305210726
48293CB00003B/1115